THE NEIGHBORHOOD

Mario Vargas Llosa was born in Peru in 1936. He is the author of some of the last half-century's most important novels, including *The War of the End of the World*, *The Feast of the Goat*, *Aunt Julia and the Scriptwriter* and *Conversation in the Cathedral*. In 2010 he was awarded the Nobel Prize in Literature.

THE NEIGHBORHOOD

A NOVEL

MARIO VARGAS LLOSA

Translated from the Spanish by Edith Grossman

FABER & FABER

First published in 2018
by Faber & Faber Ltd
Bloomsbury House
74–77 Great Russell Street
London WC1B 3DA

This export edition first published in 2018

Originally published in Spanish in 2016
by Alfaguara Ediciones, Spain, as *Cinco Esquinas*
English translation published in the United States in 2018
by Farrar, Straus and Giroux
18 West 18th Street, New York 10011

Printed and bound by CPI Group (UK) Ltd, Croydon CR0 4YY

A CIP record for this book
is available from the British Library

ISBN 978–0–571–33308–0

FSC
www.fsc.org
MIX
Paper from
responsible sources
FSC® C020471

1 3 5 7 9 10 8 6 4 2

For Alonso Cueto

Contents

1. Marisa's Dream   3
2. An Unexpected Visit   13
3. Weekend in Miami   20
4. The Entrepreneur and the Lawyer   29
5. The Den of Gossip   36
6. A Wreck of Show Business   45
7. Quique's Agony   54
8. Shorty   63
9. A Singular Affair   70
10. The Three Jokers   78
11. The Scandal   86
12. The People's Dining Room   98
13. An Absence   107
14. Conjugal Disagreements and Agreements   120
15. Shorty Is Afraid   130
16. The Landowner and the Chinese Woman   141
17. Strange Operations Regarding Juan Peineta   152
18. Engineer Cárdenas's Longest Night   166
19. Shorty and Power   173
20. A Whirlpool   189
21. Special Edition of *Exposed*   219
22. Happy Ending?   233

THE NEIGHBORHOOD

1

Marisa's Dream

Was she awake or dreaming? That slight warmth on her right instep was still there, an unusual sensation that gave her gooseflesh all along her body and revealed that she wasn't alone in bed. A confusion of memories came rushing into her head but then began to fall into place, like a crossword puzzle that one fills in slowly. The wine after their meal had made them a little tipsy, while their talk passed from terrorism to movies to gossip, when suddenly Chabela looked at her watch and jumped up, her face pale: "Curfew! My God, I can't get to La Rinconada in time! How the hours have flown." Marisa insisted that she stay and sleep there. It wouldn't be a problem, Quique had gone to Arequipa for a board meeting early that morning at the brewery, they had the Golf Club apartment to themselves. Chabela called her husband. Luciano, always so understanding, said it was fine, he'd make sure the two girls left for the school bus on time; Chabela should just stay at Marisa's, that was better than being stopped by a patrol if she violated the curfew. The damn curfew. But, of course, terrorism was worse.

Chabela stayed and slept in the bed with Marisa, and now Marisa felt the sole of her friend's foot on her right instep: a light pressure, a soft, gentle, delicate sensation. How had it happened that they were so close to each other in a bed so big that when she saw it, Chabela joked: "But tell me, Marisita, tell me how many people sleep in this gigantic bed?" She recalled that both had lain in their respective corners, separated by at least half a meter. Which one had moved so much in her sleep that Chabela's foot was now touching her instep?

She didn't dare move. She held her breath so she wouldn't wake her friend, in case she pulled back her foot and the delicious sensation that spread from her instep along the rest of her body, making her tense and concentrated, disappeared. Gradually, in the dim bedroom, she was able to make out a few strips of light through the blinds, the shadow of the bureau, the door to the dressing room, the bathroom door, the rectangles of paintings on the walls, Tilsa's desert with the serpent-woman, the chamber with the Szyszlo totem, the floor lamp, the sculpture by Berrocal. She closed her eyes and listened to Chabela's breathing, very faint but regular. Chabela was sleeping, perhaps dreaming, so she was the one, no doubt about it, who had approached her friend's body in her sleep.

Surprised, embarrassed, wondering again whether she was awake or dreaming, Marisa finally became aware of what her body already knew: she was aroused. That delicate sole of a foot warming her instep had set fire to her skin and senses, and she was sure that if she slipped a hand between her legs, she would find it wet. "Have you lost your mind?" she asked herself. "Getting excited by a woman? How long has that been going on, Marisita?" She had often been aroused by herself, of course, and had masturbated at times, rubbing a pillow between her legs, but always thinking about men. As far as she could recall, never a woman, never! And yet now here she was, trembling from head to foot with a mad desire for not only their feet but everything else to touch so she would feel, just as she did on her instep, the closeness and warmth of her friend all along her body.

Moving very gently, her heart pounding, simulating the breathing of someone asleep, she turned slightly to the side so that, although she didn't touch her, she could feel that now she was just a few millimeters from Chabela's back, buttocks, and legs. She could hear her respiration more clearly and thought she felt a hidden vapor emanating from the body that was so close, and reaching her, enveloping her. In spite of herself, as if she wasn't aware of what she was doing, she moved her right hand very slowly and rested it on her friend's thigh. "Blessed curfew," she thought. She felt her heart beating faster: Chabela was going to wake and move her hand: "Get away, don't touch me, have you lost your mind, what's the matter with you?" But Chabela didn't move and continued to seem submerged in a deep sleep. She heard her inhale, exhale, and had the impression that the air was coming toward her, entering her nostrils and mouth and warming her inside. In the midst of her excitement, how absurd, she continued to think about the curfew, the blackouts, the kidnappings—especially Cachito's—and the terrorists' bombs. What a country! What a country!

Beneath her hand, the surface of that thigh was firm and smooth, slightly damp, perhaps because of perspiration or some cream. Before she went to bed, had Chabela put on any of the creams Marisa kept in the bathroom? She hadn't seen her undress; she had handed her one of her nightgowns, a very short one, and Chabela had changed in the dressing room. When she returned to the bedroom, Chabela already had it on; it was semitransparent and left bare her arms and legs and a glimpse of buttock, and Marisa recalled having thought: "What a nice body, how well preserved in spite of two children, it must be because she goes to the gym three times a week." She had continued moving millimeter by millimeter, with the growing fear of waking her friend; now, terrified and happy, she felt, to the rhythm of their respective breathing, momentary bits of thigh, of buttock, of the legs of both women touching lightly and instantly moving apart. "No, she's going to wake up, Marisa, this is madness." But she didn't withdraw and kept waiting—what was she waiting for?—as if in a trance, for the next fleeting touch. Her right hand continued to rest on Chabela's thigh, and Marisa realized she had begun to perspire.

And then her friend moved. She thought her heart would stop. For a few seconds she stopped breathing, closed her eyes tightly, and pretended she was asleep. Chabela, without moving from her place, had raised her arm and now Marisa felt, on the hand resting on the other woman's thigh, Chabela's hand resting. Was she going to move her hand away? No, just the opposite, gently, one might say affectionately, Chabela, entwining her fingers with Marisa's, with a slight pressure and keeping hand to skin, was moving that hand toward her groin. Marisa didn't believe what was happening. On the fingers trapped by Chabela she felt the hair of a slightly raised pubis and the wet, palpitating opening against which her hand was being pressed. Trembling from head to toe, Marisa leaned in and pressed her breasts, belly, and legs against the back, buttocks, and legs of her friend as with all five fingers she rubbed Chabela's sex, trying to find the small clitoris, scratching, separating the wet lips of her sex swollen by yearning, always guided by the hand of Chabela, who, she felt, was also trembling, adjusting to her body, helping her to become entangled with her, to unite with her.

Marisa buried her face in the thick hair that she pushed aside with movements of her head until she found Chabela's neck and ears, and now she kissed, licked, and nibbled them with great pleasure, no longer thinking about anything, blind with happiness and desire. A few seconds or minutes later, Chabela turned around, searching for her mouth. They kissed avidly, desperately, first on the lips and then, opening their mouths, entwining their tongues, exchanging their saliva, while their hands removed, tore at, their nightgowns until they were naked and embracing; they turned from one side to the other, caressing each other's breasts, kissing them, and then armpits and bellies, while they rubbed each other's sex and felt them throb in a time without time, so infinite and intense.

When Marisa, in a daze and satiated, felt unable to avoid sinking into an irresistible sleep, she managed to tell herself that during all of the extraordinary experience that had just occurred, neither she nor Chabela—who also seemed overcome by sleep now—had exchanged a single word. As she sank into a bottomless void she thought again of the curfew and believed she heard a distant explosion.

Hours later, when she awoke, a grayish daylight, barely screened by the venetian blinds, came into the bedroom, and Marisa was alone in the bed. Embarrassment made her tremble from head to foot. Had it all actually happened? It wasn't possible, no, no, it wasn't. But yes, of course it had happened. Then she heard a noise in the bathroom and, feeling frightened, closed her eyes, pretending to sleep. She opened them just a little, and through her lashes she saw Chabela already dressed and ready to leave.

"Marisita, I'm so sorry I woke you," she heard her say in the most natural voice in the world.

"Don't be silly," she stammered, certain her voice was barely audible. "Are you leaving already? Don't you want some breakfast first?"

"No, darling," her friend replied: her voice certainly wasn't trembling and she didn't seem uncomfortable, she was the same as always, without the slightest flush on her cheeks and an absolutely normal gaze with no touch of mischief or impishness in her large dark eyes; her black hair was somewhat disordered. "I have to rush so I can see the girls before they leave for school. Thanks so much for your hospitality. We'll talk, here's a kiss."

She threw her a kiss from the bedroom door and left. Marisa curled up, felt desperate, was about to get out of bed but curled up again and pulled the sheets over her. Of course it had happened, and the best proof of that was that she was naked and her nightgown wrinkled and half off the bed. She raised the sheets and saw with a laugh that the nightgown she had lent Chabela was there too, a little puddle next to her feet. She began to laugh but suddenly cut it off. My God, my God. Did she feel sorry? Absolutely. Chabela had such presence of mind. Could she have done things like this before? Impossible. They had known each other for so long, they had always told each other everything, if Chabela had ever had an adventure like this she would have told her about it. Or maybe not? Would she trade this for their friendship? Of course not. Chabelita was her closest friend, more than a sister. What would their relationship be from now on? The same as before? Now they shared a tremendous secret. My God, my God, she couldn't believe it had happened. All morning as she bathed, dressed, had breakfast, gave instructions to the cook, the butler, and the maid, the same questions whirled around her head: "Did you do what you did, Marisita?" And what would happen if Quique found out that she and Chabela had done what they had done? Would he be angry? Would he be jealous and make a scene as if she had betrayed him with a man? Would she tell him about it? No, never in this life, no one else should know anything about it, how embarrassing. And yet about noon, when Quique came back from Arequipa and brought her the usual pastries from La Ibérica and the bag of large green peppers, and as she kissed him and asked how things had gone at the brewery board meeting—"Fine, fine, Blondie, we've decided to stop shipping beer to Ayacucho, it isn't worth it, the percentage that the terrorists and pseudo-

terrorists are demanding is ruining us"—she kept asking herself: "Why did Chabela say nothing at all and leave as if
nothing had happened? Why else, idiot? Because she, too, was
dying of embarrassment, she wanted to play the innocent and
to dissemble, as if nothing had happened. But it did happen,
Marisita. Would it happen again or never again?"

   She spent the entire week not daring to phone Chabela,
waiting anxiously for her to call. How strange! Never before
had so many days passed without their seeing each other or
talking. Or, perhaps, thinking about it carefully, it wasn't so
strange: Chabela must be feeling just as uncomfortable and
surely was waiting for Marisa to take the initiative. Could she
be angry? But why? Hadn't Chabela made the first move? She
had only put a hand on her leg, it could have been something
accidental, without purpose, with no bad intention. It was
Chabela who had taken her hand and made her touch her there
and masturbate her. How daring! When that thought came to
her she felt a mad desire to laugh, and a heat in her cheeks,
which must have turned bright red.

   She was this way for the rest of the week, distracted, focused on that memory almost without realizing that she was
following the routine determined by her schedule, Italian
classes with Diana, the ladies' tea for Margot's niece who was
finally getting married, two working lunches with Quique's
partners to which wives were invited, the obligatory visit to
her parents for tea, going to the movies with her cousin Matilde,
seeing a film to which she paid no attention at all because she
didn't stop thinking about it for an instant and at times still
wondered whether it hadn't been a dream. And that lunch
with her classmates from high school and the inevitable conversation, which she only half followed, about poor Cachito,
who had been kidnapped almost two months ago. They said
an expert from the insurance company had come from New
York to negotiate the ransom with the terrorists, and that poor

Nina, his wife, was having therapy to keep from going crazy. How distracted she must have been when, one night, Enrique made love to her and she suddenly realized that her husband had lost his enthusiasm and was saying to her: "I don't know what's wrong, Blondie, I think that in the ten years we've been married I've never seen you so uninterested. Is it because of the terrorism? Let's go to sleep."

On Thursday, exactly one week after the thing that had or had not happened, Enrique came home from the office earlier than usual. They were having a whiskey on the terrace, watching the sea of lights of Lima at their feet, and talking, naturally, about the subject that obsessed every household in those days, the attacks and kidnappings of the Shining Path and the Túpac Amaru Revolutionary Movement, the MRTA, the blackouts almost every night because electrical towers had been blown up, leaving entire districts of the city in darkness, and the explosions the terrorists used to awaken Limeños at midnight and at dawn. They recalled having seen from this same terrace, a few months earlier, on one of the hills on the outskirts of the city, the torches light up in the shape of a hammer and sickle, a prophecy of what would happen if the Senderistas won this war. Enrique said that the situation was becoming untenable for businesses, security measures were increasing expenses in an insane way, the insurance companies wanted to keep raising premiums, and if the bandits had their way, Peru would soon be in a situation like Colombia's, where businesspeople, driven away by terrorists, apparently were moving en masse to Panama and Miami to run their enterprises from there. With everything that signified in complications, extra costs, and losses. And just as he was telling her, "Perhaps we'll have to go to Panama or Miami too, sweetheart," Quintanilla, the butler, appeared on the terrace: "Señora Chabela's on the phone, señora." "I'll take the call in the bedroom," she said, and when she stood up, she heard Quique say: "Blondie, tell Chabela that I'll call Luciano one of these days so the four of us can get together."

When she sat down on the bed and picked up the receiver, her legs were trembling. "Hello, Marisita?" she heard, and said: "I'm glad you called, I've been swamped with so much to do and planned to call you first thing tomorrow."

"I was in bed with an awful flu," said Chabela, "but I'm better now. And missing you terribly, darling."

"Me, too," Marisa responded. "I don't think we've ever spent a week without seeing each other, have we?"

"I'm calling to give you an invitation," said Chabela. "I warn you that I won't take no for an answer. I have to go to Miami for two or three days, there are some problems at the apartment on Brickell Avenue and they can be solved only if I'm there in person. Come with me, I'm inviting you. I already have tickets for the two of us, I got them free with the miles I've earned. We'll leave on Thursday at midnight, we'll stay there Friday and Saturday, and come back Sunday. Don't say no, because I'll be furious with you, sweetheart."

"Of course I'll go with you, I'd be delighted," said Marisa; she thought her heart would leap out of her mouth. "I'll tell Quique right now, and if he has any objections, I'll divorce him. Thanks very much, darling. Great, terrific, I love the idea."

She hung up the phone and remained on the bed for a moment until she calmed down. She was overwhelmed by a feeling of well-being, a joyful uncertainty. That things had happened and now she and Chabela would leave next Thursday for Miami and for three days they'd forget about kidnappings, the curfew, blackouts, the whole nightmare. When she returned to the terrace, Enrique made a joke at her expense: "Whoever laughs alone is remembering her wicked deeds.

May I ask why your eyes are shining like that?" "I won't tell you, Quique," she flirted with her husband, putting her arms around his neck. "Even if you kill me, I won't tell you. Chabela invited me to Miami for three days, and I told her that if you won't let me go with her, I'm divorcing you."

2

An Unexpected Visit

As soon as he saw him walk into his office, the engineer Enrique Cárdenas—Quique to his wife and friends—felt a strange discomfort. What bothered him about the reporter who approached with his hand extended? His Tarzanesque walk, arms swinging and shoulders swaying like the king of the jungle? The ratlike little smile that contracted his forehead beneath hair that had been gelled and flattened against his skull like a metal helmet? The tight purple corduroy trousers that clung to his skinny body like a glove? Or those yellow shoes with thick platforms to make him look taller? Everything about him seemed ugly and vulgar.

"Delighted to meet you, Engineer Cárdenas." He extended a soft little hand that perspired so much it left Enrique's hand damp. "Finally you'll allow me to clasp those fingers after so many requests on my part."

He had a shrill, high voice that seemed to be mocking him, small shifty eyes, a rachitic little body, and Enrique even noticed that he smelled of underarms or feet. Was it his odor that made him dislike this individual so much from the very start?

"I'm sorry, I know you've called very frequently," he apologized, without much conviction. "I can't see all the people who call me, you can't imagine how crowded my schedule is. Please, have a seat."

"I can imagine very well, Engineer," said the little man; his high-heeled boots creaked when he walked, and he wore a very tight blue jacket and an iridescent tie that seemed to choke him. Everything about him was tiny, including his voice. How old was he? Forty, fifty?

"What a fantastic view you have here, Engineer! That hill in the background is San Cristóbal, isn't it? Are we on the twentieth or twenty-first floor?"

"The twenty-first," he specified. "You're lucky, the sun's out today and you can enjoy the view. Normally, at this time of year, the fog makes the whole city disappear."

"It must give you an enormous feeling of power to have Lima at your feet," the visitor joked; his little gray eyes darted about, and it seemed to Quique that everything he said revealed a profound insincerity. "And what an elegant office, Engineer. Allow me to have a look at these pictures."

Now the visitor walked up and down, calmly examining the mechanical drawings of pipes, pulleys, water tanks, and gasoline pumps with which the decorator Leonorcita Artigas had adorned the walls of his office with the argument: "Don't they look like abstract etchings, Quique?" The charm of Leonorcita, who at least had alternated those impersonal, hieroglyphic drawings with attractive photographs of Peruvian landscapes, had cost him a fortune.

"Let me introduce myself," the little man said at last. "Rolando Garro, a lifelong journalist. I'm director of the weekly *Exposed*."

He handed him a card, always with that half smile and a shrill, high-pitched voice that seemed barbed. That's what bothered him most about his visitor, Enrique decided: not his odor but his voice.

"I know who you are, Señor Garro." The businessman

tried to be pleasant. "I've seen your television program. It was canceled for political reasons, wasn't it?"

"It was canceled because it told the truth, something not tolerated in Peru today, or ever," the journalist stated bitterly, but still smiling. "They've already canceled several of my radio and television programs. Sooner or later they'll also cancel *Exposed* for the same reason. But I don't care. It's part of the job in this country."

His shifty little eyes looked at Enrique defiantly, and Enrique regretted having agreed to see this man. Why had he? Because his secretary, sick of so many calls, had asked him: "Shall I tell him then, Engineer, that you'll never see him? If you'll forgive me, I can't stand it anymore. It's driving all of us in the office crazy. He's been calling five or six times a day, every day, for the past few weeks." He'd thought that, after all, a reporter could sometimes be useful. "But dangerous, too," he concluded. He had a presentiment that nothing good would come of this visit.

"Tell me what I can do for you, Señor Garro." He noticed that the journalist had stopped smiling and stared at him with a glance both submissive and sarcastic. "If it's a matter of advertisement, let me say that we're not involved with that. We have a subcontract with a company that takes care of all the publicity for the group."

But evidently the visitor didn't want ads for the weekly. The little man was very serious now. He said nothing and observed Enrique in silence, as if searching for the words he would say next, or maintaining suspense in order to make him nervous. And in fact, as he waited for Rolando Garro to open his mouth, Enrique began to feel not only irritated but uneasy. What did this vulgar little man want?

"Why don't you have a bodyguard, Engineer?" Garro asked suddenly. "At least, there are none to be seen."

Enrique was surprised, and he shrugged.

"I'm a fatalist, and I value my freedom," he replied. "Let whatever has to happen, happen. I couldn't live surrounded by bodyguards, I'd feel like a prisoner."

Had this person come for an interview? He wouldn't give him one, and pretty soon he'd kick him out.

"It's a very delicate subject, Engineer Cárdenas." The reporter had lowered his voice as if the walls could hear; he spoke with studied slowness as, in a somewhat theatrical manner, he opened the faded leather briefcase he was carrying and took out a portfolio held shut with two thick yellow bands. He didn't hand it to him immediately; he set it on his knees and again fixed his rat eyes on him, in which Enrique thought he could now see something obscure, perhaps threatening. Whatever had possessed him to make this appointment? The logical thing would have been for one of his assistants to see him, listen to him, and get rid of him. Now it was too late and perhaps he would regret it.

"I'm going to leave this dossier with you so you can examine it carefully, Engineer," said Garro, handing it to him with exaggerated solemnity. "When you look at it you'll understand why I wanted to bring it to you in person and not leave it with your secretaries. You can be certain that *Exposed* would never publish anything as vile as this."

He paused for a long time, not moving his eyes away, and continued in his falsetto voice, which became lower and lower:

"Don't ask how this came into my hands, because I won't tell you. It's a question of journalistic obligation, I suppose you know what that is. Professional ethics. I always respect my sources, although there are reporters who sell them to the highest bidder. What I will allow myself to tell you again is that my insisting on seeing you in person was due to that. There are in this city, as you know all too well, people who want to do you harm. Because of your prestige, your power, your fortune. In Peru these things are not forgiven. Envy and resentment flourish here more vigorously than in any other country. I want only to assure you that those who wish to sully your reputation and injure you will never do so because of me or *Exposed*. You can be sure of that. I don't engage in despicable or base actions. Simply put, it's a good idea for you to know what to watch out for. Your enemies will use this and even worse obscenities to intimidate you and demand God alone knows what."

He paused to take a breath, and after a few seconds he continued, solemnly, shrugging his shoulders.

"Naturally, if I had lent myself to this dirty game and used this material, we would have tripled or quadrupled the number of issues. But there are still some journalists in Peru who have principles, Engineer, happily for you. Do you know why I'm doing this? Because I believe you're a patriot, Señor Cárdenas. A man who, through his enterprises, makes a nation. While many others, frightened by terrorism, run away and take their money overseas, you remain, working and creating employment, resisting the terror, raising up this country. I'll tell you something else. I don't want any compensation, if you offered it to me I wouldn't accept it. I've come to give this to you so that you yourself can toss this trash into the bin and sleep peacefully. No compensation, Engineer, except my having a clear conscience. I'll leave now. I know you're a very busy man, and I don't want to take up any more of your valuable time."

He stood, held out his hand, and Enrique, disconcerted, again felt the dampness left behind by contact with those soft fingers, that palm wet with perspiration. He saw the little man move toward the door with bold, certain strides, open it, go out, and without turning his head, close it behind him.

He was so confused and so irate that he poured a glass of water and drank it in one swallow before he looked at the portfolio. It was on the desk, right under his eyes, and he thought his hand trembled as it removed the bands that held it closed. He opened it. What could it be? Nothing good, judging by that individual's little speech. He saw photographs, wrapped in transparent tissue paper. Photos? What photos could they be? He began to remove the tissue paper carefully, but after a few moments he became impatient, ripped off the paper, and tossed it in the basket. The surprise caused by the first image was so great that he let go of the pile of photographs, which fell off the desk and scattered on the floor. He slid off his chair on all fours and picked them up. As he did he looked at them, quickly hiding each photo with the next one, stunned, horrified, returning to the previous one, skipping to one farther on, his heart pounding in his chest, feeling that he needed air. He remained on the floor, sitting and holding the twenty or so photographs, looking at them again and again, not believing what he saw. It wasn't possible, it wasn't. No, no. And yet there were the photos, they said it all, they seemed to say even more than what had occurred that night in Chosica and was resurrected now, when he thought he had forgotten about the Yugoslav and what had happened a long time ago.

He felt so upset, so disturbed, that as soon as he stood up he put the pile of photographs on the desk, took off his jacket, loosened his tie, and dropped into his chair, his eyes closed. He was sweating heavily. He tried to calm down, to think clearly, to examine the situation rationally. He couldn't. He thought he might have a heart attack if he couldn't manage to relax. He sat like that for a while with his eyes closed, thinking about his poor mother, about Marisa, his relatives, his partners, his friends, and public opinion. "In this country even the stones know me, damn it." He tried to breathe normally, taking in air through his nose and releasing it through his mouth.

It was blackmail, of course. He had stupidly been the victim of an ambush. But that had happened a couple of years back, maybe more, there in Chosica, how would he not remember? Was that Yugoslav named Kosut? Why had these photos turned up only now? And why by way of this repulsive individual? He had said he would never publish them and wanted no compensation at all and, of course, that was a way of letting him know he planned just the opposite. He insisted he was a man of principles in order to inform him that he was an unscrupulous criminal, determined to rob him blind, to skin him alive, terrifying him with the threat of the scandal. He thought of his mother, that dignified, noble face shattered by surprise and horror. He thought of the reaction of his brothers and sisters if they saw these photographs. And his heart shrank imagining Marisa's livid face even whiter than normal, her mouth open, her eyes the color of the sky, swollen with so much weeping. He wanted to disappear. He had to talk to Luciano immediately. My God, the embarrassment. Wouldn't it be better to consult another lawyer? No, what an idiot, he would never put photos like these in the hands of anyone but Luciano, his classmate, his best friend.

The intercom buzzed and Enrique gave a start in his chair. His secretary reminded him that it was almost eleven and he had a board meeting at the Mining Society. "Yes, yes, have the driver wait for me at the door, I'm coming down now."

He went to the bathroom to wash his face, and as he did so he thought, torturing himself: What would happen if these photos reached all of Lima through one of those papers or magazines that thrived on yellow journalism, bringing into the light of day the dirty secrets of private lives? My God, he had to see Luciano right away; besides being his best friend, his law firm was one of the most prestigious in Lima. What a surprise, and how disappointed in him Luciano would be: he'd always thought that Quique Cárdenas was a model of perfection.

3

Weekend in Miami

As they had agreed, Marisa and Chabela met at Jorge Chávez Airport an hour and a half before the departure of the LAN night flight to Miami. They went to the VIP lounge to have a mineral water while they waited for the plane. Almost all the seats were taken, but they found an isolated table near the bar. Marisa's blond hair, barely held back by a band, was loose and moving freely; she wore no makeup, and her expression was serene. Wearing caramel-colored slacks and moccasins, she carried a large bag of the same color. Chabela, on the other hand, was meticulously made up and wore a pale green skirt, a low-cut blouse, a short leather jacket, and sandals. She wore her black hair twisted into her usual long braid, which hung down her back to her waist.

"How nice that Quique said yes, how wonderful that you can make this trip with me," said Chabela, smiling, as soon as they sat down. "And how pretty you look tonight. Why is that?"

"I thought it would be difficult to get his permission, and I made up all kinds of stories," Marisa said with a laugh, blushing. "On a whim. He just said yes, right then and there, take your trip. The truth is that in the past few days my husband has been a little strange. Distracted, his head in the clouds.

Listen, speaking of pretty, you look terrific too, with that ex-otic braid."

"I know very well what's going on with Quique," said Chabela, suddenly becoming very serious. "It's the same with Luciano, with you, with me, with everybody, baby. With all these blackouts, bombs, kidnappings, and murders every day, who can live peacefully in this city? In this country? It's just as well that at least for this weekend we'll be free of all that. Is there any news yet about Cachito?"

"It seems the kidnappers have demanded six million dol-lars from the family," said Marisa. "A gringo from the insur-ance company has come from New York to negotiate. That poor man disappeared more than two months ago, didn't he?"

"I know Nina, his wife," Chabela agreed. "The poor woman hasn't recovered. She's seeing a psychologist. Do you know what frightens me most, Marisa? It isn't about Luciano or me. It's about my two daughters. I have nightmares think-ing they could be kidnapped."

And she told Marisa that she and Luciano were think-ing about hiring Prosegur, a security company, to guard the house and the family, especially the two girls. But it cost a fortune!

"Quique had the same idea after they kidnapped Cachito," said Marisa. "But we decided not to, we were told it's very dangerous. You hire bodyguards, and then they're the ones who rob you or kidnap you. What a country we were born in, Chabelita!"

"It seems it's even worse in Colombia. There they not only kidnap you, they cut off your fingers or ears and I don't know what other horrors to soften up the family."

"How lucky to spend three days in Miami, away from all this," said Marisa, taking off her sunglasses and looking at her friend, her blue eyes filled with mischief. She saw that Chabela was blushing slightly, and, laughing to cover it up, she took

Marisa's arm and squeezed it. Then Marisa extended her hand, smoothed her friend's hair, and added: "You know that braid looks fantastic on you, don't you, love?"

"I was dying of fear that you wouldn't accept the invitation," murmured Chabela, lowering her voice a little and squeezing Marisa's arm again.

"Not even if I were out of my mind," Marisa exclaimed and dared to make a joke. "You know I love Miami so much!"

She laughed and Chabela followed suit. They laughed for a while, both of them blushing, looking into each other's eyes with complicity and a touch of brazenness, hiding the confusion they felt.

As usual, business class on the LAN flight was full. They had reserved seats in the first row so that they were somewhat separated from the rest of the passengers. Neither of them wanted supper, but they each had a glass of wine. During the five hours of the flight, they talked about many things except what had occurred that night, although some allusion would remind them of it, and then, with a nervous little laugh, they would quickly change the subject. "What is going to happen in Miami?" Marisa wondered, her eyes closed, at times feeling overcome by sleep. "Will we keep avoiding it?" She knew very well they wouldn't, but there was something suggestive, disturbing, something deliciously daring in trying to imagine what would happen and how. Marisa suddenly thought that when they reached Chabela's apartment, she'd like to undo her friend's long braid very slowly, feeling her straight, deep black hair sliding between her fingers, bending down from time to time to kiss it.

They arrived in Miami in the first light of dawn. In the airport, Chabela picked up the car she had rented in Lima, and since there was little traffic at that hour, they soon reached Luciano's apartment in one of the buildings on Brickell Avenue that faced the ocean and Key Biscayne. The doorman in a

uniform and hat and who spoke like a Cuban took their suit-
cases up to the apartment, a penthouse with a panoramic view
of the beach. Marisa had been here once, on her way to New
York, but that had been a few years ago. She thought there
were new paintings on the walls—among them the Lam
they'd had in their house in Lima, as well as another by Soto,
and a drawing by Morales—and that they had redecorated.

"The place looks beautiful, Chabelita," she said. "What a
nice view of the ocean. Let's go out to the terrace."

The doorman had left their bags in the foyer. From the terrace the view at that hour of the morning was superb, with the
uncertain light, the foliage of the trees, the long line of buildings on Key Biscayne, and the white foam of the waves sym-
metrically breaking the bluish green surface of the ocean.

"If you like, let's rest awhile first and then we'll go down
to the beach for a swim," said Chabela, and Marisa, with a
sudden jolt, felt that her friend was speaking into her ear,
emitting warm breath along with her words. She had grasped
her by the hips and was pressing her against her body.

She didn't say anything, but closing her eyes, she leaned to
one side and found the mouth that had started to kiss and
gently nibble her neck, ears, and hair. She raised her hands,
held the braid, and ran her fingers through her friend's hair,
whispering: "Will you let me undo your braid? I want to see
you with your hair undone and to kiss it, darling." Arms entwined, serious now, they left the terrace and, crossing the
living room, dining room, and a hallway, came to Chabela's
bedroom.

The curtains were closed and a discreet half-light filled
the large carpeted room, which had paintings on the walls—
Marisa recognized a Szyszlo, a Chávez, the small Botero, and
etchings by Vasarely—and an attractive night table at either
side of the bed, which looked recently made. As they undressed
each other in silence, they caressed and kissed. It seemed to

Marisa, giddy with excitement and pleasure, that during that frozen, intense time a delicate melody reached them from some-where, as if it had been chosen expressly to serve as background to the atmosphere of abandonment and joy in which she was submerged. They made love to each other and took their plea-sure, and as they did so, outside the room there rose distant voices, motors, horns, the light became more intense, and Marisa even thought the waves were breaking more loudly, and closer than before. Little by little, exhausted, she slipped into sleep. Chabela's braid was undone now and her hair spread over Marisa's face, neck, and breasts.

When she awoke it was day. She felt Chabela's body close to hers; her head was resting not on the pillow but on her friend's shoulder, and her right hand rested on the smooth, flat belly close to hers.

"Good morning, sleepyhead," she heard herself say, and felt her lips brush Chabela's forehead. "Were you dreaming about angels? You were smiling the whole time you slept."

Marisa pressed against Chabela, waking her, kissing her on the neck, caressing her belly and legs with her free hand. "I don't think I've ever felt so happy in my whole life, I swear," she murmured. It was true, that's how she felt. Her friend turned, embracing her, too, and spoke with her mouth pressed against hers, as if she wanted to inlay her words within her body:

"The same for me, love. All this time I've been dreaming that we would sleep together and wake up like this, the way we are now. And I masturbated every night, thinking of you."

They kissed with open mouths, their tongues entangled, swallowing each other's saliva, rubbing their legs together, but they were both too exhausted to make love again. They started to talk, embracing, Marisa's head resting on Chabela's shoulder, one of Chabela's hands entangling her fingers, as if she were playing, in her friend's pubic hair.

"It's true, there is music," said Marisa, listening. "I heard it but thought I was dreaming. Where's it coming from?"

"The girl must have turned it on when she came to clean the apartment," Chabela said into her ear. "Bertola, a very nice Salvadoran, you'll meet her. She's impeccable, she pays the bills, keeps the refrigerator full, and is absolutely trustworthy. Are you hungry? Do you want me to fix you some breakfast?"

"No, not yet, this is delicious, don't get up yet," said Marisa, holding Chabela by the hips. "I like to feel your body. You don't know how happy I am, sweetheart."

"I'm going to tell you a secret, Marisita," and Marisa felt that her friend, as she whispered in her ear, was slowly nibbling at her earlobe. "It's the first time in my life I've made love to a woman."

Marisa lifted her head from Chabela's shoulder to look into her eyes. Chabela was very serious and somewhat embarrassed. She had deep, dark eyes, and very pronounced features, a smooth, unblemished complexion, a mouth with full lips.

"Me, too, Chabela," she murmured. "The first time. Even though you won't believe it."

"Really?" her friend replied, her expression incredulous.

"I swear." Marisa let her head rest on Chabela's neck again. "And that's not all. Shall I tell you something? I had prejudices, when I heard that a woman liked other women, that she was gay, I felt some disgust. How stupid I was."

"I didn't feel disgust so much as curiosity," said Chabela. "But it's true, you don't know yourself until things happen to you. Because the other night, when I woke up and felt your hand on my leg and your body pressing against my back, I was more excited than I had ever been before. Tingling between my legs, my heart jumping out of my mouth, I got all wet. I don't know how I had the courage to take your hand and . . ."

". . . put it here," murmured Marisa, looking for her,

opening her legs, gently rubbing the lips of her sex. "Can I tell you I love you? Do you mind?"

"I love you, too." Chabela tenderly moved her hand away and kissed it. "But don't make me come again or I'll never get out of this bed. Shall I open the curtains? You'll see how nice the ocean looks."

Marisa watched her spring from the bed naked—she confirmed once again that her friend had a young, taut body with no fat at all, a narrow waist, firm breasts—and she watched her open the curtains by pressing a button on the wall. Now a brilliant light poured in that lit the entire room. It was elegant, without excess or affectation, like her house in Lima, like the way Chabela and Luciano dressed and spoke.

"Isn't the view pretty?" Chabela hurried back to the bed and covered herself with the sheet.

"Yes, but you're even prettier, darling," said Marisa, embracing her. "Thank you for the happiest night of my life."

"You made me excited again, you bandit," said Chabela, searching for her mouth, touching her. "And now you'll pay for it."

They got up in the middle of the morning and prepared breakfast in their robes, barefoot, talking. Marisa phoned the office and Enrique said he was fine, but she thought he sounded strange and somewhat melancholy. Chabela couldn't speak to Luciano but she did talk to his mother—she stayed in the house whenever Chabela traveled—and she said that the two girls had left for school on time and would call her as soon as they got back.

"Don't worry about Quique, Marisa," her friend reassured her. "I'm certain that nothing in particular is wrong with him, just what's happening to every Peruvian because of the damn terrorists. Sometimes Luciano has those depressions too, just like Quique. For example, last week he said that if things kept on this way, it would make more sense to leave

Peru. He could go to work in New York, in the office where he trained after graduating from Columbia. But I'm not really convinced. I feel sorry for my mother, who's almost seventy. And I don't know if I'd like my girls to be brought up like two little gringas."

They had a good breakfast, with fruit juice, yogurt, boiled eggs, English muffins, and coffee, and decided to skip lunch and go to a nice restaurant in Miami Beach that night for dinner.

When Marisa asked Chabela what repairs she had to do in the apartment, Chabela burst into laughter:

"None. It was an excuse I invented to take you to Miami."

Marisa took her hand and kissed it. They put on their bathing suits, and armed with towels, creams, sunglasses, and straw hats, they went to the beach to sunbathe. There weren't many people, and though it was very hot, a cool breeze helped to mitigate that.

"What would happen if Luciano found out about this?" Marisa asked her friend.

"He would die," Chabela responded. "My husband is the most conservative, puritanical man in the world. Imagine, to this day he insists on turning off the light when we make love. And what would Quique say?"

"I have no idea," she said. "But I don't believe he'd be all that shocked. As serious as he seems, he has all kinds of dirty ideas in his head. Shall I tell you a secret? Sometimes he tells me that the fantasy that makes him most excited would be to watch me make love with a woman and then do it with him."

"Ah, caramba, perhaps we could please him," Chabela said with a laugh. "Who would have thought it, with the meek little face that husband of yours always puts on."

Then they confessed to each other that they both had been very lucky with their husbands, that they loved them and were happy with them. What they were doing now had to be kept absolutely secret so it wouldn't harm their marriages in any way; instead, it would add spice and keep them lively.

In the afternoon they would go shopping, perhaps see a movie, and have dinner with French champagne in the best restaurant in Miami Beach or Key Biscayne. It would be a truly unforgettable weekend.

4

The Entrepreneur and the Lawyer

The Luciano Casasbellas Law Offices were also in San Isidro, a few blocks from Enrique's office, and, in the past, Enrique would go there on foot, but now, because of the fear of kidnappings by the MRTA and attacks by the Shining Path, he always went by car. The driver left him at the entrance to the offices, which occupied the entire building, and Quique told him to wait. He went directly to the fifth floor, where Luciano's office was located. The secretary said he was expected and could go right in.

Luciano stood to receive him, took him by the arm, and led him to the comfortable easy chairs arranged in front of a bookcase filled with symmetrical leather-bound books behind glass panels. The Persian rug, the portraits and pictures on the office walls were, like Luciano himself, elegant, sober, conservative, vaguely British. There were photos of Chabela and his two daughters in a glass case, and of Luciano himself as a young man in cap and gown on the day of his graduation from Lima's Universidad Católica, and another, more ostentatious one of the ceremony when he received his doctorate at Columbia University. Quique recalled that at the Colegio de la Inmaculada, his friend had been awarded the coveted Prize for Excellence every year.

"It's been weeks since we've seen each other, Quique," said the lawyer, giving his knee an affectionate tap. He had his eyeglasses in his hand and was in shirtsleeves—an impeccably ironed striped shirt—and, as always, he wore a tie and suspenders; his shoes gleamed as if recently polished. He was slim and tall, with light, somewhat slanted eyes, and he had gray hair beginning to recede from his forehead, an omen of premature baldness. "How's the beautiful Marisa?"

"Fine, fine." Enrique returned his smile, thinking: "He's been my best friend since we were in short pants; will he still be my friend after this?" He felt uneasy and embarrassed and his voice sounded uncertain. "I'm the one who's not fine, Luciano. That's why I'm here."

He trembled as he spoke and Luciano, who had become very serious, noticed it. He observed him carefully.

"Everything in this life has a solution, Quique, except death." He encouraged him: "Go on, tell me all about it, as Luciana, my younger daughter, says."

"A few days ago I received an unexpected visit," he stammered, feeling his hands become wet with perspiration. "One Rolando Garro."

"The reporter?" Luciano was surprised. "It couldn't have been for anything good. That guy has an awful reputation."

Enrique recounted the visit in full detail. At times he fell silent, searching for the least compromising word, and Luciano waited, silent and patient, not hurrying him. Finally, Enrique took from his briefcase the portfolio with the two yellow bands. After handing it to Luciano, he took out his handkerchief and wiped his hands and his forehead. He was drenched in sweat and breathed with difficulty.

"You have no idea how I hesitated about coming here, Luciano," he excused himself, head lowered. "I'm embarrassed and disgusted with myself. But this is so personal, so delicate, that the truth is I didn't know what to do. Who else can I trust? You're like a brother to me."

His voice broke and he thought in astonishment that he was about to burst into tears. Luciano, leaning over the table, poured him some water from a glass pitcher.

"Calm down, Quique," he said affectionately, patting him on the shoulder. "Of course you did just the right thing coming to see me. No matter how terrible the matter is, we'll find a solution. You'll see."

"I hope you don't despise me after this, Luciano," Quique murmured. And, pointing at the portfolio, he said, "You're in for a big surprise, I'm warning you. Go on, open it."

"A lawyer is like a confessor, old man," said Luciano, putting on his glasses. "Don't worry. My profession has prepared me for everything—good, bad, and worse."

Enrique watched him open the portfolio carefully, pulling off the yellow bands and then the paper around the photographs. He saw how Luciano's face contracted a little in surprise and then, suddenly, turned pale. He didn't take his eyes away from the images to look at Enrique or make any comments while he slowly reviewed the scandalous pieces of cardboard, one by one. Quique felt his heart pounding inside his chest. Time had stopped. He remembered, when they were boys and studied together for exams, that Luciano concentrated on the books as he was doing now, pouring himself body and soul into what he was seeing. Mute and methodical, he looked through the photos again, from back to front. Finally he raised his head, looking at him with troubled eyes, and asked in a neutral voice:

"There's no doubt this is you, Quique?"

"It's me, Luciano. I'm sorry, but yes, it's me."

The lawyer was very serious; he nodded and seemed to be thinking. He took off his glasses and gave him another affectionate tap on the knee.

"It's blackmail, that's very clear," he finally declared, while, playing for time, he carefully rewrapped the photographs in tissue paper, placed them in the portfolio, and closed it with the yellow rubber bands. "They want money from you. But they wanted to soften you up first, scaring you with the threat of a huge scandal. Will you leave this with me? It's better if I keep it here, in the safe. It's not a good idea for this to fall into anyone's hands, especially Marisa's."

Enrique nodded. He took another sip of water. Suddenly he felt relieved, as if getting rid of those images, knowing they'd be kept in Luciano's office safe, had lessened the potential threat they contained.

"They were taken a couple of years ago," he specified. "More or less, I don't really remember the date, perhaps a little longer ago than that. In Chosica. Everything was organized by the Yugoslav, I think I spoke to you about him. Serbian or Croatian, something like that. His name was Kosut. Do you remember?"

"A Yugoslav? Kosut?" Luciano shook his head. "No, I don't. Did I meet him?"

"I think I introduced him to you, I'm not really sure," Quique added. "Serbian or Croatian, at least that's what he said. He wanted to invest in mines, he had letters of recommendation from Chase Manhattan and from the Lombard Bank. It's coming back to me now. Kosak, Kusak, Kosut, something like that. I must have his card somewhere. A strange, mysterious guy who suddenly disappeared. I never heard anything more about him. Are you sure you don't remember?"

"I'm sure I don't," Luciano declared. And he confronted him, speaking with severity: "He arranged the orgy? He took these pictures?"

"I don't know," said Quique. "I don't know who took them. I wasn't aware of anything, as you can imagine. I never would have allowed it. But yes, I suppose he was the one. He was there, too. Kosak, Kusak, Kosut, one of those Central European names, something like that."

"He set a trap for you and you fell in like a little angel, not to mention an ass." Luciano shrugged. "Two years ago, are you sure? And he shows up only now?"

"I thought about that, too," said Enrique. "After two or two and a half years at least. He spent several months in Lima, living in the Hotel Sheraton. I introduced him to some people. Then, one day he left me a note saying it was urgent that he go to New York and he'd be back in Lima soon. I never heard from him again. He had millions of dollars to invest, he said. I was helping him, I took him to the Mining Society, he gave a little talk. He spoke good Spanish, too. He didn't seem like a gangster or anything. I mean, Luciano, I don't know what to tell you. I was an imbecile, of course. Besides, even if you don't believe me, it was the first and last time that I . . ."

His voice broke and he didn't know how to finish the sentence. His face burned, he blinked constantly, and he felt so ashamed that he wanted to run out and never see his best friend again.

"Take it easy, Quique," Luciano said with a smile. "In these kinds of cases, the most important thing is to keep a cool head. Do you want another glass of water?"

"It took me so much by surprise," said Enrique. "As soon as I saw that reporter, I was disgusted. There's something repulsive about him, his fawning manner, his little rat's eyes. This can only be blackmail. Of course that's what I thought."

"He brought you the photographs to frighten you about a scandal," Luciano agreed. "I see he's succeeded. For the moment, I'll tell you that the worst thing would be for you to start negotiating with people like that. They'll get money from you over and over again, they'll never give you all the negatives of those photographs. It'll never end. The first thing that occurs to me is to give the reporter a good scare. But that dog must be only an intermediary, a tool. Yugoslav, did you say?"

"Kosuk, Kosok, or Kosut," Quique repeated. "I must have his card, copies of the recommendations he brought. He wanted to invest in mines, he was looking for Peruvian partners. He gave lunches and spent lavishly, as if he were very rich. Then, without warning, the note saying it was urgent that he leave for New York. And he disappeared. Now he comes back to life with these photos. Two or two and a half years later. It doesn't make any sense, does it?"

Luciano had become thoughtful and Enrique stopped talking.

"What are you thinking, Luciano?"

"Was there anyone else besides him and the girls at that little party?" he asked. "I mean, anyone you knew."

"Just him and me," Quique declared. "And the girls, of course."

"And the photographer," Luciano corrected him. "Didn't you realize you were being photographed?"

"I never would have allowed it," Quique protested again. "I wasn't aware of anything. It was very well prepared. It didn't occur to me it could be a trap. Can you imagine what would happen if those photos appeared in *Exposed*? I'm sure you've never even looked through that rag. A puddle of filth, of gossip, of despicable things. A scandal sheet of pestilential vulgarity."

"Yes, I've seen it occasionally, I must have," said Luciano. "Look, here in the firm we have two magnificent criminal lawyers. Let me talk to them, maintaining absolute discretion, of course. I'll present the matter to them and see what they think. I'll do it this afternoon. And I'll call you. In the meantime, try to stay calm. Don't even think about saying anything to anybody. If necessary we'll go all the way to Fujimori. Or to

Dr. Montesinos himself. And, naturally, don't see Garro again. Don't even talk to him on the phone."

He stood and accompanied him to the door. There they exchanged conventional phrases about Marisa and Chabela, who, apparently, seemed very happy with their little weekend jaunt to Miami. They all had to get together and go out one of these days, Luciano repeated, as if nothing had changed between them. Of course, of course.

Enrique left Luciano's office more dejected than when he came in. He felt sad, convinced that in his life things would never be as they had been before that horrifying visit.

5

The Den of Gossip

"I asked for monstrous tits, a belly, an enormous ass." Rolando Garro was angry, shaking the photographs as if about to throw them into the face of the intimidated photographer, who took a step back. "And you bring me a fine-looking young lady. You didn't understand me, Ceferino. Was what I said so difficult that your tiny little brain couldn't get it?"

"I'm sorry, señor," stammered Ceferino Argüello. The photographer for *Exposed* was an ageless, skinny mestizo crammed into old blue jeans and a pair of rubber flip-flops, with lank, straight hair that fell to his shoulders, and heavy eyebrows. He looked at the editor of the magazine with nervous eyes, dying of fear. "I can go back to the show tonight and take some others for you, señor."

Garro didn't seem to have heard him. He attacked him with his stare and the fury in his voice.

"I'm going to explain it to you again and see if this time the subject gets into that brontosaurus head of yours," he said with muffled rage. From his desk he dominated the entire small room that was the editorial office of the magazine, in a big old two-story house on Calle Dante, in Surquillo, and he could observe that the half dozen editors and reporters all had their heads buried in their computers or papers; none of them, not even Estrellita Santibáñez, the nosiest of them all, even dared to turn their eyes to spy on the hard time he was giving the photographer. At that hour of the morning there was already the noise of trucks, the shouts of peddlers, and an intense going and coming of pedestrians in the area around the nearby market.

"Of course, I understand you very well, señor," the photographer murmured. "I give you my word I do."

"No! You didn't understand a thing!" Rolando Garro shouted, and Ceferino Argüello moved back another step. "It isn't a question of giving her publicity or raising the one-eyed cow's fees. It's a question of sinking and defeating her, of discrediting her forever. It's a question of their throwing her out of the show because she's ugly and old and can't move her ass. These pictures are going to illustrate an article where we say that the one-eyed cow is turning the show at the Monumental into a hodge-podge that nobody can stand. Because besides not knowing how to dance or sing, she's turned into a hideous monster and doesn't belong on the stage; she belongs in horror movies. Do you understand or don't you get it yet?"

"Of course I understand, señor," the photographer repeated. He was livid and could barely speak, and it was obvious he wanted to get out of there right away. "I swear on my mother I do."

"Fine." The editor threw the photos in his hand to the floor. He pointed at them and said to Ceferino Argüello, "Throw this trash in the trash, please."

He saw the photographer squat down to pick them up, and then awkwardly withdraw. Total silence reigned in the crowded space, which must have been the house's dining room before it was transformed into the editorial office of a weekly magazine. Because of the lack of space, the rough desks touched one another, and the peeling walls were crowded with faded covers of old issues of *Exposed*, with spectacular

nudes and shrieking headlines. Rolando Garro sat down
again at his desk, which was up on a platform, affording him
a complete view of all the personnel. He tried to calm down.
Why did the bad photos of the one-eyed cow irritate him so
much? Had he been too hard on poor Argüello, who, without
realizing it or meaning to, had performed a great service by
bringing him the photos from Chosica? Maybe. He had humiliated him in front of the entire office. Anybody with a little
dignity would have quit. But he was too poor to afford the
luxury of dignity, and besides, he was probably married with
kids, so he'd swallow the humiliation and stay at *Exposed* because the pittance he earned here was what allowed him to
survive. True, he'd hate him a little more. On the other hand,
the question of the photos from Chosica kept Ceferino tied to
him. Bah, he said to himself, amused; if things went well, he'd
give him a nice present. That people hated him wasn't anything that kept Rolando Garro awake. It even gave him a
certain satisfaction: being hated meant being feared, being
acknowledged. Something that Peruvians did very well: lick-
ing the boots that kicked them. The proof: Fujimori and the
Doctor. Well, forget about the broken-down Ceferino and get
to work.

In fact, he was angry not with him but with the one-eyed
cow. Why? Because he had seen and heard her on television a
couple of months ago, on a program as popular as Magaly's,
no less, saying it was a shame that magazines like *Exposed*
existed, where artists were subjected to campaigns designed
to discredit them and to slanders concerning their private
lives. And the one-eyed cow said all this while widening her
big bulging eyes and vigorously denying that the police had
found her making love to some guy in a taxi, as the yellow-press
magazine of Señor Rolando Garro had stated. He imagined
the one-eyed cow naked in an old jalopy; he imagined screw-
ing a piece of human garbage like her. Sickening! Who was

the poor bastard whose cock wound up inside a fat pig like her? From that day on, he had it in his head to wreck her life and make her lose her job. But he needed a good investigation to finish her off. That was taken care of. The woman he called Shorty had done some excellent research, as always. The world would fall down around the cow's ears, they'd throw her out, and she'd have to work as a whore to keep from starving to death. Garro had warned the administrator of the Monumental, spelling it out for him: "As long as you keep the one-eyed cow dancing in the show, I'll make things hot for you, compadre." It was a formula that made scriptwriters for radio and television tremble, not to mention producers and dancers in music hall shows or on the small screen, and of course, all the animal life that the one-eyed cow called "artists."

He stood up and called Julieta Leguizamón. Shorty was so small that, seen from the back, anyone would have taken her for a child. She was dark, with kinky hair, always dressed in sweatpants or jeans, a wrinkled blouse, and basketball sneakers, skinny and frail, but still there was something impressive about her: her big eyes were incisive and intelligent, imbued with a strange immobility and fearlessness, which Rolando Garro thought he had seen only in certain animals. They seemed to bore into people, making them feel uncomfortable, as if all their shame were visible to anyone looking at them.

"How's the article coming along, Shorty?"

"It's coming, I don't have much left to do," she said, staring at him with those eyes that never blinked, that were generally cold with everybody except him, for Shorty evinced a doglike devotion to Rolando. "Don't worry; I've found out lots of new things about One-Eye. They'll make life pretty hot for her, I swear. When she was young she was in reform school for some minor crime. It's false that she was a professional singer and dancer in Mexico. There's no proof. She's had two abortions with a very popular midwife, a black woman I know from Five Corners. They call her Dreamer, just imagine. And, best of all, One-Eye's daughter is in the women's prison for trafficking drugs."

"That's terrific, Shorty." Rolando patted his star reporter on the arm. "More than enough material to send her to hell."

"I'm almost finished." Shorty smiled at him and went back to her desk.

"She always comes through," Rolando thought, watching her sit down in the chair to which she had added a cushion so she would reach the top of the desk. Shorty was his great discovery. She had showed up at the magazine a couple of years back in frayed jeans, her sneakers with no laces, and some handwritten sheets that, with no preamble, she handed to him as she boldly said: "I want to be a reporter and work at *Exposed*, señor." Rolando asked about her credentials: where she had studied and past work experience in the field.

"I don't have any," Shorty confessed. "I brought you this piece that I wrote. Read it, please."

There was something about her that he liked, and he read it. In those four pages dedicated to a television star, there was so much poison and animosity, so much spite, that Garro was impressed. He began to give her small jobs, inquiries, follow-ups, minor tasks. Julieta never disappointed him. She was a born reporter of his stripe, capable of killing her mother for a scoop, especially if it was dirty and salacious. Her article on the one-eyed cow would be brilliant and lethal, because Shorty always adopted as her own the phobias and predilections of her editor.

He began to diagram the next issue of *Exposed* with the material he had. He still had twenty-four hours to take all of it to the printer, but it was better to do a little work in advance so that the last day, the day the magazine closed, wouldn't be the usual madhouse. But it would be, no way around it, inevitably there were last-minute things to change or add to what had been planned.

How old was Rolando Garro? Garro didn't know, and probably no one else did either. Or what his real surname was. In the orphanage where his mother had abandoned him, they named him Lázaro because, apparently, it was on San Lázaro Day that nuns from the Convent of Las Descalzas found him whimpering on the ground at the entrance to the institution they administered at the corner of Junín and Huánuco Alleyways, in the Barrios Altos district of Lima. Albino and Luisa Torres, who adopted him, didn't like the name and changed it to Rolando. He remembered having been named Rolando Torres as a child, but at a certain point and for mysterious reasons, his surname was changed and he began to be called Rolando Garro. That was the name on his identity card and his passport. He didn't think about his mysterious origins much except in extraordinary circumstances; for example, the days in his house in Chorrillos when he had to take the pills that sedated him and made him sleep for ten hours straight (he awoke as confused and bewildered as a zombie). He tried not to take them except on days when he was perturbed or depressed, but the psychiatrist had told him that, given his devilish psychological constitution, those states of mind were not a good idea, for he ran the risk of really going crazy or becoming permanently withdrawn. What would happen if he lost his mind? He would have to live like a beggar on the streets of Lima. Because Rolando, ever since he had run away from his adoptive parents when they told him he wasn't their biological son but that they had found him in an orphanage, had been as solitary as a toadstool. And surely he would continue that way for as long as he lived, for although he'd had some adventures with women, he had never been able to maintain a stable relationship with any of them: they all broke it off because of his perverse character, unless he was the one who sent them on their way first.

His adoptive parents revealed that he had been an abandoned baby when he was in the fifth year of secondary school at the Colegio Nacional Ricardo Palma, in Surquillo, right here, not far from where *Exposed* was located. That night he ran away from home, stealing all the money his adoptive father kept hidden in his bedroom in a leather briefcase, hidden behind a loose brick. A little more than six hundred soles allowed him to sleep for a few days in run-down boardinghouses in the center of Lima. To survive he took every possible kind of job, from washing cars in parking lots to unloading trucks in La Parada Market. One day he found his vocation at the same time that he discovered his talent: journalistic blabbermouth.

It happened in a boardinghouse on Ocoña Avenue where he would have lunch for a few soles; it was a fixed menu: soup, rice and beans, and compote. A reporter from *Late News* whom he would see in the dining room told him he was tracking down a possible adultery involving Sandra Montero and her partner in crime Felipe Cailloma, about which contradictory rumors were flying in the world of show business. Wouldn't he like to give him a hand? His instinct told Rolando it would be a good idea. He said yes. He stationed himself like a guard dog at the door of the building where the female television host and entertainer lived, and in less than twenty-four hours he had followed Sandra and discovered that she was meeting Felipe (they were both married to other people, so they were committing a double adultery) at a house of assignation in Pueblo Libre, at a corner of the Plaza Bolívar. The information allowed *Late News* to photograph the adulterers in their underwear.

This was how the journalistic career of Rolando Garro

had begun: as a tipster on scandals for *Late News*, the paper
that, with Raúl Villarán at its head, introduced yellow journalism to Peru. He moved from informant to a reporter who
specialized in show business, that is, the gossip and scandals
kept alive in the world of showgirls, minor singers, radio ac-
tresses and actors, owners of cabarets, music hall impresarios,
and dancers in parades, a form of life that Rolando Garro, as
he moved up and became a columnist, a director of radio and
then television programs, had come to know like the palm of
his hand: to use as he pleased and help to ruin without pity.
He had a public delighted to follow his revelations, accusing
singers and musicians of being faggots, his morbid explorations
of the private lives of public persons, his "first fruits" exposing
the base and shameful acts that he always exaggerated and at
times invented. He succeeded in everything he undertook. But
he never stayed too long with any one thing, because the scandals, the great secret of his popularity—he found them out or
provoked them—usually got him into judicial, police, and
personal trouble that he sometimes emerged from the worse
for wear. The directors of newspapers, radio stations, and
television channels eventually threw him out because of the
protests and threats they received and because Garro was capable at times, in the frenetic performance of his duties, of
making them the victims of the very scandals he fostered and
stirred up. Sometimes he earned a great deal of money, which
he squandered with both hands and then he lived, down and
out, on his scant savings, and sometimes on the street. He
didn't have friends, he had transient accomplices, and, of
course, masses of enemies, which meant he lived in a state
of permanent turmoil that did not fail to flatter his vanity.

   Exposed had already lasted three years. Things were going
well for him now, people said it was thanks to the Doctor,
who, according to the rumors, had become a Maecenas to the
weekly, the secret master of its rather marginal existence. The

magazine was a relative success as far as sales were concerned but had almost no advertisements, so it could barely pay its expenses. Rolando Garro increased his personal income by extorting showgirls and producers with threats to reveal their secret peccadilloes, and receiving money from people who wanted to harm other people—competitors and enemies—by discrediting and ridiculing them. Many suits had been filed against him, but he had survived all those risks, which he considered inherent to the type of journalism he practiced and in which, no doubt, he had achieved a twisted kind of brilliance.

But all that was nothing compared with what, thanks to Shorty and the poor wretch Ceferino Argüello, he now had in his hands. He closed his eyes and remembered the shocked face of the engineer Enrique Cárdenas when he handed him the package of photographs. He had always thought that some-day an opportunity would make him famous, powerful, rich, and perhaps all three at the same time. And he was sure this was the marvelous gift from the gods that had finally fallen from heaven into his hands.

"I finished the article, boss. One-Eye will shit fire," said Shorty, handing him some pages and staring at him with those eyes that emitted a cheerful, cold wickedness.

6

A Wreck of Show Business

Juan Peineta walked out of the Hotel Mogollón, on the third block of Huallaga Concourse, followed by Serafín. It was still early and the center of Lima was half deserted. He saw street sweepers, emollient peddlers—"relics of a past time," he imagined—night owls after a long night, and the usual beggars and vagrants dozing at the corners and in doorways. Some early-rising turkey buzzards picked at the garbage scattered on the street, cawing. He tried one more time to remember what his name had been when he was very young, before he began to use the artist's surname that everyone knew him by (well, back when he was known): Was it Roberto Arévalo? No, nothing like that. He still had some papers in the pile of documents that he kept in a cardboard box in his small room at the Mogollón, his birth certificate, for example, with his old name, but he didn't want to read it, he wanted to remember it. He had been struggling against this forgetfulness. His memory failed so often that he dedicated a good part of his time to what he was doing now: trying to fish, in the confused mess his head had turned into, for some lost word, some indistinct faces, names, anecdotes. The only thing he never forgot was the name Felipe Pinglo, the immortal bard, one of his idols since he was a boy, and the name Rolando Garro, the man who had ruined his life; for that reason, two or three times a week, he wrote notes attacking him to the papers, radio stations, and magazines, which rarely published them. But he had made himself known through those persistent notes, and in the world of show business, everyone laughed at him.

They had reached the corner of Emancipación, and Serafín, as he always did at streets and avenues with heavy traffic, stopped and waited for Juan to pick him up. Juan did, carried him across the avenue, and deposited him on the ground on the other side. His relations with Serafín were some three years old. "The years of my decline," he thought. No, his real decline—changing his job, betraying his vocation—came from further back, ten years at least, perhaps more. One day he went into his room in the Hotel Mogollón—well, calling it a room was a great exaggeration, it was a hole, really, a den— and he saw a cat lying on his bed. The one small window in the room was open. That's how the cat got in. "Out, out!" He shooed him away with his hands, and the cat, frightened, jumped to the floor; then Juan noticed that the animal could barely walk; he dragged his hind legs as if they were lifeless. And half stretched out on the floor, he had begun to cry the way cats cry, with long, low meows. He felt sorry for the animal, picked it up, put it on the bed, and even shared the little bottle of milk he drank at night before going to sleep. The next day he took him to the Municipal Veterinary Clinic, which was free. The veterinarian who examined the animal said that the kitten's legs weren't broken, only bruised by a blow he had received, perhaps from those street urchins who amused themselves using their slingshots to stone stray animals in Lima; he'd be better soon, with no need for remedies or splints. That was when, after naming him Serafín—for Serafín Álvarez Quintero, a poet who was one of his specialties when he was a professional reciter of poetry—he adopted him. The little cat became his companion and friend. A very special companion, of course, a libertine; at times he would disappear for several days and then return suddenly as if nothing had happened. Juan Peineta would always leave the small window in his dismal little room open so that the cat could come and go as he wished.

A strange little animal, Serafín. Juan Peineta had never been able to tell whether the cat loved him or was indifferent to him. Perhaps he loved him the way cats love, that is, without the slightest sign of sentiment. At times he would curl up in his arms, but it wasn't a demonstration of affection; the fact was he was enjoying his greatest pleasure: having Juan scratch his neck and belly. Sometimes he would recite what remained in his memory of the old poems from his repertoire: José Santos Chocano, Amado Nervo, Gustavo Adolfo Bécquer, Juan de Dios Peza, Juana de Ibarbourou, Gabriela Mistral—remnants of poems that hadn't wandered away from his mind—and usually Serafín would listen with an attention that moved him, "an attention equivalent to applause," he told himself. But at other times, with an indifference that resembled scorn, Serafín would turn away and leave him reciting to ghosts while the cat applied himself to smoothing his whiskers and falling asleep. "He's an egoist and ungrateful," Juan Peineta thought. Yes, no doubt about it, but he'd become fond of him. In fact, he was the only living creature for whom he felt affection—that is, except for Willy the Ruletero and fat Crecilda, another victim of the slanderous Rolando Garro—because all the others had been dying and leaving him more alone with each passing day. "That's what you are, Juan Peineta," he repeated to himself for the hundredth time: "an orphan."

What he did remember very clearly was his old love for the genius of Peruvian song, Felipe Pinglo, and his own age: seventy-nine. There he was, resisting the avalanche of time. Unfortunate, perhaps, but healthy, his only ailments those inherent to his age—some deafness; poor vision; dead sex; a slow, uncertain step; a cold or flu in the winter—nothing to worry about from the physical point of view, though mentally his memory was worse each day, and it wasn't impossible that he would end up transformed into a phantom of himself, not knowing who he was, or what his name was, or where he was. He laughed when he was alone: "What a sad ending for the famous Juan Peineta!"

Had he been famous? In a certain sense he had, especially during the time when he recited in coliseums, between performances of folkloric dances and singers. The applause was enormous after they heard Bécquer's "The Dark Swallows Will Return," Chocano's "He was a sad Inca with a dreaming brow, / ever sleeping eyes, and a smile of bitter gall," Neruda's "Tonight I can write the saddest verses," or "I like it when you're silent because it's as if you were absent," or the lyrics to the waltzes of Felipe Pinglo, his specialty. They would ask for his autograph. "Señor Poet," they called him, but he corrected them right away with the modesty that always characterized him: "Not a poet, señora, just a reciter." He also recited on the radio, though never on television, the mortal enemy of poetry. At times he had recited in private homes, at parties or receptions—first communions, weddings, birthdays, funerals— occasions when they tended to pay him very well. But Juan had never cared too much about earning money; what he liked was reciting, transmitting the words of poets, those sensitive geniuses, such beautiful sentiments accompanied by the lilting music of good poetry. He recalled that at times he recited with so much emotion that his eyes would fill with tears.

He had inherited his love and unbounded admiration for Felipe Pinglo from his father, who knew Pinglo and even was his companion at musical gatherings and songfests of the bard, who in his brief life—born in 1899, he died at the age of thirty-seven—had elevated Peruvian music with his compositions to heights not attained by the waltz, the polka, or the *marinera* or *tondero* folk dances either before or after his

prolific existence. Juan had known him only through the stories and anecdotes of his father, who, in spite of not being a
singer or playing any instrument, had been part of the bohe-
mian life and Peruvian songfests in Barrios Altos. There, in that
neighborhood, Felipe Pinglo had thought up a good number
of the compositions that would make him famous. Juan's
father told him that he had been in the Alfonso XIII Theater
in Callao in 1930 when the singer Alcides Carreño gave the first
performance of Pinglo's most famous waltz, "El Plebeyo."
When Juan Peineta and Atanasia were married, they went to
lay the bride's bouquet of gardenias at the foot of the statue
that immortalized the Peruvian bard in front of the little
house where he had been born, on the fourteenth block of
Junín Alleyway, a few steps from Five Corners, the navel of
Barrios Altos. When he died, Felipe Pinglo had left some three
hundred waltzes and polkas. Juan Peineta knew a good number of them by heart, and he had copied many others into a
thick student notebook. A source of artistic pride had been
including in his reciter's repertoire some texts of the waltzes
of Felipe Pinglo, who, in his opinion—he always said this to
the audience before reciting—was as great a poet as he was a
musician and composer. The truth is that Juan had a good
deal of success reciting, as if they were poems without music,
the lyrics of "Hermelinda," "El plebeyo," "La oración del
labriego," "Rosa Luz," "De vuelta al barrio," and "Amelia,"
Pinglo's first well-known song, composed when he was still a
boy. Before reciting their lyrics, he would entertain the audience by recounting anecdotes (both true and invented) about
the immortal bard: his sad, sickly life, his poverty, the modesty
of his daily existence, the way he introduced cadences from
the North American fox-trot and the one-step, which were
very popular at the time, into Peruvian music and, above all,
that the first musical instrument he played was the harmonica
and how, because he was left-handed, he had to play the guitar

backward, which, he said, had allowed him to discover new tonalities and accents for his compositions.

Juan Peineta had met Atanasia while he was reciting. He didn't like to think about Atanasia, because he lost control of his feelings, became sad and depressed, and none of that was good for his health. But now it was difficult to remove Atanasia from his memory: there she was, in the first row at the Club Apurímac de Lima, in her little gray skirt, her green blouse, her white shoes, listening to him with fervor and applauding madly. She had eyes that gave off sparks; when she laughed, she had dimples in her cheeks and you could see her small, even teeth. After his number he had introduced himself to her, and she said she was a telephone operator at the Central Post Office in Lima, single, and not seeing anyone. The party at the Apurímac went on for a while, they drank, danced to waltzes, boleros, a few *huaynitos*, and this was the beginning of the relationship that would end in their engagement and a marriage that had lasted for many years. Juan Peineta felt that fat tears had begun to run down the wrinkles in his face. This usually happened when Atanasia, taking advantage of some carelessness on his part, suddenly got into his head.

He reached the Church of the Nazarenes, and Serafín, who knew that cats were not allowed in the church—the pious old women there had made his life very difficult—immediately climbed the little tree at the entrance to wait for him. Mass hadn't begun and Juan sat in the first row—there weren't very many people yet—and, saddened by the memory of Atanasia, dozed off. A little bell awakened him. They were reading the gospel of the day, and he wondered whether being tardy to the service would be acceptable in the eyes of God, or have no effect at all on the balance sheet of good and bad deeds that would decide his future in the next life. He had been very Catholic ever since he was a boy, but his religiosity had increased substantially with old age and forgetfulness. He had always gone to Mass on Sundays; now he also went to processions, rosaries, rogations, and the holy sermons on Friday in the parish church of the Good Death.

When he left the church, Serafín appeared, wrapping himself around his feet. During his return to the Hotel Mogollón—some three-quarters of an hour at his prudent, very slow pace—he thought about the episode of *The Three Jokers*, a key moment in his artistic career. Like everyone else in Lima, he knew the program. Atanasia and he would watch it on Saturday nights in the small house in Mendocita where they had lived since their marriage. With what he earned through his recitals and her salary as a telephone operator, they had been able to rent this house, which Atanasia arranged and furnished with her invariable good taste. Things were going pretty well for Juan as far as contracts were concerned; he always had performances at clubs in the district, at a few Peruvian-music clubs, and sometimes even in a nightclub. Moreover, he kept his little weekly program, *The Poetry Hour*, on Radio Libertad. He liked his work, and since his marriage to Atanasia, he had been happy. At night, when he prayed, he thanked God for being so generous to him.

It was a great surprise when the manager of Radio Libertad told him that América Television had called, asking for him. And had left an urgent message for him to call the producer, no less a personage than Don Celonio Ferrero, the magician and master of the small screen, who invited him to take some refreshment with him in a cafeteria near the television station. Señor Celonio Ferrero was tall and well dressed, wearing a waistcoat, tie, and rings; his nails were buffed, his watch gleamed with diamond chips, and he was so sure of himself that Juan Peineta felt constrained and dwarfed next to that demigod.

"I don't have much time, Juan Peineta, my friend, so I'll get right to the point," he said as soon as they sat down and had ordered two coffees. "Tiburcio, one of the Three Jokers, is dying. Cancer of the liver. Bad luck, poor man. Or maybe too much alcohol. So young. He'll be able to work only until the end of the month. A problem, because he's left me with an opening in the most popular program on Peruvian television. Do you want to replace him?"

Surprise made Juan Peineta's jaw drop. Was he suggesting that he, an artist of poetry, replace a vulgar and utterly tasteless clown?

"Close your mouth before a fly goes in," Señor Celonio Ferrero said with a laugh, giving him a little pat. "Yes, I know, my offer is like winning the lottery. But I've got it in my head that you are the ideal person to replace that mestizo Tiburcio. These intuitions of mine are never wrong. I heard you recite not too long ago at the Club Arequipa, and I laughed out loud. That's when I told myself: 'This guy could be one of my Three Jokers.'"

Juan Peineta was so offended, he felt like standing and telling this arrogant man that he was an artist and his proposal had wounded his professional honor, and end the conversation then and there. But Don Celonio Ferrero beat him to it:

"I'm sorry, my friend, but I don't have much time," he repeated, consulting his aerodynamic watch. "I'm offering ten thousand soles a month to start. If you work out, we can talk about a raise, if you don't work out, our agreement ends after the fourth week. I'll give you a couple of days to think it over. It's been a pleasure to meet you and shake your hand, Señor Juan Peineta."

He paid the bill, and Juan watched him walk away with long strides toward the television station. Ten thousand a month? Had he heard correctly? Yes, that's what he had said. Juan had never seen so much money. Ten thousand a month? He went back home, his head in a whirl, knowing deep down that it would be impossible not to accept a job that would pay him a fortune like that.

"That was when you ruined your career as an artist," he thought once again, as he had been doing for many years. "You sold yourself out of greed, you renounced poetry for playing the clown, you stabbed art out of sheer avarice. That's when your decline began."

They had reached the Hotel Mogollón in time to sit down in the small lounge at the entrance, next to Sóceles, the hotel guard, to listen to Radio Popular and the nastiness and venom of Rolando Garro on his program *Red Hot: Truth and Lies About Show Business*.

Before he went to sleep, Juan Peineta wrote a letter in his tremulous, tortuous hand to Radio Popular, protesting in his own name and in the name of many listeners the "pestilential vulgarity that the man named Rolando Garro vomits in his program; he should more appropriately be called the Slanderous Gossipmonger. How shameless, what a discredit to the station!" He signed his name and placed the letter in an envelope. He'd mail it tomorrow.

7

Quique's Agony

"Something's wrong with you, darling, something very serious," Marisa said to him. "I'm sorry, but you have to tell me about it."

"Nothing's wrong, Blondie." He tried to reassure her, forcing a smile. "Like everybody else, I'm concerned about the nightmare we're living in this country, that's all."

"We've had terrorism in Peru for a long time," she insisted. "I may be a fool, but not as big a fool as you think, Quique. You're not eating, you're not sleeping, you're falling apart. Just yesterday your mother said to me: 'Enrique's getting very thin; has he been to see the doctor?' What's going on? I'm your wife, aren't I? I can help you. Whatever it is, you have to tell me."

They were eating breakfast on the covered terrace of the penthouse in San Isidro, she in robe and slippers, and Enrique already showered, shaved, and dressed, ready to leave for the office. There was fog, and you couldn't see the ocean in the distance, or the gardens of the Golf Club at the foot of their building. The orange juice, boiled egg, buttered toast, and marmalade that Quintanilla, the butler, had set in Quique's place were untouched; he'd had only a cup of coffee. He saw Marisa's face twist with worry; he saw her blue eyes shining as if she were about to cry, and he felt sorry for his wife. He approached her and kissed her cheek. Marisa put her arms around his neck.

"Tell me, Quique," she pleaded. "Whatever it is, tell me about it, sweetheart. Let me share it with you, help you. I love you."

"I love you, too, Marisa darling." He embraced her. "I don't like to alarm you. But, well, since you insist, I'll tell you about it."

Marisa moved away from him, and Enrique saw that his wife had grown pale; her lips were trembling. Mechanically, she arranged her blond hair and looked at him with wide eyes, waiting. In his confusion, he said to her: "You look as beautiful as ever, more than ever. It must be the first time since we married that we haven't made love for ten days.

"Nothing's happened yet, but something might." As he spoke, very slowly, he searched eagerly for what to invent. "I've received threats, Blondie. Anonymous ones, of course."

"From terrorists?" she stammered. "From the Shining Path? From the MRTA?"

"I don't know yet. Perhaps from terrorists, that's possible. Or common criminals. They want money, of course. But don't be frightened. I've consulted Luciano, we're taking steps to see what it's about. For the sake of what you love best, don't say a word to anyone, darling. It might be much worse if word about this gets out."

"How much have they asked for?" she asked.

"They haven't told me an amount, not yet," he said. "Just threats for the moment. I swear that from now on I'll keep you up to date on everything. Besides, it might be a bad joke from some lowlife who wants to sour our lives."

"Have you gone to the police?" Marisa had taken his hand and was pressing it. "Have you reported it to them? They ought to give us protection, you especially. You can't expose yourself this way, Quique. My God, I knew that sooner or later what happened to Cachito would happen to us."

"Now you're the one who's frightened," he said, caressing her cheek. "Do you see why I didn't want to say anything to you, Blondie?"

He looked at his watch: 8:15. He stood up.

"I have an appointment with Luciano precisely to talk about this," he said, kissing the top of her head. "I beg you not to worry, Marisa. Nothing's going to happen, I swear. I'll keep you in the loop about everything, I promise."

He went down to the garage. The driver was waiting for him, he got into his car, and when they drove out to the street they encountered one of those gray overcast days typical of Lima's winter; the dampness blurred the windows of the Mercedes-Benz, and made his clothing feel wet. Enrique had the impression it was entering every pore of his body. On the Zanjón, traffic was already very heavy. Had he done the right thing telling Marisa those lies? Well, perhaps they weren't lies. Maybe that lout of a reporter was connected to the Shining Path or the MRTA. Anything was possible. Agustín, the chauffeur, drove with his usual prudence, and Enrique's mind was elsewhere, hypnotically concentrating on his problem. He had been like this ever since Rolando Garro's visit to his office. The worst thing was the uncertainty. Continue to wait. What was he waiting for? For that son of a bitch to finally let him know how much they wanted. Him or his accomplices. Because this couldn't be the work of that poor bastard alone. Who the hell could be behind him? The Yugoslav? Was that possible? He had organized the Chosica trap. But why was the hare jumping two years later? Not knowing what they wanted, what might happen to him, had kept his nerves on edge ever since that damn visit. Ten days now. Ten days without touching Marisa. It hadn't happened since they'd been married. "How could I have been such an idiot when I have a wife

who's so beautiful, so sensitive?" he thought for the hundredth
time. "Marisa will never forgive me." Each time he thought
about the orgy, he felt the same nausea he'd felt then among
those fat whores, as heavily made up as clowns. "You have to be
stupid, Quique, completely stupid to have done what you did."

Agustín drove very steadily, and now Quique was nervous, looking all around, afraid something would happen to
him, thinking that in fact, why not, they could kidnap him
just as they did Cachito. His kidnapping had frightened all
of Lima society. Could it be true they were asking for a six-
million-dollar ransom? Apparently the insurance man who
came from New York to negotiate with the kidnappers was
very tough and would not give in to their demands. The result
might be that Cachito would end up a corpse. It could have
happened to any businessman, himself included. Ever since
the terrorism had begun, this was an idea that from time to
time would get into his head, much more so since Garro's visit
with those photographs.

Luciano was waiting for him, and in his office were two
cups of recently poured coffee.

"Take it easy, Quique," said his friend. "You look awful.
The worst thing is to let yourself be defeated like this before
you've even begun the battle."

"My nerves are shattered, Luciano," he agreed, dropping
into an armchair. "Not on my account, or Marisa's, or because
of what this could cost me. But if those photos are published,
it would kill my mother. You know how conservative, how
Catholic she is. I swear to you that if she saw them, she'd have
a heart attack or lose her mind, I don't know which. Well, let's
get down to business. What do your two criminal lawyers have
to say?"

"First of all, take it easy, Quique. We'll do everything possible and impossible to prevent their publication," the attorney
said encouragingly. "They both agree that it's better to wait

for them to make the first move. What do they want? How much do they want? In the final analysis, we'll have to negotiate. The most important things are the guarantees for recovering the negatives. And in the meantime, of course, denying categorically that you're the man in the photographs."

"Do they know this Garro? What do they know about him?"

"They know him very well," Luciano agreed. "A yellow journalist specializing in show business. A toady, apparently, of little importance at the outset, who has made a career of blackmailing or offering publicity to actors, scriptwriters, announcers, program presenters. He lives on scandals. He's been sued several times for libel and slander, but the association of journalists protects him, and in the name of freedom of the press the judges almost always file away the lawsuits or acquit him. There are lots of stories about him, including one that says he could be one of the Doctor's undercover reporters hired to throw dirt at critics of the government, destroying their reputations, inventing scandals about them. The two criminal lawyers in the firm don't believe Garro is the head of this operation. He's just a minor player, a messenger, a tool of the real bosses. They're surprised he went in person to blackmail an entrepreneur as well known as you. We've requested an appointment with the Doctor. We'll go with the presidents of the Confederation of Entrepreneurs and the Mining Society to impress him. So he'll know that not only you but the entire business sector feels threatened by this blackmail. Do you agree, Quique?"

"Yes, of course," he said. "I hate the idea of so many people knowing about this, but it's true, it's better to go right to the top. The Doctor can stop it by frightening Garro and obliging him to inform on his accomplices."

"According to the criminal lawyers, this is a high-flying operation. Perhaps an international mafia."

He smiled at him affectionately, but Enrique didn't return the smile. This stupid comment was all that these criminal specialists could tell him? He'd known that someone was behind Garro from the very beginning.

"What's the worst that could happen to me, Luciano?"

Luciano became very serious before answering.

"The worst, my friend, would be if the person behind this operation is the one you've already imagined."

"I haven't imagined anyone, Luciano. Please, speak more clearly."

"None other than the sinister Doctor," said Luciano, lowering his voice. "He's very capable of plotting something as dark as this. Especially if he thinks there's a lot of money involved."

"Fujimori's own adviser?" Quique was surprised.

"The strongman in this government, the one who makes and unmakes careers, the real boss of Peru," Luciano reminded him. "Lawyers are absolutely certain that the man does things like this. He's greedy, with an excessive thirst for money. There are indications that many small businessmen have been black-mailed, and it seems to come from him. They'd be surprised at his setting up something like this against a person as impor-tant as you. That's why it's a good idea that when we go to see him, the directors of the Confederation of Entrepreneurs and the Mining Society accompany us. Their presence may frighten him a little, if in fact he's involved. On the other hand, I've al-ready told you there are rumors that one of the gossip colum-nists the Doctor uses to ruin the reputations of his political enemies is this Garro. You know he finances a good number of those obscene sheets full of filthy words and naked pictures that bathe critics of the government in shit. Are you listening to me, Quique?"

Enrique had begun to think that if Dr. Montesinos, the head of the regime's Intelligence Service, was behind those photos, there was no way out. He was lost. How could he confront so powerful a man, the Machiavellian adviser to the president? He recalled the only time he had seen him, at a dinner for entrepreneurs, when the famous Doctor had suddenly appeared without being invited. Very pleasant, somewhat unctuous and servile with all of them, in a tight blue suit, and with a potbelly that struggled to be noticed, he told them that private enterprise would be secure in the country as long as Engineer Fujimori remained in the government. And that the regime needed at least twenty years to complete the program of reforms that was taking Peru out of underdevelopment and raising her to first-world-nation status. Regarding terrorism, he talked at some length, justifying his "hard-fisted" policy with an example that made the hair of some of those present stand on end: "It doesn't matter if twenty thousand die, including fifteen thousand innocents, if we kill five thousand terrorists." When he left, the entrepreneurs had joked about the presumption of this character, a fawning, ostentatious braggart who wore yellow shoes with a blue suit.

"If he's behind this, Luciano, I'm fucked, plain and simple," he murmured.

"Nobody's saying it's him, take it easy," his friend reassured him. "It's just one conjecture among many. Don't be frightened ahead of time. And don't think the Doctor has as much power as he believes he has."

"What should I do, then?"

"The fact that they've waited two years since they took those pictures means something," said Luciano. "Try to remember every possible detail of your relationship with the Yugoslav who organized the thing in Chosica. Look for every letter and message from him still in your files. One way or another, this individual is at the root of it all. Do this for the time being, and we'll wait. The criminal lawyers advise not taking any action until they show themselves. And above

all, not going to the police. Let's see what comes of our nego-
tiation with the Doctor. And please, try not to look so nervous. Garro brought you the photographs to frighten you, to
soften you up. The hare will jump very soon. When he does,
and we know what kind of blackmail is involved, we'll know
what to do. Then we'll decide on a plan of action."

They talked for another moment and Luciano suggested
that he get away with Marisa for a few days. Quique rejected
that idea out of hand. He had a thousand matters pending, an
unusual amount of work because of the country's difficult
situation. Leaving Lima, rather than calming him, would make
him even more upset than he was already. They agreed that,
in any event, this week the two couples would have lunch
together—Sunday, for example, at La Granja Azul—and
Luciano walked with him to the door.

When Quique reached his office, the head of security at
the Huancavelica mine, and a pile of messages, letters, and
e-mails, were already waiting for him. Señor Urriola—wrinkles
like furrows, a big mustache, a boxer's hands, and a stereo-
typed smile that never left his face—did not give him good
news. There had been more thefts of explosives in the past
month, due to complicity among thieves, clerks, and workers,
perhaps with the help of the police guards stationed there.
Happily, no shoot-outs or victims. The watchmen, of course,
hadn't noticed anything.

"I must sound like a broken record," Señor Urriola said as
he ended his report. "But you should have the Guardia Civil
withdraw from the mines. I assure you my people would stop
these thefts cold. The guards earn miserable salaries, and now
terrorism gives them the perfect alibi for stealing from us and
blaming the Path and the MRTA."

After Urriola, three more people came in, and there was a
long phone call from New York. It was difficult for Quique to
concentrate, to listen to them or answer them. He could not

get out of his head the sinister images that had hounded him since Garro's visit. He couldn't even recall that damn party in Chosica with any precision. Had the Yugoslav given him some drug? He remembered how unwell and dizzy he'd felt, his nausea and vomiting. Finally, at about twelve, when the last visitor left, he told his secretary not to forward any more calls, because he had urgent matters to attend to and needed complete privacy.

In reality he wanted to be alone, to let up for a while on his exhausting efforts to split himself in two, trying to pay attention to office matters when all he could think of was his personal problem. He spent almost an hour seated in one of the easy chairs where he received visitors, staring at but not seeing the vast expanse of Lima at his feet. What could he do? How long would this uncertainty last? At one point he felt drowsiness overcoming him, and though he tried to resist, he fell asleep. "It's anguish," he thought as he dropped off. Perhaps it would be good if he did what he had never wanted to do: learn to play golf, the sport of the Japanese and the lazy. Perhaps it would be a good relaxant for his nerves. He woke with a start: at 1:15 he had a lunch appointment at the Club de la Banca. He washed his face, combed his hair, and called his secretary.

She gave him a long list of messages, which he barely listened to.

"And that reporter you saw the other day called, too," she added. "Garro? Yes, Rolando Garro. He was very insistent and said it was urgent. He left me a phone number. What shall I do? Make an appointment or put him off?"

8

Shorty

As soon as she felt that the individual behind her, on the bus from Surquillo to Five Corners, was too close and had bad intentions, Shorty took out the long needle she wore in her belt. She kept it in her hand, waiting for the vehicle to make its next stop, since the wise guy took advantage of the stops to bring his fly close to her buttocks. He did just that, in fact, and then she turned to look at him with her enormous, intense eyes—he was an insignificant little man, along in years, who immediately looked away—and, holding the long needle up to his face, she warned him:

"The next time you push into me I'll stick this in that filthy little prick of yours. I swear to you it's poisoned."

Some people in the bus laughed, and the little man was confused; he dissembled and pretended to be surprised:

"Are you talking to me, señora? What is it?"

"You've been warned, asshole," she concluded, drily, and turned her back.

The man absorbed the lesson, and, uncomfortable and shamed by the mocking glances of the passengers, no doubt, got off at the next stop. Shorty recalled that these warnings didn't always work, in spite of the fact that she, on two occasions, had carried out her threats. The first, on a bus on this same line, right by the Barbones military base; the boy, who was stabbed by the needle in the middle of his fly, had given a shriek that startled all the passengers and made the driver brake suddenly.

"Now you'll learn to only rub up against your mother, faggot!" Shorty had shouted, taking advantage of the fact that the bus had stopped to jump down onto the street and start running toward Junín Alleyway.

The second time she had plunged the needle into the fly of someone rubbing against her was more complicated. He was a hulking mulatto whose entire face was covered with pimples; he shook against her frenetically and would have hurt her if other passengers had not stopped him. But the matter ended at the police station; they let her go only when they discovered that she was carrying a reporter's identity papers. She knew that in general the police were more afraid of journalists than of outlaws and holdup men.

As the bus drove toward Five Corners, she returned to what she had been thinking before she became aware of the man pressing into her back: had the *emolienteros*, the vendors of herbal drinks, disappeared? Whenever she saw someone pushing a cart on the street she approached for a better look. Usually he was selling ice cream or sodas or candy bars. Rarely, very rarely, herbal drinks. They must be dying out, another sign of supposed progress in Lima. Soon there wouldn't be a single one left, and Limeños of the future wouldn't even know what an *emoliente* was.

Her childhood was inseparable from that traditional Peruvian drink, made with barley, flax seed, *boldo* leaves, and horsetail; throughout her childhood, she had watched her father prepare it with an assistant, a twisted cripple nicknamed Fish. Back then, the *emolienteros* were all over the center of the city, especially at the entrances to factories, in the vicinity of the Plaza Dos de Mayo, and along Argentina Avenue. "My

best customers are drinkers and laborers," her father would
say. As a little girl and an adolescent, she had gone with him
on his rounds thousands of times, pulling the cart with the big
pots of *emoliente* that he and Fish had prepared in the small
house where they lived then, in Breña, at the end of Arica
Avenue, where the old part of the city ended and the waste-
land that stretched all the way to La Perla, Bellavista, and
Callao began. Shorty remembered very well that her father's
most faithful customers were, in fact, the night owls who had
spent hours drinking in the little bars in the center of the city,
and the workers who at dawn entered the factories on Argentina and Colonial Avenues, and in the area of the Ejército
Bridge. She would help, serving the small glasses to the customers with a little piece of cut paper to use as a napkin. When
her father left her at the little neighborhood school and the
life of the city began with the appearance of street sweepers
and the traffic police, the *emolientero* had already been working at least four hours. Hard work; a killing, dangerous job. Her
father had been mugged and robbed of all the day's earnings
several times, and, worst of all, he risked so much to earn no
more than a pittance. Thinking about it carefully, it wasn't
strange that *emolienteros* were disappearing from the streets
of Lima.

She'd never asked her father about her mother. Had she
left him? Had she died, or was she still alive? He never said a
word about her, and Julieta respected his silence, not asking
even once about her. He was an introverted man who could
go for days without saying a word, but although he was never
very effusive with her, she remembered him with affection.
He had been good to his only child; at least, he had been concerned about her finishing school so that in the future, he
told her, she wouldn't have the kind of hard life he'd had
because he was illiterate. Not knowing how to read or write
infuriated him. The happiest day of his life was the afternoon

when his only child showed him the journalist's card that Rolando Garro had obtained for her after hiring her as a reporter on his magazine.

They were in Five Corners now, and Shorty got off the bus. She walked the seven blocks between the bus stop and her house on Teniente Arancibia Alleyway, passing all the places she knew by heart and responding with movements of her head or her hand to the greetings of people she recognized: the spiritualist from Piura who saw his clients only at night, an auspicious time to converse with souls; the pharmacist who occupied the little house where, they said, Felipe Pinglo, the great composer of waltzes, was born; Heeren Manor, which, apparently, had been a redoubt of the most elegant mansions of Lima during the nineteenth century and was now a collection of ruins fought over by turkey buzzards, bats, drug addicts, and fugitives from justice; the house of Limbómana, the abortionist; the Church of Carmen and the small convent of the Franciscan Sisters of the Immaculate Conception. It was still early, but since robberies and muggings had increased a great deal in the neighborhood, the shopkeepers already had their grates up and waited on customers through a slit barely large enough for small packages to pass through. Half-built houses and filthy alleys with a single water tap, vagrants and beggars on the corners that, at night, filled with drug dealers and transient prostitutes, their pimps lurking in the darkness. Her house was at the back of a dilapidated courtyard; its buildings, all one-story, were small and seemed fitted inside one another except for hers, which, because it was the last one, stood somewhat apart from the others. The house had a bedroom, a living-dining room, a small kitchen, and a bathroom; it was furnished with the bare essentials but was filled with piles of newspapers and magazines in every room. Shorty had been collecting them since she was a girl. Beginning in primary school, she had been a compulsive reader of papers and magazines and had begun to keep them long before she knew that one day she would be a reporter and could benefit from the enormous collection. Although in personal matters she wasn't very orderly, her mountains of newspapers and magazines were rigorously organized. Small pieces of paper, written on in her tiny hand, indicated the most important years and subjects. She devoted her free time to putting them in order, just as other people dedicated their time to sports, chess, knitting, embroidery, or watching television. She had an old, small television set that she turned on—when the electricity hadn't been cut—only for programs dedicated to gossip and scandals; that is, to topics related to her work.

She went into her house and in the kitchen prepared a packet of dried soup and reheated a plate of rice and tripe she had left in the oven. She never ate very much, and she didn't drink or smoke. She was nourished above all by her work, which was also her vocation: finding out other people's secret shames. Bringing them to light produced both professional and personal satisfaction. It excited her to do it, and she intuited in a somewhat confused way that by doing what she did, she was taking her revenge on a world that had always been so hostile to her and her father. Although she was young, her achievements were already enviable.

Her teacher had been Rolando Garro, and for this reason she felt an absolute loyalty to him. Was she in love with him? In the editorial office of *Exposed* they sometimes joked with her about this, and she denied it so emphatically that all her colleagues were sure she was.

As far back as she could remember, the idea of one day being a reporter had always pursued her; but her idea of journalism had little or nothing to do with what is called serious journalism: objective reports and political, cultural, or social analyses. Her idea of journalism came from the small yellow scandal sheets displayed in the newsstands in the center of town, which people stopped to read—or rather look at, because there was almost nothing to them beyond the large, glaring headlines—and to contemplate the naked women showing off their breasts and buttocks with fantastic vulgarity, and the panels in strident red letters denouncing the filthy things, the pestilential secrets, and the real or supposed vile acts, thefts, perversions, and trafficking that destroyed the reputations of the most apparently worthy and prestigious people in the country.

Shorty—they had given her the nickname in school, where the girls in her class sometimes also called her Chubby—recalled with pride the success that had crowned her first forays as a reporter, when she was still a high school student at the María Parado de Bellido School. It had occurred to the director that the students should publish a bulletin-board newspaper. Julieta, not imagining the effect it would have, began to send in articles written by hand in her even, tiny writing. She soon became the star reporter of the bulletin-board paper, because unlike the other contributors, who spoke of the nation, of national heroes like Grau and Bolognesi, of religion, the pope, or the land problem in Peru, she limited herself to recounting the most salacious gossip and rumors circulating about students and teachers, concealing their names when it was a matter of really risqué items such as casting suspicion on a man's masculinity or a woman's femininity. With success came a sanction. She was called to the office, admonished—she had been warned earlier for using curse words—and threatened with expulsion if she continued along that path.

She did—but was already out of school. With an audacity inversely proportional to her size, she began to investigate, passing herself off as a reporter for *The Latest*, *The Chronicle*, *Masks*, *Express*, and even *Commerce* in theaters, radio stations, nightclubs, television stations, recording studios, or the private houses of people in show business, extracting from them, with her ingenuous little girl's voice and large, unmoving eyes, an entire report naturally marked by mendacious distrust and an unfailing intuition for the morbid, sinful, and ill-gotten that attracted her so deeply. In this way she came to *Exposed*, met Rolando Garro, and became the weekly's star reporter and best-loved disciple of the country's most famous journalist in matters of infidelity and scandal.

"How will the damn story of those photographs end?" she wondered before she fell asleep. "Well or badly?" Since the beginning, that is, since Ceferino confessed he had them, she had sensed that the topic could do them more harm than good, especially when Rolando Garro took them to Enrique Cárdenas, that snob of a miner. But what her boss said and did she respected without saying a word.

9

A Singular Affair

When Enrique saw Rolando Garro walk into his office, he felt the same distaste as the first time. Garro was dressed in the same clothing he had worn two weeks earlier, and he walked swinging his arms and coming down hard on the heels of his high platform shoes, as if wanting to come up in the world. He reached his desk—Enrique hadn't stood to receive him—and extended the flaccid wet hand that Enrique remembered with revulsion. It was ten in the morning: he was right on time for their appointment.

"Since I imagine that this conversation will be recorded, I propose we don't discuss you-know-what," Garro said as he came in, in the high-pitched, arrogant voice Enrique remembered from their previous meeting. "Except for what brings me here. And since I know you're a very busy man and I don't want to waste your precious time, I'll propose it to you with no preambles. I've come to offer you a business deal."

"A business deal?" The engineer was surprised. "You and I?"

"Yes, you and I," the journalist repeated with a defiant laugh. "I, the dwarf who doesn't exist, and you, the god of the Peruvian entrepreneurial Olympus."

He laughed again, an anomalous little laugh that narrowed

his mocking eyes, and after a strategic pause, added with a great deal of conviction:

"*Exposed* is a small weekly with limited circulation only because of a lack of means, Señor Cárdenas. But this could change radically. If an entrepreneur of your prestige and power decided to invest in it, the magazine would reach all of Peru. It would be unstoppable, and even the stones would read it. I'd take care of that, Engineer."

Was this how the blackmail would go? Asking him to invest in the filthy yellow scandal sheet? Enrique looked at this individual dressed in his outlandish, gaudy clothes, and thought what a contrast he made to his own modern, elegant office with its functional, discreet Scandinavian furniture and the etchings on the walls, the mechanical drawings, the pumps, pulleys, and pipelines that the decorator Leonorcita Artigas had combined with beautiful views of deserts, the foaming waves of the coastline, and the imposing, snow-covered Andes.

"Explain in more detail what you're saying, Señor Garro," he said, hiding his repugnance. But in spite of his efforts, he was sure the aversion he felt toward the poor devil in front of him was evident in his voice.

"A hundred thousand dollars to start," the journalist said with a shrug, as if the sum were laughable. "A trifle for you. Later, when you can confirm how well this investment is going and what an excellent deal you've made, the amount of capital would have to increase. For the moment, I'd allow myself to double the number of printed copies and the staff. Improve the paper and the printing. I wouldn't even see the money. You'd put in place the manager, administrator, spy, or whatever you want to call him. Someone you trust absolutely. The matter is very simple. More than your money, I'm interested in your name, your prestige. If you're associated with me, the grudge that advertisers and their agencies have against me will disappear in an instant. The weekly will become respectable and full of ads. I assure you, Engineer, it will be an excellent investment."

His little eyes glittered as he spoke, and Enrique saw that his teeth were stained with nicotine. And he was chewing something, perhaps a piece of gum. Or could it be a tic?

"Before you continue, I want to tell you something, Señor Garro," he said, hardening his voice and staring into his visitor's shifty eyes. "I don't know why you brought me that gift on your last visit. The person who appears in those photos isn't me."

"So much the better, Engineer." The journalist applauded theatrically, delighted at the news. "I'm very glad. I already imagined as much, as a matter of fact. But I told you I didn't want us to discuss that now. Not only because you're surely recording this conversation but because there's no connection between this visit and my previous one. I've come to propose a business deal, nothing more. Don't look for complications where none exist."

"Journalism isn't my field, and I don't like to invest in things I don't know about," said Enrique. "In any event, if you have a project, with market and feasibility studies, leave it with me and the technical department will study it with the seriousness it deserves. Was that all, Señor Garro?"

"Naturally I've brought you the proposal in writing," said Garro, touching the faded leather briefcase he held on his knees. "But I'd like to explain a little more in my own words what we could do with the expansion of *Exposed*. It won't take more than ten minutes, I promise you."

Enrique, resisting the urge to get this ridiculous little man out of the office once and for all and never see him again, agreed without saying a word. He had allowed him this appointment because those were the instructions of the two criminal lawyers in Luciano's firm, though it went against his own better judgment. A dull rage was taking hold of him.

"Morbid curiosity is the most universal vice in the world," the little man pontificated in his strident, cocksure voice, not taking his eyes off Enrique. "In all peoples and all cultures, but especially in Peru. I suppose you know this all too well: we're a nation of gossips. We want to know people's secrets, preferably the ones having to do with bed. In other words, and excuse my language, who's fucking whom, and how they're doing it. Poking into the private lives of well-known people, the powerful, the famous, the prominent. Politicians, entrepreneurs, athletes, singers—and if there's anyone who knows how to do it, and I say so with all the modesty in the world, it's me. Yes, Engineer, Rolando Garro, your friend and, if you agree, from now on your partner, too."

He spoke for fifteen minutes, not ten, and with so much cynicism and eloquence that the entrepreneur, who listened openmouthed, could not interrupt him. Enrique was alarmed, but he wanted to know how far Rolando Garro's brazenness would take him, so he let him talk and talk.

Several times he was about to silence him but he controlled himself, fascinated by what he was hearing, like a bird paralyzed in midair by the gaze of the snake before it swallows him. He couldn't get it into his head that anyone would reveal himself in that way, displaying the intentions his brain devised with a total lack of scruples. Garro said that until now, *Exposed* had concentrated on the world of show business because it was the one that Rolando Garro and his team knew best, but also because of a lack of means. With an increase in capital, his sphere of action would extend like concentric waves and incorporate into his exposés, "coming right to the point, Engineer"—politicians, and entrepreneurs, too, of course, but certainly Engineer Cárdenas would always have the right to a veto. His prohibitions and advice would be sacred to the weekly. And so, on a national scale, *Exposed* would reveal—"bring to light"—that entire shadowy world of adultery, homosexuality, lesbianism, sadomasochism, bestiality, pedophilia, corruption, and thievery which thrived in the basements of society. All of Peru would be able to satisfy its morbid curiosity, its appetite for gossip, the immense pleasure produced in the mediocre, which is most of humanity, knowing that the famous, the respectable, the celebrated, the decent are made of the same dirty clay as everyone else. After a short pause, the journalist gave him examples, in the United States and in Europe, of publications similar to the kind he wanted to use as models for the transformed *Exposed*.

Had he finished? Rolando Garro was smiling at him, with an air of being very satisfied with himself, waiting for his response with a beatific expression.

"So you've come to propose that I invest in a paper that would be dedicated to spreading yellow journalism and scandal throughout the entire country," Enrique Cárdenas finally said, speaking very slowly to hide the rage that bubbled up inside him like lava.

"That's the journalism that sells the best and is the most modern in today's world, Engineer," Rolando Garro explained, with pedagogical gestures. "*Exposed* will earn you a lot of money, I assure you. Isn't that what matters to a capitalist? Earning dividends, the nice jingling of soles. But besides that, and this is perhaps the most important thing, it will make you a feared man, Don Enrique. Thanks to *Exposed*, your competitors will be terrified that you'll plunge them into disgrace with just a flick of your little finger. Think what this means, this weapon that I'll place in your hands."

"The weapons of the Mafia, of blackmail and extortion," said Enrique; he was trembling with indignation and had to spell out the words as he spoke. "Do you know: I hear you speak and can't believe that anyone can say the things you're saying to me, Señor Garro."

He saw the reporter abandon his arrogant smile for a moment, become very serious, spread his arms, and exclaim in astonishment, as if addressing a hall filled with spectators:

"Are we talking about morality, Engineer? About ethics and scruples?"

"Yes, Señor Garro," he exploded in fury. "About morality and scruples. Things you don't even know exist, to judge by what I'm hearing."

"No one who saw the photographs I gave you the other day would say that you're so scrupulous a moralist, Engineer." Now the voice of Rolando Garro was cold, piercing, and aggressive, a voice Enrique didn't know he had. He'd stopped chewing. His eyes drilled into him.

"I don't intend to invest a single cent in your filthy rag, Señor Garro," said the entrepreneur, getting to his feet. "I'm asking you to leave and not set foot in my office again. As for those faked photographs you're trying to use to frighten me, I assure you that you're mistaken. And that you'll regret it if you insist on this blackmail."

The journalist didn't stand up. He remained seated, defying him with his eyes, as if pondering what Enrique would say to him.

"In fact, Señor Garro, this conversation is being recorded," the engineer added. "In this way, the police and the judges will know the kind of deal you came to propose to me. The kind of revolting animal you are. Leave immediately, or I'll throw you out myself."

This time the journalist, who had changed color with each of the engineer's insults, got to his feet. He nodded a few times and then, with his habitual Tarzanesque strides, walked unhurriedly to the door. But before he left, he turned to look at Enrique and said with the mocking little smile he had recovered, and in his shrill voice:

"I recommend the next issue of *Exposed* to you, Engineer. I swear you'll find it very interesting, from beginning to end."

As soon as the little man left his office, Enrique called Luciano at his firm.

"I've done something very obtuse, old man," he blurted out, even forgetting to greet him first. "Do you know why that piece of trash came here? To propose that I invest one hundred thousand dollars in his rag. So that he can add politicians, businessmen, and society people to the list of showgirls he concerns himself with now and bring all their dirty secrets to light. I couldn't control myself. He nauseated me. I threw him out of the office, threatening him with a beating if he ever came back. It was dumb, wasn't it, Luciano?"

"You're committing the worst stupidity now, Quique," his friend replied. He maintained his usual calm. "Suppose this conversation is being taped? It's better if we speak of this in person. Never again by phone, I've told you that. It seems you don't know what country we're in, old man."

"He threatened to dedicate the next issue to me," Enrique added. He noticed that he was sweating profusely.

"We'll talk about this later, in person, not by phone," Luciano interrupted very energetically. "I'm sorry, but I have to cut this short."

And Enrique heard a click and then silence. Luciano had hung up.

He stayed at his desk for a long while, with no energy to take care of the thousand things waiting on the day's schedule. Luciano was afraid that their conversation was being recorded. By whom? And to what end? The famous Doctor? It wasn't impossible, of course. Luciano had told him about the meeting he'd had with the two criminal lawyers, the presidents of the Confederation of Entrepreneurs and the Mining Society, and the head of the Intelligence Service. The Doctor seemed indignant at the blackmail attempt. He assured them that he'd set the blackmailer straight; he knew that journalist all too well and would make him reveal his accomplices, if he had any. Would he keep his word? Enrique no longer trusted anyone. For a long time everything had been possible in Peru. A country, it seemed to him, that only now he was beginning to understand deep down, even though he was almost forty years old and had spent all those years here except for the four when he'd been a student at MIT in Cambridge, Massachusetts. Since those photographs had fallen into his hands, his eyes had been opened, revealing a hell even worse than the bombs of the Shining Path and the kidnappings of the MRTA. "Where were you living until now, Quique?" he asked himself. Hadn't poor Cachito been kidnapped months ago? He hardly knew him, but he had always seemed like a nice person. They had played tennis a few times in Villa. Sebastián Zaldívar, Cachito to his friends, ran his manufacturing business efficiently, though without much imagination. He wasn't very ambitious. He was satisfied with what he had, his games of tennis, his saddle horses, his little trips to Miami from time to time to do some shopping, go on a spree, and sleep peacefully with no blackouts. Poor man! What tortures were they inflicting on him? Could this pig's threat be true? Would he dare to publish the photos? He imagined his mother bent over the cover of *Exposed* and shuddered. Perhaps he had been hasty to threaten and insult a worm like that. Would he have to retreat? Beg his pardon and tell him he'd invest the hundred thousand in that repulsive sheet he published?

10

The Three Jokers

When he opened his eyes, the first thing he saw was the silhouette of Serafín outlined in the recess of the only window in his room at the Hotel Mogollón, which he always left open in case the cat wanted to go out or come in. "Ah, you came back, you rascal," he said, spreading his arms; the cat immediately jumped from the window to the bed and came to curl up beside him. Juan Peineta scratched the back of Serafín's neck and his belly, feeling how the animal stretched with contentment. "You were gone three days, what ingratitude," he scolded. "Or was it four, or five? What unspeakable things you must have been up to out there." The cat looked at him as if he were sorry and curled up, begging his pardon. "We'll have breakfast later, Serafín. I feel lazy, I'm going to stay in bed a little longer."

His experience with the Three Jokers had been, depending on how you looked at it, a great success or the worst mistake of his life. A success because he had earned more money than he ever had before. He and Atanasia could indulge their whims, including a vacation in Cusco and a trip to Machu Picchu, and he had become better known than in all his years as a reciter. All over Peru! They published his photograph in the papers, people recognized him and approached him on the street to ask for his autograph. He never imagined that anything like this could happen to him. But it was a catastrophe because, instead of feeling happy playing the clown, he felt unfortunate and always had to endure an oppressive sense of guilt: he had betrayed poetry, art, and his vocation as an orator.

The worst thing was that in the program *The Three Jokers*, they even had him recite. That is to say, begin to recite on any pretext, just so the other two jokers could shut him up by slapping him with blows that knocked him to the floor and made the audience that attended the taping of the program roar with laughter, not to mention the myriad viewers they had throughout Peru. These were the worst moments of each program for Juan Peineta: making a laughingstock of divine poetry. "The dark swallows will return," and wham, "Shut up, asshole," a hard slap to the face, down to the floor, and laughter. "Green, oh I love you, green, green wind," and wham, "There the faggot goes again with his little verses," a hard slap, down on the floor with legs spread wide, and booming laughter.

They had taught him all the tricks of clowning, and he had learned them with no difficulty. Clap his hands when they slapped him so that it seemed they were hitting much harder than they really were, and fall down bending his legs and arms to lessen the impact. Break into booming laughter with his mouth wide open or sob like a baby and even really cry when necessary according to the demands of the script. He complied with everything and did the best he could, like a good professional. But he never got used to that moment in all the episodes of *The Three Jokers*, when he, on any pretext, began to recite at the top of his voice—"Tonight I can write the saddest verses"—and his companions, who'd had enough, sent him to the floor with a punch to the nose. He thought it was contemptible, that he was committing a crime against poetry, dealing a low blow to the best in himself.

He never became a friend of the other two members of the Jokers. They never accepted him as an equal, they were constantly bringing up Tiburcio, the one who had disappeared, making innuendos, rubbing it in that Juan was not and never would be as good a comedian or as good a person or as good a buddy as the other man. But perhaps Juan recognized at times that he hadn't done very much to win the sympathy and friendship of the other two. The truth is, he felt contempt for them because they were uncouth and coarse, because they didn't even know about the art or feel the least respect for the occupation by which they earned a living. Eloy Cabra had been a provincial circus clown before joining *The Three Jokers*, and he lived and worked to get drunk and go to brothels where, he boasted, the girls gave him discounts because he was on television and famous. The other "joker," Julito Ceres, had been a guitarist who played Peruvian music and had won the Competition for Mimics on América Television, where he had pocketed two thousand soles imitating the president of the republic, Chabuca Granda, and two Hollywood actors. He wasn't as coarse and primitive as Eloy Cabra, but, in spite of being better mannered, he expressed the greatest contempt for Juan Peineta's profession; he thought recitation was for fairies and faggots, and he always let Juan know this with wounding gibes that he added to the script when it was time to record the program.

Juan Peineta didn't get along well with the scriptwriter, either. He was named Corrochano, but at the station everyone called him Maestro, perhaps because he always wore a scarf and a tie. He wrote scripts for several programs, using different pseudonyms, and had a tiny office that he called the Sanctuary, because no one was allowed to enter without the permission of the all-powerful writer. How could a man like him, a lawyer, so well dressed, and so pleasant and well spoken with everybody, write scripts that were so vulgar and ridiculous, so obnoxious, so tasteless, so stupid? The explanation was that this was what people liked: the program's ratings broke all records, and it had led the polls ever since its creation.

Why didn't he give up playing a comic in *The Three Jokers* when he felt disgusted with himself for doing what he did? For practical reasons. With the ten thousand soles a month, which increased to twelve thousand and then fourteen thousand, he and Atanasia could buy clothes, go to movies and restaurants, even save for the trip to Miami, his wife's great dream, even greater than her other dream: having a child. But this never happened; the doctors told them it was impossible. Atanasia suffered from a defect in her reproductive system that caused the eggs to disintegrate as soon as they were formed. In spite of her diagnosis, she insisted on receiving treatment, which was very expensive and did no good.

Juan had reached the point of crying with impotence and frustration after taping shows that were particularly humiliating for him. And he never lost his nostalgia for the good times when he was a reciter. At times he declaimed one of the verses he knew by heart—there were many of them—in front of a mirror (Campoamor's "Write me a letter, Father / I know who it's for") or his wife, and his heart contracted with sadness when he thought how he had been brought down as an artist, moving from reciter to comedian.

With this in his past, he must have felt pleased with the campaign that, without his knowing how or why, was unleashed against him in *The Latest*, a campaign that, after a few months of great anguish, would end his career as a television clown. The story of the campaign was incredible. In spite of so much time having gone by, it still kept him awake at night. But with his loss of memory, he didn't remember it very well, and at times he had the sensation that his mind distorted things.

The proverb said, "Welcome, trouble, if you come alone," and Juan Peineta could affirm that in his case it was absolutely true. Because the attacks against him in *The Latest* coincided with Atanasia's headaches. At first they responded to acetaminophen, but since, in the end, the tablets did nothing for her, they went to the Hospital del Seguro. After they'd waited close to two hours, the doctor who examined her said it was a problem with her vision and transferred her to an oculist. And, in fact, this doctor diagnosed farsightedness and prescribed eyeglasses that, for a time, relieved her migraines.

How did the attacks in *The Latest* begin? Juan Peineta's memory was confused. Someone told him that in Rolando Garro's column, which everyone in radio and television read religiously, he had said that *The Three Jokers* on América Television had deteriorated since Tiburcio had died and been replaced by Juan Peineta, a coliseum reciter who was boring when he told jokes and wasn't even good at taking the slaps that his two companions gave him ("deservedly so") whenever he threatened to recite on the program.

He didn't see that column or the other ones where, apparently, that reporter continued to criticize him until one day Eloy Cabra warned him, at the end of a taping: "These attacks aren't good for us, either, they can fuck up our ratings. You have to do something to stop them." And what could Juan Peineta do to make that individual stop attacking him?

"A nice visit and a little gift for Señor Garro," Eloy Cabra murmured, winking at him.

"Ah, caramba," he said, surprised. "Is that how things work?"

"That's how things work with mercenary reporters," Eloy Cabra explained. "Better take care of it soon. That Garro is very influential and can make our ratings fall. And we're not going to allow that, not us, or the producer, or the channel. Listen to what I'm telling you, my friend."

Eloy Cabra's threat irritated him so much that instead of giving the little gift that his colleague on *The Three Jokers* had advised, Juan Peineta wrote a letter to the editor of *The Latest* complaining about "the unjust and unjustified attacks" on him, the victim, by the television columnist. He said that if the campaign did not cease, he would have recourse to the courts.

Later he would recognize that he had been imprudent, that all by himself he had plunged into the quicksand that would swallow up his career as a comedian. Because, instead of stopping, from then on the reporter's attacks against him multiplied, not only in his column in *The Latest* but also on a program he had on Radio Colonial, where every day he called him the most inept "pseudo-actor" on Peruvian television, who was ruining *The Three Jokers*, the most popular comedy program when "the inadequate Juan Peineta replaced the sorely missed and much-admired Tiburcio Lanza and left the show without viewers."

During that same period they discovered that Atanasia had a brain tumor, the real cause of her periodic headaches. Suddenly she became mute. She opened her mouth, moved her lips—her eyes full of despair—and emitted guttural sounds instead of words. Finally, the doctor who examined her, a general practitioner, sent her to a neurosurgeon. He said that everything indicated the presence of a brain tumor, but this would have to be verified with an MRI. Since the wait for this test in the Public Health System was several weeks—or perhaps months—Juan took Atanasia to a private clinic for the MRI. Yes, it was a tumor and the neurosurgeon said they had to operate. But first she had to receive chemotherapy to shrink it. Juan recalled that period of chemotherapy as if it were a slow nightmare. After each treatment Atanasia was so weak she could barely move. She never recovered her voice, and soon she couldn't get out of bed. The Public Health neurosurgeon said then that, given the señora's condition, he wouldn't risk putting her under the knife. They had to wait until she recovered a little.

They were in the midst of this when Juan Peineta was summoned again by Señor Ferrero and his gold rings and fluorescent watch to have coffee near América Television. He told Juan then that he had to leave the program. He said, with characteristic brutality, the ratings were falling, the announcers were complaining, the surveys were categorical: Juan had lost the favor of the public and was dragging down his colleagues. He tried to protest, saying that it was all the result of Señor Rolando Garro's campaign against him, but Señor Ferrero was very busy, he couldn't waste time with idle gossip, and said he should go today to the cashier's office to arrange his termination. The channel, he added to raise his spirits, would give him more money than he was entitled to as a special bonus.

Six months later Atanasia died without having surgery and Juan Peineta could not find another job as either a reciter or a comedian. He never had regular employment again, just miserable occasional jobs, paid sometimes in tips. From then on he would say to the few friends he had left—he kept losing them at the same time that he lost his memory of all of them except for a few: Ruletero and Crecilda—that the misfortunes of his life were due to a son of a bitch named Rolando Garro, a reporter whose mug he hadn't ever seen in person.

From then on he devoted himself to revenge. That is, to making life difficult for the cause of all his ills. He became something like an ineradicable vice. He listened to all of Garro's radio and television programs and read everything he published in order to criticize him knowledgeably. He sent letters— signed with his own name—to the owners and directors of television and radio stations, magazines, and newspapers, accusing Garro of everything from minor gaffes to defamation and vileness, which he revealed, and a thousand evil deeds that were true or that he imagined, threatening the reporter with legal actions he couldn't even initiate. Did these missives have any negative effect on the professional life of Rolando Garro? Probably not, judging by the popularity of his disclosures, gossip, and betrayals among the lowbrow public for whom he produced his columns and programs. At times Juan Peineta went to the extreme of showing up alone with a placard in front of América Television, accusing Garro of taking his job and killing his wife. The guards at the station would push him away. Among people in show business, none of whom remembered his good periods, Juan Peineta began to be known, humorously, as "the lunatic with the letters, the sworn enemy of Rolando Garro."

11

The Scandal

Every day, from Monday to Friday, Chabela was the first to hear the alarm clock. Yawning, she got up to brush her teeth and wash her face, and then she went to their bedroom to wake her two daughters and get them ready for school. The girls had stayed up late doing homework, and it was harder than usual for their mother to wake them. When she went downstairs with them to the first floor, the cook and Nicasia, the maid, had prepared breakfast. Luciano appeared a short while later, showered, shaved, dressed, his shoes gleaming, ready to leave for the office. But before that he took the girls outside to wait for the bus from the Franklin Delano Roosevelt Academy, which stopped at the door of the large house in La Rinconada, surrounded by a garden filled with tall trees—ficus from India, sequoias from North America, and even a couple of Andean pepper trees—where the tiles in the pool were already sparkling. Chabela watched from the living room, still in her robe, as the girls climbed into the bus; punctual as always, it stopped at the front door at 7:30 every morning. Luciano returned to the house to pick up his briefcase and say goodbye to his wife. Also as usual, he was as well groomed as a fashion model.

"Why don't we go to the movies this afternoon?" she said,

nuzzling her cheek up to his. "It's been ages since we've seen a film on the big screen, Luciano. It's not the same always watching them on TV. Let's go to Larcomar, it's so nice."

"Once and for all, I have to build that screening room at the back of the garden," said Luciano. "So we can have our cinemateque and watch movies right here at home."

"You've promised me that so often, I don't believe it anymore," Chabela said with a yawn.

"I swear I'll build it this summer," her husband responded, moving toward the street door. "I'll try to leave the office early, though I can't promise. Find a good film, just in case. I'll call you, in any event. Ciao, darling."

She watched him back the car out of the garage and drive away, waving goodbye, and she waved, too, from behind the curtain. It was a gray, damp day, the sky dark with leaden clouds and so ugly it seemed to foretell something sinister. Chabela thought sadly that there were still so many months to go before summer returned. She missed her little beach house in La Quipa, swimming in the ocean, long walks in the sand. She hadn't slept very well the night before and felt tired. Should she take a short swim in the heated pool? No, she'd go back to bed for a while. She went up to her bedroom, took off her robe, and slipped between the sheets. The curtains were still closed and there was semidarkness and a profound silence throughout the house. At ten she had Pilates and then yoga at the gym, so she still had time; she closed her eyes to doze for a little while longer.

Two days earlier, she and Marisa had had lunch together, and when they got back from El Central, in Miraflores, after a delicious meal, they had gone to Marisa's bedroom, in her penthouse in San Isidro, and made love. "Also delicious," she thought. And that same night, she and Luciano had made love. "What excess, Chabelita," she laughed, half-asleep. The truth was that things were going pretty well in her life; there were no complications at all stemming from her new relationship with her best friend. If it hadn't been for terrorism and kidnappings, in reality one would have lived very well in Lima. She and Marisa continued to see each other, as they had before, but now they also shared their little secret: they took their pleasure together. Too bad Marisa was so tense because of Quique's nerves, what could be worrying him and eating him alive, he wouldn't open his mouth and tell his wife what was wrong. Marisa had dragged him to Dr. Saldaña, at the Clínica San Felipe, but after examining him the doctor found him in excellent health and simply prescribed some mild pills to help him sleep. Could Quique have a girlfriend? Impossible, anybody but him; as Marisa would say, "My husband was born a saint, so it's no credit to him that he's faithful." "Not to mention Luciano," Chabela thought. "They'll both go straight to heaven."

She fell asleep, and when she awoke it was already 9:15. She had just enough time to get to the gym for the Pilates class. She was putting on her sweat suit and sneakers when Nicasia, the maid, came to tell her that Señora Ketty was calling, and it was urgent. "She's so tiresome," Chabela thought. But "urgent" piqued her curiosity, and instead of declining to take the call, she picked up the receiver.

"Hello, Ketty darling," she said hurriedly. "What is it? Let me say that I'm in a terrible hurry, I don't want to miss my Pilates and yoga classes."

"Have you seen *Exposed*, Chabelita?" Ketty greeted her in a voice from beyond the tomb.

"*Exposed*?" asked Chabela. "What's that?"

"A magazine," said Ketty, sounding alarmed. "You're not going to believe it, Chabelita. Send out for it right now. You'll faint, you'll be so shocked, I swear."

"Will you please stop all the mystery, Ketty," Chabela protested, feeling apprehensive. "What's happened? What's in that magazine?"

"I'm embarrassed to tell you, Chabela. It has to do with Enrique. Yes, Quique. You won't believe it, I swear. I know you and his wife are very good friends. What poor Marisa must be going through, I feel sorry for her. How mortifying, Chabela. I've never felt as embarrassed as I was when I saw that magazine, I'll tell you. Incredibly obscene, you'll see!"

"Will you tell me what the hell you've seen?" Chabela interrupted in a fury. "Stop beating around the bush, Ketty, please."

"I can't tell you, you'll have to see it with your own eyes. And don't swear at me, please, my ears are ringing," Ketty complained. "I'm embarrassed, I'm horrified. It's awful, Chabela. They're not talking about anything else in Lima. Two friends have already called me, in shock. Send somebody to buy it right now. *Exposed*, yes, that's what it's called. I didn't know it existed either, until now."

She hung up, and Chabela was left holding the receiver. She was very worried and began to dial Marisa's cell phone but stopped herself. Better to find out first. On the intercom she called the chauffeur and told him to go out and buy a magazine called *Exposed*. She finished getting ready to go to the gym but, since the chauffeur took so long to return, she decided to forget about Pilates and yoga and, summoning her courage, called Marisa. The line was busy. She called ten times in a row and it was still busy. Finally, the chauffeur returned holding the magazine, on his face an expression of surprise and mockery that he didn't try to hide. On the cover was a large photograph in which Chabela instantly recognized Quique's face. My God! It couldn't be! Quique—no doubt it was him— naked! Naked from head to toe. And what was he doing, she couldn't be seeing what she was seeing. Her face burned and her hands were trembling.

The phone rang. Chabela continued looking at the cover as if in a trance, not managing to read the caption that accompanied the photograph. She saw that Nicasia was coming into her room and saying that Señora Marisa was on the phone. Her friend could barely speak.

"Have you seen what's going on, Chabela?" she heard her stammer. A sob cut off her voice.

"Calm down, darling," she consoled her, stammering as well. "Shall I come to see you? You have to get out of your house, the reporters will drive you crazy. I'll come for you right now, okay?"

"Yes, yes, please, come quickly." Marisa sobbed into the telephone. "I can't believe it, Chabela. I have to get out of here, yes. The calls are driving me crazy."

"I'm leaving right now. Don't answer the phone, don't open the door to anyone. Those awful people must be all around the entrance to the building."

She hung up, and though she wanted to take a fast shower, she couldn't move. Astonished, disconcerted, she flipped through the pages of the magazine and didn't believe, didn't accept, wasn't convinced she was seeing what she saw. Could they have faked the photos? Yes, certainly they had. That's why poor Quique had been so troubled recently. Poor? What an animal if those photographs were true. What a scandal, what ugly gossip would pour down on poor Marisa's head. She had to get her out of the house right now. She tossed the copy of *Exposed* to the floor, ran to the bathroom, showered quickly, threw on the first thing she found, tied a kerchief around her head, got into the car, and sped to Marisa's house. It took more than half an hour to reach San Isidro because traffic was very heavy at that time of day on Javier Prado Avenue and the Zanjón. Poor Marisa. Incredible, my God. This was why she'd been in that state for so many days, of course. Poor Quique, too. Or not, what a despicable little man, what a hateful wretch that meek little hypocrite had turned out to be. Of course, naturally. What a dirty trick on poor Marisa!

When she reached the building where Marisa and Enrique lived, near the Golf Club, she saw a small group of people crowded around the entrance with their flashbulbs and cameras. She didn't stop but drove on and parked around the corner. She walked back, said excuse me to the photographers and cameramen, and one of them asked: "Are you coming to see the Cárdenas family, señora?" She didn't stop and shook her head no. The doorman, who blocked the door with his body, recognized her right away and stepped aside to let her in. The elevator was free, and she rode up alone to the penthouse. Quintanilla, who opened the door for her, had a mournful face and, not saying a word, pointed to the bedroom.

Chabela went in and saw Marisa standing at the window, looking down at the street. When she heard her, a livid Marisa turned and came toward her. She threw herself into her arms, sobbing. Chabela felt her friend's entire body shivering, and she couldn't speak for weeping. "Calm down, darling," she whispered in her ear. "I'm going to help you, and be with you. You have to be strong, Marisita, tell me what happened, how this could have happened."

Marisa finally began to calm down. Taking her by the hand, Chabela led her to a sofa, sat her down next to the Berrocal sculpture, and then sat beside her. Her friend was in her robe, her hair uncombed, and she must have been crying for a long time, because her eyes were swollen and her lips bluish, as if she had been biting them.

"How did this happen? Have you talked to Quique?" Chabela asked, smoothing Marisa's blond hair, caressing her, putting her face next to hers and kissing her check, holding her white hands in hers. They were icy. She rubbed them, warming them.

"I don't know anything, Chabela," she heard her stammer; she never had seen her so pale. Her blue eyes seemed liquefied. "I can't talk to him, he isn't in the office or he's told them to say he isn't. This is horrible. Have you seen those photos? I still can't believe it's true, Chabela. I don't know what to do, I want him to explain it to me. How can it be possible, I feel so ashamed, I've never felt so wounded, so betrayed, how awful. My parents, my brothers and sisters have called, horrified. I don't even know what to say to them."

"They might be faked; nowadays photographers can falsify anything," Chabela said, trying to comfort her.

In half a voice, as if she hadn't heard her, Marisa said that her husband had gotten up very early, as usual, they'd had breakfast together, and he had left for the office before eight o'clock. And at that very moment, Marisa had received the first phone call. Her cousin Alicia, who was taking her little boy to the Colegio San Agustín, had been horrified when, at a traffic light, a newsboy had pushed that filthy magazine into the car. And, of course, she had bought it when she saw Quique on the cover. And naked, just what you're hearing, naked! Her cousin also thought it was a fake, that they had doctored those photos, it was impossible for Quique to have done things like that. Marisa had someone buy the magazine and still could not believe what those disgusting pages showed. The entire magazine devoted to an orgy in Chosica! She retched, she threw up. And the calls didn't stop, every damn gossip in Lima seemed to know the story. And soon radio stations, newspapers, television stations began to call, too. A magazine that Marisa didn't even know existed until now. Yes, it had to be a falsification, didn't it? Because, she repeated over and over again, as if to convince herself, it wasn't possible that Quique would do those things. The worst part was that she still couldn't speak to him. He had disappeared from his office, or they said he had; his secretary contradicted herself, claiming he hadn't come in yet or that he had just left in a hurry. Surely the damn reporters were looking for him and the poor man had hidden somewhere to get rid of them. But how was it possible he hadn't called to calm her down, to offer some explanation, to say it was all a lie and that soon the refutations would come and everything would be cleared up?

"Take it easy, Marisa." Chabela took her by the shoulders. "You have to get out of here. They'll drive you crazy if you don't. Get dressed and I'll have Luciano's driver come for us. I'll tell him to stop at the garage so the reporters don't see you go out, because they'll follow us. Let's go to my house, it'll be quiet there and we can talk calmly and find Quique. I'm sure this is a trick, a fake by that disgusting rag, he'll explain everything. The important thing now is to get you out of here, agreed, darling?"

Marisa nodded and now she embraced her. They barely kissed on the lips. "Yes, yes, let's do that, Chabelita, you don't know how grateful I am that you're here, I was going crazy before you arrived."

Now Chabela kissed her on the cheek and helped her stand. "Pack a small bag with what's absolutely necessary, Marisa. The best thing will be for you to spend a few days with me until the storm passes. We can call Quique from my place. While you get ready, I'll call Luciano."

Marisa went into the bathroom and Chabela called Luciano at the office. As soon as she heard his voice she knew that her husband knew about everything.

Even so, she asked if he had seen *Exposed*.

"I don't think there's a single person in this country who hasn't seen that stinking rag," said Luciano in an acid voice. "I'm trying to locate Quique but can't find him."

"Neither can Marisa," Chabela interrupted. "But what matters now is to get Marisa out of here, Luciano. Yes, I'm at her house. As you can imagine, there's a crowd of reporters at the entrance to the building. Send the driver with the car. Have him go to the garage, and I'll have them open the door for him. We'll be waiting. We'll see each other at home. Can you come and talk to her?"

"Yes, yes, I'll go to lunch and talk to her at home," said Luciano. "But the most important thing now is to find Quique. I'll send the chauffeur over right away. If Marisa finds Quique, have her tell him to get in touch with me right away and not to even think about making any statement to anybody before talking to me."

They did just as Chabela had planned. Luciano's chauffeur drove directly into the garage, the two women got in the car, and Marisa slumped down in her seat so the reporters wouldn't see her. The car passed in front of them and they thought Chabela was the only passenger. None of them followed the car. Half an hour later they were in La Rinconada and Chabela helped her friend settle into the guest room, in a wing completely independent from the rest of the house. Then she led her to the living room and had the cook prepare hot chamomile tea. She sat next to her and dried her tears with a handkerchief.

"This is what kept him from sleeping or eating, what was wearing him down for more than two weeks," said Marisa after taking a few sips from the cup. "He told me that some blackmailers had threatened him on the phone. Now I'm sure it was because of this, the photographs this magazine published."

"These photos are faked, Marisa." Chabela took her hands and kissed them. "You don't know how sad it makes me that you're going through this, darling. Quique will come and give you an explanation, you'll see."

"Do you think it hasn't occurred to me that they could be faked?" Marisa squeezed her hands. "But have you looked at them carefully, Chabela? I really hope they're falsified, retouched. Sometimes I doubt it. But even if they are, the scandal's out there, nobody can stop it now, there's no turning back. Can you imagine what my life will be like after this? And I swear it will kill my mother-in-law. She's so proud and straitlaced, she won't survive something like this."

As if confirming her words, Nicasia came in to tell them that the *Exposed* photographs were being talked about on the radio and on television.

"We're not interested in hearing about it," Chabela interrupted her. "Turn off the radio and the television and don't pass through any phone call unless it's Luciano or Señor Enrique."

A few minutes later, Luciano called.

"I just spoke to Quique," he told his wife. "He's at his mother's. They'd already brought the magazine to the poor woman, can you imagine, what awful people. He had to call her doctor. Quique is still with her, he can't leave until he knows whether it's anything serious. Tell Marisa not to even think about going to her mother-in-law's house. The reporters are prowling around there, too. I'll go as soon as I can. Try to calm Marisa down; tell her that as soon as his mother's better, Quique will see her and explain everything."

Chabela and Marisa spent the rest of the morning talking. The only topic was those disgusting photographs, of course. "My mother-in-law's going to die," she kept repeating. "Did Luciano tell you who brought her the magazine? The people of Lima are the most perverse in the world, Chabela. I don't think the poor woman will survive the scandal. She's virtue personified, the poor old woman must have had a terrible shock when she saw the photos. Didn't you think it was incredible to see Quique there, naked in the middle of those prostitutes, doing those disgusting things?"

"It probably isn't him, darling, probably all those photographs have been doctored to harm him. Calm down, please."

"I am calm, Chabela. But don't you realize what's going to happen now to my life, to my marriage? How can a marriage survive something like this?"

"Don't think about that now, Marisa. First talk to Quique. I'm sure this is all a scheme to hurt him. Some envious person,

one of those enemies you make in this country simply because
your business is doing well."

Marisa didn't eat a mouthful at lunch. They turned on
the television to watch the news, but since the first thing to
appear on the screen was the cover of *Exposed*, and the
announcer almost shouted the news item—"Scandal in high
society!"—they turned it off. Luciano arrived at about four.
He embraced and kissed Marisa and read them a communiqué that, he said, had been distributed to the press in Quique's
name. Engineer Enrique Cárdenas Sommerville said he was
the victim of a publication that specialized in yellow journalism and scandal, which in its most recent edition published
photographs that had been doctored and falsified in an
attempt to undermine the businessman's good name. This
reprehensible effort would have its response and sanction according to current law. Lawyers had already presented an ap-
peal for protection to the Judicial Branch, asking for the
immediate seizure by the police of the libelous and insulting
paper, as well as precautionary measures so that Rolando
Garro, the editor of *Exposed*, the reporter Julieta Leguizamón,
co-author of the defamatory article, and the corresponding
photographer would be prevented from fleeing the country in
order to escape the punishment they deserved for attempted
blackmail, libel, falsification of documents, and affronts to
honor and privacy. The judicial suit had already been filed,
and Engineer Enrique Cárdenas Sommerville would soon hold
a press conference in response to this cowardly, base attempt
by gutter journalism to harm his person and his family.

Chabela looked at Marisa. She had listened to Luciano
reading the communiqué, as white as a sheet, looking down,
motionless in her chair. When he finished, she made no comment. Luciano folded the text and approached Marisa, whom
he embraced and kissed again on the forehead.

"All this is moving ahead, Marisita," he said. "It may be

too late to withdraw the magazine from every kiosk. But I assure you that the rat who has done this will pay dearly for it."

"Where's Quique?" Marisa asked.

"He stopped at his office for a moment to see to some urgent matters. He told me to wait for him here. He'll come very soon. It's better for you and Quique to stay with us for a few days until the storm dies down. You have to be brave, Marisa. Scandals seem terrible when they happen, but they quickly pass and soon nobody even remembers them."

Chabela thought that her husband didn't believe a word he was saying. Luciano was so proper he didn't even know how to hide his lies.

12

The People's Dining Room

Juan Peineta began the morning, as he did almost every day, writing in pencil, in his trembling hand, a letter against Rolando Garro. He addressed it to the newspaper *El Comercio*. In it he protested because the dean of the national press hadn't published his three previous letters "against that outlaw, the enemy of art and of quality, Señor Rolando Garro," who continued "doing his dirty business in his slanderous rags and programs, destroying reputations and committing offenses against everything that is decent, creative, and talented in the nation's artistic world, in which he is nothing but a pestilential excrescence." He signed it and put it in an envelope on which he placed a stamp and then put it in his pocket so he could drop it in the first mailbox he passed. He hoped he wouldn't forget, because sometimes that happened and some of his letters vegetated for many days in his pockets without his remembering to mail them.

Three or four times a week he went to have lunch at the people's dining room that the Barefoot Carmelites had in their convent of Our Lady of Carmen, on the eighth block of Junín Alleyway, in Carmen Alto. The food wasn't substantial, but it had the advantage of being free. He had to wait in a long line among crowds of poor people; better to get there early, since admission was limited, no more than fifty at a time, and many people never got in. That was why Juan would leave the Hotel Mogollón in good time. It wasn't too long a walk from there to Barrios Altos; all the way up Abancay Avenue, then around the Plaza de la Inquisición and the Congreso de la República, and up Junín Alleyway almost to Five Corners. But it was long for him because, with his varicose veins and his distractions, he had to walk very slowly. It took him close to an hour, and he had to stop at least a couple of times along the way.

Serafín didn't accompany him on these trips. He would leave the Hotel Mogollón with him, but when he realized that Juan was going up to Barrios Altos, he silently disappeared. Why was he so afraid of that impoverished area in the center of Lima? Perhaps because, with the natural intelligence of cats, Juan Peineta's friend had concluded it was a dangerous neighborhood where he could be kidnapped and turned into fricassee or "cat stew" and become a meal for those in the district who ate cats, and there must have been many of them. Eating a domestic animal so close to Juan Peineta seemed to him a form of cannibalism, almost like eating a human being.

He arrived at the Convent of Las Descalzas early, but even so there was already a long line of poor people, beggars, vagrants, the unemployed, little old men and women who looked as if they had just arrived in Lima from remote mountain communities. They could be recognized because they tended to look bewildered, as if they had lost their way and were afraid they'd never find it again. After standing in line for half an hour, Juan saw that they were opening the large doors to the people's dining room, and those in the first shift were beginning to go in. From the doorway, he could make out the bulky, shapeless silhouette of his friend Crecilda; he waved to her but she didn't see him. He had known her for many years, when she'd had a school of tropical dance in the Magdalena

Vieja district. But they had become friends only here, in the people's dining room, where the Carmelite Sisters had been preparing free lunches since time immemorial.

The menu was almost always the same, served on old, dented tin dishes: noodle soup, stewed greens with rice, and for dessert, apple or lemon compote. The dishes were already on the tables when they arrived; the food was served to them with large spoons by women in smocks with kerchiefs on their heads, but when they finished eating, it was the poor people themselves who carried the dishes to a sink, where the same women who had served them from large pans took the dishes and washed them. Crecilda directed all of this with a gentle but energetic hand; that was why she was always moving from one side to the other, agile in spite of her corpulence: enormous breasts, muscular legs, and dancing buttocks. This time she saw him first, sitting next to an Ayacuchan couple who were speaking Quechua. She came to say hello and to tell him not to leave immediately after eating but to stay and have a little maté with her and chat for a while.

Juan Peineta had come to esteem Crecilda—and he thought she felt the same for him—especially when he learned that she had been involved in the world of show business for many years and that, like him, her career as a dancer had ended because of that demon in trousers, that Satan, Rolando Garro. Crecilda's story made him sad because, like him, she was alone in the world. She'd had a son, but he'd left her years ago and she no longer had any contact with him at all; the boy had gone to find his fortune in the jungle, which made Crecilda very apprehensive, thinking that he probably was involved in something bad, maybe smuggling or, even worse, drug trafficking. But then, too, he also felt sad because of how disfigured her face was after she'd had that surgery to remove wrinkles. She had told him the story, and it really was very sad; a friend had a facelift with the surgeon Pichín Rebolledo, and looked much younger. Crecilda decided to do the same; she even took out a bank loan to pay in advance, as he required. And just look at how he had left her! So swollen and disfigured she could barely close her eyes, for he had tightened her eyelids. Her whole face, down to the beginning of her neck, had lost its color and acquired a bluish cast, like the face of someone with tuberculosis, or a corpse. "That surgeon and Rolando Garro are the tragedy of my life," she would say mischievously. "And I didn't fuck either one of them." She wasn't embittered or resentful, just the opposite: she maintained a lively spirit and knew how to fend off adversity without losing her coarse, vulgar sense of humor. It was one of the things about her that Juan Peineta liked best: Crecilda knew how to put on a brave face in hard times and defy misfortune with her delicious laughter.

When the first shift for lunch was over, Crecilda came to find Juan and took him with her to the small locutory from which one could observe everything that happened in the place. They sat down to drink two cups of tea that she had already prepared, and as they chatted, Crecilda kept glancing at the huge dining room to see that everything was in order, that nothing and no one demanded her presence.

"And what would happen if the good sisters discovered that you were once a music hall dancer and performer, Crecilda?"

"Nothing would happen. The sisters are very good people," she replied. "They know that's all over and forgotten, and now in my old age I behave like a saint. I come to Mass and take Communion every Sunday. Don't you see how I'm dressed? Don't I look like a nun, too?"

She did. She wore a tunic of rough cloth that covered her from her shoulders to her feet, encased in house slippers.

"They ought to have meat on the menu sometime, Crecilda," said Juan, enjoying his sugared tea. "I already know that scramble of vegetables all too well. Even now when my memory is a disaster, every day I forget something else."

"If you only knew: it's a miracle they keep producing that lunch, Juanito." She shrugged. "A real miracle. The donations become skimpier every day. And with all the talk about the crisis, even the poor sisters are half-dead with hunger with the little they eat. I wouldn't be surprised if this dining room closed any day now."

"And what would happen to you then, Crecilda?"

"I'd have to devote myself to begging, Juanito. Because I doubt very much that I'd find another job. The time for me to devote myself to a wayward life is past."

"Well, one possibility is that you marry me and come live at the Hotel Mogollón."

"I think I prefer begging to that proposal of marriage," Crecilda said with a laugh, indicating a negative response with her hand. "Do you think the three of us would fit in that cave you live in?"

"Three of us?" Juan was surprised.

"Your cat," she reminded him. "Don't tell me you've forgotten him, too. His name's Serafín, isn't it?"

"Yes, Serafín. Do you know why I think he doesn't follow me when I come here? He's afraid the vagrants in the neighborhood will kidnap him and turn him into 'cat stew.'"

"They say it's delicious when it's well prepared," Crecilda acknowledged. "But no matter what they say, I'd rather die than eat a cat. Listen, Juan, changing the subject, have you seen the latest issue of *Exposed*?"

"As you can imagine, Crecilda, I haven't bought and never will buy one of Señor Rolando Garro's magazines."

"Neither have I, compadre," she replied, laughing and again making a negative sign with her right hand. "But I read it sometimes when I see it hanging in the magazine kiosks. So you haven't seen the latest scandal he's uncovered. Photos of a millionaire in that awful orgy in Chosica. I never thought they'd publish photos like these. They even show him doing sixty-nine with some girl."

"Sixty-nine?" Juan Peineta said with a sigh. "You know, Crecilda, I never got to do that with my Atanasia. At least, I don't remember our doing it. We were both a little puritanical, I think."

"A little stupid, you mean, Juanito," Crecilda said with a laugh. "You don't know what you missed."

"Yes, maybe you're right. And who is the millionaire in the photos? From here, a Peruvian?"

She nodded:

"Yes, yes, his name is Enrique Cárdenas and he's a miner, really rich, it seems. Photos that are really shocking, Juanito. I think this time that midget bastard Garrito has gone too far. And maybe now they'll make him pay for all the bad he's done."

"From your lips, Crecilda," Juan Peineta said with a sigh. "I only hope that miner hires a killer to take care of him. They say there are very cheap Colombian assassins who've come to Peru because back in Colombia there's no work for them. And apparently they'll take care of anybody for just two or three thousand soles."

"I'd rather they threw him in jail, Juanito. What do we get if he dies? It's better if he suffers, if he pays for all the bad he's done with years in jail. Death isn't enough for guys like him. But rotting for years and years in a cell, yes, that's a real punishment."

"Yes, yes, they should torture him," Juan Peineta laughed. "Pull out his nails, his eyes, cook him over a slow fire, the way the inquisitors did with heretics."

They were laughing as they imagined evil things happening to Rolando Garro, the man responsible for their respective misfortunes, until the second shift for lunch was over. Crecilda had to go to supervise the dishwashing and the cleanliness of the place. Juan Peineta said goodbye and thought that on his way back to the Hotel Mogollón he'd look for a kiosk where *Exposed* was on display, he wanted to see that millionaire naked and doing the famous sixty-nine that he and Atanasia, out of excessive piety, had never done. Or had they? He couldn't remember. But yes, he did recall that Atanasia refused to suck him off, claiming that her confessor had said that doing those filthy things, even though they were married, was a mortal sin. And he, who loved her so much, had he been resigned? He wasn't very certain. He tittered: "Juanito, you'll die without ever knowing what a sixty-nine and a suck-off were like." Bah, hadn't he and Atanasia been happy without experiencing that kind of foolishness?

He found the kiosk where *Exposed* was on display and it took him some time to approach the issue of the magazine hanging from a couple of hooks in the ceiling of the magazine kiosk. Two pages of the weekly were on view: the cover and the double spread in the middle. A handful of people had crowded around him, contemplating the scandalous photographs; some stood on tiptoe, trying to read the captions and the other information that the photos illustrated. Juan Peineta recognized the face of the great gentleman who appeared here naked, in every imaginable position, and how well accompanied! He couldn't find the photo of the sixty-nine. It must be on one of the inside pages, what a shame. Juan Peineta told himself he would have to confess to having spent so much time looking at such filth. He reflected in astonishment that Crecilda probably was right. This time Rolando Garro had gone too far. That guy was important, one of Peru's fat cats. Photographing him like that, in those positions, with those women, was too much. Garro would pay; this time he wouldn't get his way as easily as he had so often in the past.

And he immediately began to plan the letter he would write as soon as he was back at the Hotel Mogollón.

He resumed his walk, always taking small steps, unable to get the images in *Exposed* out of his head. It meant that those things were not only dreamed about, they were lived in reality, too. Well, by the fat cats, not by poor men. He'd never gone in for that kind of bizarre thing. Or had he, one night when he'd been drinking? He wasn't sure about that, either. His forgetfulness created problems for him when it was time to confess. The priest became exasperated: "Now you don't even remember your sins. Have you come here to mock me?" Perhaps he didn't try those things because he was very happy making love in a nice, normal way with poor Atanasia. He remembered how his wife would tremble all over when they made love, and her eyes would grow wet.

When he was only three blocks from the Hotel Mogollón, he discovered that Serafín had silently reappeared and was walking between his feet. "Hi, pal," he said, happy to see him. "Well, today at least you escaped their kidnapping you and throwing you into a pot to make a 'cat stew' out of you. Don't worry, while you're with me nobody will touch a hair on your head, Serafín. Now, in the hotel, I'll give you a little of the milk I've been keeping in the bottle. I hope it hasn't gone sour."

In his room in the Hotel Mogollón, after sharpening his pencil, he wrote a letter to "Señor Rolando Garro, Editor of *Exposed*." He reproached him for having violated the privacy of that degenerate miner who engaged in sexual depravities with prostitutes, and for having offended the honor and morality of his readers by publishing that obscene filth, which, if it fell into the hands of children and minors, could shock and pervert them. Undoubtedly there were laws he had violated with those scandalous photographs and he hoped the national public prosecutor would intervene in this matter and proceed to close the aforementioned magazine and fine and prosecute its twisted editor.

He reread the letter, signed it, and, satisfied with himself, prepared to go to sleep. Early tomorrow—if he remembered—he would mail it.

13

An Absence

Shorty prepared her frugal breakfast every morning—café con leche and brown corn bread—but today, she didn't know why, she had the impulse to have it in a coffee shop in Five Corners located at the bus stop. After thirty or forty-five minutes of shaking and crowding, the bus carried her each morning down the very long Grau Avenue, the Zanjón, and Panamerican Avenue to Surquillo, in the vicinity of *Exposed*. They did not have corn bread in the coffee shop, so she ordered some kind of biscuit along with her café con leche and they brought her sweet bread. She was sorry she had gone there: the coffee shop was dirty and the walls were stained and the waiter who served her, a cripple with rheumy eyes, had black, very long nails.

But the good weather improved her spirits. In spite of its being the middle of winter, there was a luminescence this morning in Lima that seemed to announce the sun. "The sky is celebrating our success too," she said to herself. Because the issue of *Exposed* with the photographs of Engineer Enrique Cárdenas had been a rousing success, announcing on the first page, in a large headline in red and black letters above the spectacular image: "Naked Magnate Having a Snack!" Three successive reprints in a single day! The night before, a euphoric Rolando Garro had been negotiating a fourth with the printer even though it was barely a thousand more copies.

What would happen now? she had asked her boss when the letter from Engineer Enrique Cárdenas's lawyers had reached the magazine's editorial office, denying, of course, that he was the man in those photos and accusing them of libel and slander. Apparently they had filed for an order of relief, asking for the sequestration of the issue, including the first copies.

"What's going to happen?" Rolando Garro asked himself, shrugging. And he answered his own question, giving one of his sarcastic little laughs: "Nothing, Shorty. Does anything ever happen when a scandal breaks in Lima? I wish something would, I wish a judge would close down *Exposed*. We'd put out a new weekly called *Gotcha* maybe, and sell as many copies as we did this week."

Shorty thought her boss's calm was faked. Because this time the subject of the scandal wasn't a model, a dancer, an actor, or one of those poor show-business types like that idiot Juan Peineta with his animosity toward Rolando Garro, who couldn't do him or the magazine much harm no matter how they tried and who, like the ex-Joker, dedicated their lives to that useless plan. Engineer Enrique Cárdenas, an important entrepreneur, rich, powerful, wouldn't just sit still after an issue in which he appeared naked among whorish tits and asses. He'd take his revenge, and if he persisted, he certainly could have the weekly closed down. Well, we'd soon see, she didn't much like the idea of losing her job overnight. Rolando Garro seemed so sure of himself that probably, just as in the other exposés they'd done, there would be no consequences this time, either. Just think of how poor Ceferino Argüello's photographs had ended up; instead of making them all-powerful, as Rolando believed, they would be just another scandal in *Exposed*.

She paid for her meager breakfast and took the bus; it

wasn't too crowded, she even was able to find a seat. It took three quarters of an hour to reach the stop on the Panamericana, in Surquillo, a few blocks from Calle Dante. She was walking to her office when Ceferino Argüello, the weekly's photographer, approached her. As always, his skeletal body was crammed into blue jeans and a dirty polo shirt, wrinkled and open at the neck. He looked more frightened than usual.

"What is it, Ceferino? Why that face, who died this time?"

"Can we get something to drink, Julieta?" The photographer, very upset, paid no attention to her question. "My treat."

"I have an appointment with the boss," she said. "And I'm running late."

"Señor Garro isn't in yet," he insisted, pleading with her. "Just for a moment, Julieta. I'm begging you, please, as a colleague and an old friend. Don't turn me down."

She agreed and they went to the little café near *Exposed*, Peruvian Delight, where the reporters on the magazine had coffee, and on the days they put the issue to bed, would eat a sandwich with an Inca Kola for lunch. They ordered two sodas.

"What is it, Ceferino?" Shorty asked. "Go on, tell me your troubles. I imagine they don't have anything to do with love."

Ceferino Argüello didn't want to joke; he was very serious, and there was a great deal of fear in his dark eyes.

"I'm shitting, I'm so scared, Julieta." He spoke very quietly so that no one would hear him, and it was absurd, nobody could hear him because at that moment, they were the only customers in Peruvian Delight. "This is getting too big, don't you think? Last night all the channels opened their news reports with photos of the magazine. This morning, radio and television stations pounded away at the same subject."

"What do you expect, you idiot, you're finally becoming

famous like the rest of us, thanks to this issue." She mocked the photographer. "We haven't had this much success with an exposé for a long time. Now, for sure, at the end of the month we'll all get our full salary."

"This isn't a joke," Ceferino remonstrated with her. He paused, looked around, and continued in a voice so low it was almost a whisper. "That Cárdenas is very important, and if he decides to take his revenge he can fuck up our lives. Don't forget that you signed that article too, Shorty."

"On the other hand, your name doesn't appear anywhere, Ceferino, so take it easy," she said, making an effort to get up. "Pay, and let's get out of here. And please, don't be such a big sissy. You're scared of everything."

"Even though I'm not named in the article, I took those photos, Julieta," he insisted; his anguished expression looked almost comic. "And I'm the only photographer listed on the masthead. I can get involved in a big mess. Señor Garro should have consulted me before doing what he did with my photographs."

"It must be your fault, Ceferino, you brought it on yourself," Shorty attacked him. But she took pity on the terror she saw in his eyes and smiled at him: "Nobody will know you took them. So cut the bullshit and don't think about it anymore."

"Swear you haven't told anybody that I took them, Julieta. And that you never will."

"I'll swear anything you want, Ceferino. Forget about it. Nobody's going to find out, nothing's going to happen to you. Don't worry."

The photographer, his face constantly tormented, paid, and they left. Rolando Garro wasn't at *Exposed* yet. While they waited for him, Shorty devoted herself to reviewing all the day's papers. Caramba, what excitement! There were references to the scandal in every paper, without exception, from serious publications to the most insignificant dailies. Shorty laughed to herself: the engineer must be feeling like a puddle of spit right now. When she finished going through the papers it was eleven in the morning. Strange that Rolando Garro hadn't showed up or called to give a reason for being late. She called his cell phone and it was turned off. Could he still be asleep? It was unusual, the boss never missed an appointment, even with his reporters, without giving a reason for being late. Shorty looked around; there was a strange silence in the editorial room; nobody was typing on a computer, nobody was talking. Estrellita Santibáñez looked at her desk as if hypnotized; old man Pepín Sotillos had the butt of his cigarette dangling from his lips as if he'd forgotten he was smoking. Lizbeth Carnero, distracted from her stars, bit her nails, not bothering to hide her uneasiness. Up at one of the Theatine windows, a turkey buzzard was sitting, seeming to observe them with his fierce stare as if they were strange beasts. Everyone was very serious, waiting, looking at her, not hiding their concern. Poor Ceferino Argüello looked as if he were about to mount a scaffold.

A short while later a messenger arrived from the Criminal Court of the Lima District with two announcements of judicial actions filed against the magazine for this week's issue. One came from the Luciano Casasbellas Law Offices, representing Engineer Enrique Cárdenas, and the other from a religious association, Good Habits, denouncing them for "public obscenity and corruption of youth." Julieta left the citations on Rolando Garro's desk, which she confirmed was, as always, maniacally neat. She returned to her desk to look over her notebook. She made a list of subjects that could be investigated with a view to an article and began to take notes, navigating past the snares, on a case of trafficking boys and girls in Puno, near the Bolivian border. There were accusations that a gang of bandits was kidnapping children born in indigenous

Bolivian communities and selling them to Peruvian gangsters at the border who, in turn, resold them to couples, generally foreigners who couldn't have children and didn't want to wait the many years that procedures for legal adoptions required in Peru. At about one o'clock she looked up from the computer because she saw that the entire editorial staff had congregated around her desk: the three reporters, the two fact-checkers, and, of course, the photographer for *Exposed*. Their expressions were grave. Ceferino, very pale, was gasping for breath.

"It's past the time for giving out assignments, which was twelve o'clock," said Pepín Sotillos, the oldest of the reporters on the weekly, showing her his watch. "And it's after one."

"It's strange, yes, I agree," said Shorty. "I had an appointment with him at eleven. Nobody's talked to the boss this morning?"

No, nobody. Sotillos had called him several times on his cell, but it was turned off. Shorty saw her colleagues' long, uneasy faces. It was really very strange, the boss might have many defects but lack of punctuality wasn't one of them; he was obsessive about always arriving on time, even early. And especially for the meeting that planned the work for the week. Julieta decided to mobilize the entire editorial staff. She gave Sotillos the task of calling hospitals and clinics in case he'd had an accident; she told Estrellita Santibáñez and Lizbeth Carnero, the horoscope editor and the adviser in sexual and romantic matters, to check the police stations and find out whether Señor Rolando Garro had been the victim of an accident. And she would run over to the chief's little house in Chorrillos; the address was in his engagement book.

She went out and was going to take a cab but checked her wallet and thought that the little she had with her might not be enough to go and come back, and so she went to wait for the bus. It took almost an hour to reach the little house on José Olaya Avenue where the editor of *Exposed* lived. It was one of the old Chorrillan ranch houses of the previous century, a kind of cube made of cement and wood with a large grating that separated the door from the sidewalk. She rang the bell for some time but no one answered. Finally she decided to ask in the nearby houses if anyone had seen him. Her search was hopeless. The house to the left was empty; on the right, it took a very long time for anyone to come to the door. The woman who opened a peephole said she didn't even know that her neighbor was named Rolando Garro. When Shorty returned to the magazine offices it was already 2:30. No one had learned anything. The only thing certain was that there was no record in hospitals, clinics, or police stations of the chief having suffered an accident.

They spent a long time in confusion, exchanging ideas, not knowing what to do. Finally they decided to go home and meet again at four to see whether by then there would be any news about the editor.

Shorty had taken just a few steps toward the bus stop when she felt somebody grab her arm. It was the photographer. Ceferino was so nervous he could barely speak:

"I always knew this was dangerous, that this exposé could give us a lot of problems," he said, stumbling over his words. "What do you think happened, Julieta? Are they holding the boss prisoner? Have they done anything to him?"

"We don't know yet that anything's happened," she responded, in a fury. "Let's not get ahead of ourselves. Maybe something urgent turned up suddenly, some plan of his, or a party, I don't know. A little patience, Ceferino. We'll see this afternoon. He'll probably turn up and everything will be explained. Don't get ahead of yourself, and above all, don't do anything stupid. You'll have time to be scared later. Now, let go of me, please. I'm tired and I want to go home. To think calmly and rest a little. It's better to have a cool head for what may happen."

The photographer let her go but still managed to murmur as she was walking away:

"This smells very bad to me, Julieta. His disappearance means something serious."

"Shit-eating coward," she thought without responding. An hour later, when she reached her house in Five Corners, instead of preparing something to eat she lay down in her bed. She was alarmed, too, though she would have hidden that from Ceferino and the reporters on the weekly. Rolando Garro never just disappeared like this without letting anybody know, least of all on the day when work assignments were made for the week, and materials for the next issue were discussed. Could his disappearance be connected to the exposé of Engineer Cárdenas? If this was a real disappearance, most likely he was safe. Now she felt very tired. It wasn't the morning's activity, however, but concern, misgivings, suspicions regarding what could have happened to the boss that had her stupefied with fatigue.

When she awoke and looked at the clock, it was four in the afternoon. She had slept close to an hour. The first time in her life she had taken a siesta. She washed her face and returned to the offices of *Exposed*. All her colleagues were there, with long faces. None of them had heard anything at all about Rolando Garro.

"We'll go to the police and file a complaint," Shorty decided. "Something's happened to the chief, no doubt about it. Let's have the police look for him, then."

The entire editorial staff of *Exposed* moved to the Surquillo police station, which was very close to the offices of the magazine, right on Calle Dante. They asked to speak to the chief. He kept them standing in the little courtyard at the entrance, next to a large statue of the Virgin, for close to half an hour. Finally he had them come into his office. It was old man Sotillos who explained that they were upset because Señor Rolando Garro, their boss, had not been seen for the past twenty-four hours; there was no precedent for his disappearing like this, without saying a word, precisely on the day when he met with all the reporters to hand out assignments for the week. The mustached chief, a police colonel who put on airs, had them file a complaint, which all of them signed. He promised that he would begin the inquiry immediately and would let them know as soon as he had any information.

When they left the station, fearing that the mustached colonel wouldn't do anything, they decided to go to the firm of the lawyer for *Exposed*. Both Sotillos and Shorty knew Dr. Julius Arispe, who received them immediately in his office on España Avenue though it was close to seven in the evening. He was an amiable man who shook hands with everybody. He would brush his nose from time to time, as if he were frightening away a fly. He listened carefully to what Shorty said and said yes, the matter was alarming, especially when it had to do with a prestigious journalist like Señor Garro; he would alert the minister of the interior, who, aside from everything else, was a personal friend of his.

When they left the law offices, night had fallen. What else could they do? At that hour, nothing. They agreed to meet the next day at ten o'clock at the *Exposed* offices. They said goodbye and Shorty heard Ceferino Argüello approaching to talk to her alone. She stopped him dead:

"Not now, Ceferino," she said in a hard voice. "I know you're scared to death. I know you think the boss's disappearance has to do with your photos of the orgy in Chosica. I'm worried too, and frightened. But for now, there's nothing more to say about the matter. Not a single word until we know what to do about Señor Garro. Understood, Ceferino? I'm very nervous, so don't bother me anymore, please. We'll talk tomorrow."

She walked away from him and, remembering that she hadn't eaten anything all day, when she reached Five Corners sat down in the same filthy coffee shop where she'd had breakfast that morning. But before ordering anything, she got up and continued walking to her house. Why order anything if she wasn't hungry? She wouldn't be able to swallow any food she put in her mouth. She walked very quickly along the Junín Alleyway because it was dark, and this was the time for buying and selling drugs, prostitution, and holdups in the neighborhood. As she walked past a grate, a dog came out to bark, and frightened her.

In her house, she turned on the television and kept changing channels to see whether they said anything about her boss on the news. Not a word. After she turned off the TV, she continued to sit in the living room, lit by a single bulb that shed a greasy light among the piles of newspapers and magazines that crowded the room. What could have happened to him? A silvery cobweb hung from the ceiling, over her head. A kidnapping? Difficult. Rolando Garro didn't have a cent, what money could they get out of him? Blackmail by the terrorists? Unlikely. *Exposed* didn't get involved in politics, though it sometimes did publish personal exposés of politicians. Could it be true that the editor did these by order of the Doctor, the head of Fujimori's Intelligence Service? That rumor had been making the rounds for a long time, but Shorty had never dared to ask Rolando Garro about something so delicate. If the Shining Path or the MRTA wanted a journalist, they would have taken the editor of *El Comercio*, or a television channel, or the RPP conglomerate, not the owner of a publication as small as *Exposed*.

She was sitting there, in the shadows, without the energy

to go to bed, when a minute or an hour later—she had no idea how much time had passed—she heard someone knocking at her front door. She started in her chair with fright and her hands were wet with perspiration. They knocked again, this time in a peremptory way.

"Who is it?" she asked, not opening the door.

"Police," said a man's voice. "We're looking for Señorita Julieta Leguizamón. Is that you?"

"Why are you looking for her?" she asked. Her heart had begun to beat very rapidly.

"We're from the Ministry of the Interior, señorita," the same voice replied. "Open up, please, and I'll explain everything. You have nothing to fear."

She opened the door, very frightened, and saw a man in uniform with another man in civilian clothes. In the distance, behind the small houses in the lane, on the street, there was a police car with all its lights on.

"Captain Félix Madueño, at your service," said the official, raising his hand to his kepi. "Are you the journalist Julieta Leguizamón?"

"Yes, that's me," she concurred, trying to control her voice. "What can I do for you?"

"You have to accompany us to make an identification," the captain said. "We're sorry to bother you at this hour, señorita, but it's very urgent."

"An identification?" she asked.

"A group of you filed a complaint this afternoon regarding the disappearance of Señor Rolando Garro, the editor of *Exposed*, in the Surquillo police station. Isn't that so?"

"Yes, yes, our boss," said Shorty. "Do you have news about him?"

"Perhaps," the captain intimated. "That's why we need to make this identification. It won't take very long. Don't worry: we'll bring you back home."

Only when she was sitting in the back seat of the car, which pulled away toward Grau Avenue, did Shorty have the courage to ask something that she suspected:

"Where are we going, Captain?"

"To the morgue, señorita."

She didn't say anything else. She felt she didn't have enough air, she opened her mouth and tried to fill her lungs with the cool breeze coming in through the partially opened small window. They drove along dark streets and finally she recognized Grau Avenue near the Dos de Mayo Hospital. She felt dizzy, as if she were suffocating, and was afraid she might faint at any moment. At times she closed her eyes, and as she did when she had insomnia, she counted numbers. She barely noticed that the car had stopped; she was vaguely aware that Captain Félix Madueño was helping her out and, holding her arm, led her down some damp, dismal passageways with walls that smelled of cresol and medicines, an odor that nauseated her and obliged her to control her retching. At last they entered a brightly lit room where there were many people, all men, some in white lab coats and face masks. Her legs trembled and she knew that if Captain Madueño let her go, she'd fall to the floor.

"Here, this way," someone said, and she felt herself carried, pushed, held up by men who scrutinized her with a mixture of insolence, compassion, and mockery.

"Do you recognize him? Is this Rolando Garro?" another voice asked, one that Shorty hadn't heard so far.

It was a kind of table or board on two sawhorses, lit by a very white reflector light; the silhouette of the man under her eyes was stained all over with blood and dried mud.

"We know this is difficult for you, because, as you'll see, they bashed in his face with stones, or kicked it in. Can you recognize him? Is he who we think he is? Is this the journalist Rolando Garro?"

She was totally paralyzed, she couldn't move or say a word, she couldn't even nod, her eyes fixed on that muddied, bloody, pestilential silhouette.

"Of course she's recognized him, of course it's him," she heard Captain Félix Madueño say. "But Doctor, it would be a good idea for you to give her a tranquilizer or something. Don't you see what's happened to her? Any minute now she'll faint on us."

14

Conjugal Disagreements and Agreements

"Let me come back home, darling," Quique pleaded; his voice was weak and his face upset. Marisa noted that in these few days her husband had lost several kilos. He wasn't wearing a tie and his shirt was badly ironed. "I'm begging you, Marisa, I'm on my knees."

"I agreed to your coming here to talk about practical matters," she replied drily. "But if you insist on talking about that subject, which is absolutely closed, you'd better go."

They were in the small reception room next to the terrace where they used to eat breakfast. It was growing dark. Lima had turned into a gloomy stain and a myriad of tiny lights lost in the distance, dissolving in the incipient fog. In front of him, on the little glass table, Quique had a half-full glass of mineral water.

"Of course we're going to talk about practical matters, Blondie," he agreed, somewhere between plaintive and mournful. "But I can't go on living at my mother's when all my things are here. Please, reconsider, I beg of you."

"Just take them to your mother's, Quique." She raised her voice; she spoke with determination, not hesitating for a moment, staring into his eyes, not blinking. "You're not returning to this house, at least while I'm living here. Get used to the idea once and for all. Because I'll never forgive you for the despicable thing you did to me. I've already told you. I want a separation. I'm already separated from you . . ."

"I didn't do anything to you, I'm not the man in those photos, you have to believe me," he pleaded. "I'm the victim of a monstrous slander, Marisa. I can't believe that instead of helping me, my wife is supporting my enemies and taking their side."

"It's you, don't be such a liar and so cynical, Quique." She cut him off with a flashing look. She was wearing a very low-cut blouse, her shoulders bare with a glimpse of breast, her skin very white, her blond hair loose, her feet in open sandals. "It's fine if for legal reasons you deny that you're the man in the photos. But you won't deceive me, my boy. Have you forgotten how often in my life I've seen you naked? It's you, doing those disgusting things and, even worse, letting yourself be photographed in those awful poses with those revolting whores. You're the laughingstock of all Lima, and so am I, because of you. The most famous deceived wife in Peru, as *Exposed* says. Do you know how my parents and brothers and sisters feel with everything you've put me through recently?"

Enrique took a sip from the glass of mineral water. He tried to take his wife's manicured hand, but she pulled it away, making a disgusted face.

"I'm never going to separate from you, because I love you, darling," he pleaded, almost whimpering. "I've always loved you, Marisa. You're the only woman I've loved. And I'm going to win back your love, whatever it takes, I swear. Do you think I don't regret in my soul that we're involved in this scandal? Do you think that . . . ?"

He was interrupted by the ring of the cell phone in his pocket. He took it out and saw that Luciano was calling him.

"Excuse me, Blondie," he said to his wife. "It's Luciano, it could be something urgent. Hello? Yes, Luciano, go on, I'm here with Marisa. Yes, of course you can talk. Is there any news?"

Marisa saw that her husband, as he listened to what Luciano was saying, grew even paler; his face contorted, he opened his mouth, and a thread of saliva trickled out of the corner without his realizing it or wiping it away. What could have happened to make Quique behave this way? He blinked incessantly and his expression was idiotic. Luciano must have noticed that something strange was happening to Enrique, because Marisa heard her husband murmur twice: "Yes, yes, I hear you." Finally she heard him say goodbye in a faint voice: "Yes, Luciano, I'll go there right now." But instead of standing up, Quique, as white as a sheet, continued to sit in the easy chair across from her, his eyes lost, stammering: "It can't be, my God, it can't be, on top of everything else."

Marisa was frightened.

"What is it, Quique? What did Luciano say?" she asked. "Even more problems?"

Enrique looked at her as if only now was he aware that she was sitting across from him, or as if he didn't recognize her.

"Rolando Garro's been murdered," she heard him say in a voice from beyond the grave. He had the deranged eyes of a madman. "With horrible savagery, it seems. I don't know how many stab wounds, and besides that, his face was smashed in. They just found his body dumped on the street, in Five Corners. Do you know what this means, Marisa?"

He attempted to stand but slipped; he tried to hold on to the back of his chair, he couldn't, and he collapsed, falling first to his knees and then stretched out on the rug in the reception room. When Marisa kneeled down to help him she saw that Quique's eyes were closed, his forehead wet with perspiration, and he was frothing at the mouth and shivering.

"Quique, Quique!" she shouted, holding his face, moving him. "What is it? What's wrong?"

Her voice was very loud, and Quintanilla, the butler, and the maid came running into the reception room.

"Help me lift him," she told them. "Let's put him on the sofa. Nice and slow, let's not bang him. We have to call Dr. Saldaña. Hurry, hurry, please look up his number in the address book."

The three of them picked him up, and when the butler and the maid were putting a cold towel on his forehead and Marisa was trying to reach Dr. Saldaña on the phone, Quique half opened his eyes, in a daze. "What happened, what happened?" he asked, his voice husky. Marisa dropped the phone, ran to the sofa, and embraced her husband. She was pale and weeping.

"Ay, Quique, what a fright," she said. "You fainted, I thought you were dying. I was calling Dr. Saldaña. Do you want me to call an ambulance?"

"No, no, I'm feeling better now," he stammered, grasping his wife's hand and kissing it. He kept it at his lips and added: "It was the tension of these past few days, darling. And then this terrible news."

"There's nothing terrible about it, it's news we should celebrate," Marisa exclaimed; she had left her hand in her husband's and allowed him to keep kissing it. "Why do you care that they've killed the wretch who got us involved in this mess, the editor of that filthy magazine? I'm glad they killed him."

"I love you, I need you, my love," he said, raising his head and searching for Marisa's cheek to kiss. "We shouldn't wish for anybody's death, darling. Not even that crook's. But imagine what his murder means for me. Right now, this is going to revive the damn scandal."

"How do you feel?" she asked, touching his forehead; rage had disappeared from her face; she looked at him with concern and compassion. "No, you don't have any fever."

"I'm better now," he said, sitting up. "Luciano's waiting for me at his office, I have to go see him."

"Fix yourself up a little, Quique," she said, smoothing his shirt with both hands. "You're all disheveled from the fall. And your shirt and suit are shameful, they're all wrinkled."

"You were afraid," he said, smoothing his hair and brushing off his jacket and trousers. "Yes, don't say you weren't, darling. You were afraid when I passed out. Which means you still love me a little, don't you, Blondie?"

"Of course I was frightened," Marisa conceded, pretending to a severity she no longer felt. "But I don't love you at all. I'm disappointed in you and always will be. And I'll never forgive you."

She said this so mechanically, in a way that was so unconvincing, that Quique dared to take her by the waist and pull her toward him. Marisa didn't offer much resistance. He brought his mouth up to her ear. Seeing what was happening, Quintanilla and the maid exchanged a glance and decided to withdraw.

"I'm going to see Luciano to talk about this infernal matter," he whispered, kissing her and nibbling at her ear. "And then I'm coming back here to make love to you. Because you look very beautiful and I've never wanted to hold you naked in my arms as much as I do right now, Blondie."

He found her lips and his wife let him kiss her on the mouth, but she didn't respond and kept her lips closed while he kissed her.

"Are you going to do the same disgusting things that you did to those whores in the photographs?" Marisa asked as she walked with him to the front door.

"I'm going to make love to you all night, because I don't think you've ever looked as beautiful as you do today," he whispered, opening the door. "I'll be back very soon, don't fall asleep on me, please, for the sake of what you love most."

He left with the chauffeur—he hadn't driven himself since the *Exposed* scandal—and told him to drive to Luciano's office. He thought that because of this tragedy he'd at least be able to return to his Golf Club apartment, his bed, his home, his things, and to making love with Marisa. What he had just told his wife wasn't pretense. It was true; Blondie had become more beautiful with this crisis; while they argued, he had suddenly desired her and now, he was certain, tonight he would take his pleasure with Marisa again as he had in the best times. How long since they had made love? Three weeks at least, since the awful day when Rolando Garro brought those photographs to his office. And now that worm was dead, killed in an awful way in Barrios Altos. What was going to happen? Whatever it was, the scandal would surface again, and once again he'd be on the front pages of the newspapers, on the radio stations and television channels. He shivered: once again that bath of revolting publicity, repugnant insinuations, having to be careful about what he said, where he went, whom he saw, just to evade people's damned morbid curiosity.

"Did you finally make up with Marisa?" Luciano asked as soon as he greeted him in his office. "At least now she's letting you back in the house again."

"Yes, at least in that I've made some progress," Quique agreed. "What about Garro's murder? Do they know who did it or why he was killed?"

Luciano had received a call from the Doctor himself and had already had two interviews with him because of the scandal of the photographs and Garro's attempt at blackmail.

"He called to tell me that they found him stabbed to death with his face bashed in on a rubbish heap in Five Corners, up in Barrios Altos, at the entrance to a gambling den," Luciano explained. "The police haven't said anything yet. He wanted to warn me: because of this, it's inevitable that the matter we're trying to bury will flare up again. I'm sorry, but I'm afraid that's how it will be, Quique."

"Have they announced Garro's murder yet?"

"Not yet, but according to the Doctor, the police were going to make it public now, in a press conference. The item will appear on all the news programs tonight. You mustn't make any statements. And by all means keep them from connecting this death to the scandal. Although, of course, they will."

Luciano stopped talking and was looking at Quique in a way that his friend thought was strange, scrutinizing him with a solemn, suspicious face. Had the head of the Intelligence Service said something else to him that Luciano was hiding?

"What is it, Luciano? Why are you looking at me that way?"

The lawyer came up to him, held him by both arms, and looked at him for a moment very seriously, in silence; his narrow, somewhat Asian eyes revealed alarm and doubts.

"I'm going to ask you a question, Quique, and I need you to be absolutely frank with me." He patted his arms affectionately. "I'm not asking this as your attorney. I'm asking because of all the years we've been friends."

"I can't believe you're going to ask me that question, Luciano," he murmured, horrified.

"I'm going to ask it all the same, Quique," Luciano insisted. "Did you have anything to do with this?"

Quique felt dizzy and thought he would pass out again. He felt a strong pressure in his chest, everything around him was blurred, and he began to sway. He grabbed the edge of the desk.

"You think that?" he stammered. "I can't believe it, Luciano. You're asking me whether I killed that worm? If I had him killed? You're asking me that? Do you think I'm capable of such a thing?"

"Answer me, Quique." Luciano had not let go of his

shoulders. "Just tell me you had nothing to do with the murder of Rolando Garro."

"Of course I had absolutely nothing to do with the murder, Luciano! I can't believe that you, who've known me my whole life, can think I'm capable of killing someone, of having someone killed."

"It's all right, Quique." Luciano sighed with relief. He attempted a smile. "I believe you, of course I believe you. But I wanted to hear you say it."

Luciano let go of his arms and indicated that they should sit in the easy chairs under the English engravings and the shelves of leather-bound books.

"I have to know in full detail what you've done during these past forty-eight hours, Quique."

Luciano was still very serious, he spoke very calmly and held a notebook and pencil. He had recovered his usual serenity and calm; unlike Quique, who was so disheveled, Luciano wore a perfectly pressed red-and-white striped shirt, a wine-colored tie, and shoes that shone like mirrors. His cufflinks were silver.

"But why, Luciano, will you tell me what's going on once and for all?" Quique was very frightened now.

"What's going on, Quique, is that you're the prime suspect for this crime," said his friend, very calmly, speaking again in his usual affectionate voice, taking off his glasses and holding them. "You can't be foolish enough not to realize that. Garro involved you in this major scandal, which has even had repercussions in other countries. He ruined your life, in a sense. He destroyed your marriage, your name, your prestige, you name it. Now all the dirty yellow press is going to pounce again, claiming that you paid an assassin to get your revenge. Don't you understand?"

Dazed, imbecilic, Enrique listened to him and had the feeling that Luciano was talking about someone else, not him.

"I need you to sit there, at my desk, right now, and make me a list, as complete as possible, of the people you've seen, the places you've been during the past forty-eight hours. Right now, Quique, yes. We're at the threshold of a new scandal and it's better to be prepared to confront it. It's absolutely necessary to establish all your alibis in case the worst happens. Go on, sit there, and make that list now."

He obeyed Luciano docilely and, sitting at his desk, for close to half an hour, Quique tried to put into writing everything he had done for the past two days. He thought it would be very easy, but as soon as he began to write, he discovered that he was especially confused about the times, and that there were gaps in his memory. When he finished, he handed the list to Luciano, who examined it carefully.

"It may be that nothing will happen and this is all my imagination, Quique," he reassured him. "I hope so. But, since you never know, we have to be prepared. If you remember anything else, even if it's an insignificant detail, call me."

"In other words, the whole damned nightmare will come back," the engineer said with a sigh. "Just when I thought the storm was beginning to calm down, this happens. Welcome, trouble, if you come alone, as the saying goes."

"Do you want a whiskey?" Luciano asked. "It might do you good."

"No, I prefer to get into bed," said Quique. "I feel as if I just ran the New York marathon, old man."

"Okay, rest, Quique." Luciano said goodbye. "And make peace once and for all with Marisa. We'll talk tomorrow."

When he reached his apartment, Quique said good night to the chauffeur and went up to the penthouse, somewhat uneasy, thinking that Marisa had probably set the alarm and locked the door. But no, he was able to enter his home without difficulty. The servants told him the señora had gone to bed and asked if he wanted them to fix him something to eat. He said he wasn't hungry and wished them good night. Quintanilla, an Ayacuchan who had been with them for many years, murmured as he passed: "How good that you've come back, Don Enrique."

The bedroom was dark and he didn't turn on the light on the night table. He undressed in darkness and, without putting on pajamas, slipped under the sheets naked. The presence and scent of Marisa excited him all over again, and without saying a word he slid to where she was and embraced her.

"I love you, I love you," he murmured, kissing her, joining his body to hers, embracing her. "Please forgive me for the difficult times you've had on my account, Marisa, my love."

"I don't think I can ever forgive you, you wretch," she said, turning so as to face him, kissing and embracing him as well. "You'll have to do something distinguished for that to happen."

15

Shorty Is Afraid

Hadn't Captain Félix Madueño, the one who came for her in Five Corners and took her to the morgue in the patrol car, called her "Julieta Leguizamón"? Well, he was very well informed. Yes, Julieta was her name, but very few people knew that her last name was Leguizamón. It had sounded very strange to hear herself named that way, because everybody used her nickname: Shorty. Or, at most, Julieta. That's how she signed her articles, with her nickname or her first name. The patrol car that brought her back to Teniente Arancibia Alleyway didn't carry the officer or the civilian, just the civil guards. During the trip neither the driver nor his companion said a word to her, and again she noted that they were perfectly familiar with the narrow potholed alley in Barrios Altos where she lived.

When she arrived home, Shorty went to the kitchen, drank a glass of water, and got into bed in her clothes, removing only her shoes. She was very cold. And then she felt grief, a deep, tearing grief, as she recalled what she had seen in the morgue: what remained of Rolando Garro. She didn't usually cry, but now she felt that her eyes were wet and fat tears were rolling down her cheeks. How perverse, how cruel, they had crushed his face with a stone and riddled his body with stab wounds. That wasn't the work of an ordinary rat, one of those poor devils who snatched purses or watches. That had been an act of vengeance. A well-planned and, surely, very well-paid murder. A murder by assassins, by professional criminals.

She shuddered from head to toe. And who could have planned that act of revenge but Enrique Cárdenas, the millionaire whose naked photographs in an orgy with whores Rolando Garro had published, photographs by Ceferino Argüello. Motherfucker, damn, son of a bitch. It would put the fear of God into poor Ceferino when he found out what they had done to the editor of *Exposed*. It was to be expected, because if his boss had been destroyed like that, what would they do to the creator of those photos? She'd better let him know so he could disappear for a while, certain they were looking for him. But she didn't even know Ceferino's address, and she didn't have his cell phone number so she could warn him. As for the rest, Shorty didn't intend to show up tomorrow at the offices of *Exposed*. She wasn't crazy. She wouldn't set foot there for a long time. Besides, who knew whether the magazine would survive; of course not, it would disappear just like poor Garro. Was she in danger, too? She tried to reason coldly. Yes, no doubt about it. Everybody knew that for a long time she'd been the boss's right arm, that Shorty was the star reporter of *Exposed*. And though Rolando himself had written the article that accompanied the photographs of the naked millionaire, she had obtained a good part of the information and her signature was right next to the chief's, so she was compromised as well.

"What kind of mess have you gotten me into, boss?" she said aloud. She was afraid. She had always expected those complications, that revealing the intimate dirt of well-known, famous people would put her at risk one day, perhaps even the risk of jail or death. Had her time come? Day and night her life had been a balancing act: Didn't she live in Five Corners, one of the most violent neighborhoods in Lima, with assaults, fights, and beatings all around her? She and her boss had often joked about what they were risking with their expert scandalous disclosures. "One day they'll put a bullet in us, Shorty, but cheer up, we'll be two martyrs to journalism and they'll put up a statue to us." And her boss would let out that laugh that was like stones falling in his throat. He didn't believe what he was saying, of course. And now he was a stinking corpse.

Poor man. The world seemed empty without Rolando Garro. Her boss. Her teacher. Her inspiration. Her only family. You're all alone now, Shorty. And her secret love. But nobody knew that, only she did, and she kept it buried deep in her heart. She had never let him even suspect she was in love with him. One night she heard him say: "Two people who work together shouldn't go to bed; love and work are incompatible, 'go to bed with' almost rhymes with 'contend with.' So now you know, Shorty. If you ever notice me making advances, instead of paying attention to me break a bottle over my head." "Better if I stab you in the heart with this, boss," Shorty replied, showing him the small knife she carried in her purse, in addition to the needle in her hair or belt in case of emergency. She closed her eyes and remembered once again the bloody corpse and destroyed face of Rolando Garro. Grief froze her from her head down to her feet. She remembered that, a few months ago, her boss had gone too far. The only time. At the opening of that club that didn't last very long, El Pingüino, in a basement on Tacna Avenue, to which Rolando had been invited. And he took her. There were a good number of people when they arrived at the club, small, filled with smells and smoke, *chilcanos*, or pisco and ginger ale, and pisco sours, which was what they were offering to drink. Trays of small glasses were being passed around, and some people were already drunk. They turned down the lights. The show began. Half-naked black girls came out to dance to the rhythms of a small band playing tropical music. Suddenly, Shorty noticed that her boss, standing behind her, was touching her breasts. With anyone else she would have reacted with her usual ferocity and stuck him with the needle in her hair or made his face swell up with a hard slap. But not Rolando Garro. She stood motionless, feeling something strange, a pleasure mixed with displeasure, something dark and pleasing, those small hands indelicately groping her breasts made her quiet and docile. She turned to look at him and saw in the semidarkness that her boss's eyes were glassy with alcohol, for he'd already had several *chilcanos*. Rolando Garro, immediately after they looked at each other, let her go. "Forgive me, Shorty," she heard him say. "I didn't realize it was you." Never again did he even allude to that episode. As if it had never happened. And now he was in the morgue, his face smashed in by stones and his body riddled with stab wounds. The policeman said they had found him in Five Corners. What could Rolando Garro have been doing in this neighborhood? Had he come looking for her? Impossible, he'd never set foot in this house. Some woman, maybe. Not her in any case, because her boss had no idea where she lived. In spite of working with him and seeing him every day for years, Shorty knew nothing about her boss's private life. Did he have a wife? Children? Probably not, because he never mentioned them. And he spent all day and all night preparing issues of *Exposed*. He was always as alone as she was and had no life except his work.

She slept very badly. She fell asleep and the nightmare was

immediately reborn; with a background of catastrophes, fires, earthquakes, she was rolling down a steep slope, a bus was bearing down on her, and, paralyzed by terror, she could not move away, and when it was about to run over her, she awoke. Finally, when the gray light of dawn appeared at the windows, she dozed off, disturbed by the bad night.

She had showered and was getting dried when she heard someone knocking at the door. Frightened, she gave a start. "Who is it?" she asked, raising her voice a good deal. "Ceferino Argüello," the photographer said. "Did I wake you? I'm really sorry, Shorty. It's urgent that I speak to you."

"Wait a minute, I'm getting dressed," she shouted. "I'll be right there."

She dressed and let the photographer in. Ceferino's face was devastated with worry and his eyes were irritated and red, as if he had been rubbing them very hard. He was wearing wrinkled trousers, sneakers without socks, and a black polo shirt decorated with a red lightning flash. His voice sounded different, he spoke as if it was very difficult for him to articulate each word.

"Forgive me for bothering you so early, Shorty," he said, standing in the doorway. "They've killed the boss, I didn't know whether you knew."

"Come in, Ceferino, sit down." She pointed to one of the chairs that emerged from among the piles of newspapers in the living room. "Yes, yes, I know. The police came to see me last night. They took me to the morgue to identify the body. It was horrible, Ceferino. I'd better not tell you about it."

He had dropped into the chair and looked at her, very pale, eyes staring, mouth open with a thread of saliva hanging from it, waiting. Shorty knew very well what was passing through Ceferino's head and she felt fear again, a fear as great as the one reflected in the photographer's face.

"They found him up here in Five Corners, it seems," she explained. "With his body full of knife wounds. And those sons of bitches destroyed his face with stones."

She saw that Ceferino Argüello was nodding. His hair was on end, like a porcupine. His pockmarked face was livid.

"It's what the papers and the radio stations are saying. That they were very brutal with him."

"Yes, yes, real butchery. Something that sadists, that savages would do, Ceferino."

"And now it'll happen to us, Shorty." The photographer's voice broke. She thought that if he started to cry she'd insult him, call him a "damn faggot," and throw him out of her house.

But Ceferino didn't cry, his voice just broke, and he sat looking at her as if hypnotized.

"I don't know what can happen to us." Shorty shrugged and decided to put on the finishing touches. "They might decide to kill us, too, Ceferino. Especially you, you're the one who took those pictures."

The photographer stood up and spoke with troubled solemnity, raising his voice with each sentence that he said:

"I knew this was very dangerous, damn it, and I told you, and I told the boss." He was shouting now, beside himself. "And they can kill us for goddamn greed, to get money out of that millionaire, damn it. You're guilty too, because I trusted you and you betrayed me."

He dropped into the chair, covered his face with his hands, and sobbed.

Shorty, seeing him like that, so defenseless and drowning in panic, felt sorry for him.

"Make an effort and try to think clearly, Ceferino," she said gently. "You and I need to have cool heads if we want to get out of this safe and sound. Don't waste your time looking for the person who's to blame for what's happened. Do you know who's to blame? Not you and not me, not even the boss. It's the work we do. And that's enough."

Ceferino took his hands away from his face and nodded. His eyes weren't crying but they were very irritated and shining; a stupid grimace distorted his face.

"When I told you I had those photographs, it was only to ask your advice, Julieta," he said in a quiet voice. "That's the only thing I wanted to remind you of."

"You're lying, Ceferino," she replied, not raising her voice either, as if she were advising him. "You told me you'd held on to them for two years because you wanted to see whether you could get anything out of them. I mean, publishing them and making a little money with them."

"No, no, I swear that's not true, Shorty," Ceferino protested. "I didn't want them published. I knew something very ugly could happen, like what's happened now, exactly like this. I guessed this would happen, I swear."

"If you didn't want them published, you would have burned them, Ceferino." Shorty was becoming angry. "I mean, cut the bullshit. I told you that the person who'd make the most out of them was the boss. And you authorized me to tell him everything. Didn't you take those photos to see what he could do with them? Don't you remember that now?"

"Okay, okay, let's not argue about what can't be helped." The photographer softened, again putting on his usual face of a whipped dog. "Now we have to decide what to do. Do you think the police will call us to testify?"

"I'm afraid they will, Ceferino. And the judge, too. There's been a murder. We worked with the victim. It's logical that they'd call us to testify."

"And what am I going to tell them, Julieta?" Suddenly the photographer seemed desperate again. His eyes were sunken, and his voice, hoarse now, was quavering.

"Don't be stupid enough to admit that you took those pictures," said Shorty. "That's all we'd need."

"Then what am I going to tell them?"

"That you don't know anything about anything. You didn't take those pictures and the boss didn't tell you who did."

"And what are you going to say when they call you to testify?"

Julieta shrugged.

"I don't know anything either," she declared. "I wasn't at that orgy, I didn't know about it until we prepared the information for *Exposed*. Isn't that the truth?"

Julieta advised Ceferino not to go to the offices of the weekly; she wouldn't either. If Engineer Cárdenas had hired killers, that's the first place they'd look. And it would also be prudent if he didn't sleep at home for a few days.

"I have a wife and three children, Shorty. And not a cent in my pocket. Because they haven't even paid us this month."

"And they won't pay us, Ceferino," she interrupted. "With the boss's death, *Exposed* will pass on to a better life. You can be sure of that. So now you can begin to look for another job. So will I, of course."

"So you think we won't even get paid for this month, Julieta? This is a tragedy for me, don't forget I always live paycheck to paycheck."

"For me, too, Ceferino. I don't have any money either. But since I don't like the idea of one of Engineer Cárdenas's hired killers coming after me, I'm not setting foot in *Exposed* again. I advise you to do the same. I'm saying this for your own good. Explain the problem to your wife, she'll understand. Stay out of sight with someone you trust. At least until the situation becomes clearer. That's the only advice I can give you. Because it's what I'm going to do myself."

Ceferino stayed a while longer in Julieta's house. From

time to time he'd say goodbye, but as if an irresistible force kept him from leaving, he would sit down again among the pyramids of newspapers and magazines, complain again about his bad luck, and curse the Chosica photographs, whose negatives he had kept, not to try to make any money—he swore to God!—but in the hope that the gentleman who hired him to take the pictures would reappear and pay him the amount they'd agreed on. He'd been stupid—yes, stupid—and he'd regret it the rest of his life.

Finally, after sniveling for a long time and complaining about his bad luck, he left. Shorty dropped into the easy chair among mountains of newspapers. She was exhausted and, worst of all, Ceferino Argüello had infected her with his confusion and panic.

She looked at her knees and saw they were trembling. It was a small movement, from right to left and left to right, almost imperceptible, rhythmic and cold. When she raised a foot, the trembling stopped, but only in that knee; it continued in the other one. She felt invaded by fear, from the roots of her hair to the soles of her feet. Ceferino Argüello's cowardice was contagious. She tried to calm down, to think objectively. She had to do what she had recommended to the photographer: leave her house immediately, stay with someone she trusted, until the storm let up. Who? She reviewed the people she knew. There were a lot of them, of course, but no one close enough to ask that they put her up. She had no relatives or hadn't seen them for years. Her friends were journalists, radio and television people with whom she had very superficial and occasional relationships. In reality, the only person whom she trusted enough for a matter like this was Rolando Garro. This murder had deprived her of the only real friend she had.

A small hotel or a boardinghouse, then. Nobody would

know where she was. But how much would that cost? From a bureau she took the notebook where she carefully recorded her expenses and income. The amount at her disposal was ridiculous: less than three hundred soles. She would have to borrow the money. She knew very well that, with the boss's death, it would be very difficult this month for her to receive her salary at *Exposed*. The magazine's funds were probably in the possession of Garro himself or had been placed under judicial sequestration because of his death. The manager of the weekly always said it was about to fall into insolvency, which perhaps was true now. In other words, there was nothing to hope for from that quarter.

Then what are you going to do, Shorty? She felt depressed, cornered, paralyzed. She knew very well that it was dangerous to remain in the house, where they'd look for her first if they wanted to do her harm. She knew that sooner or later she'd find another position with no difficulty: wasn't she good at her job? Of course she was, but now wasn't the best time to visit newspapers, radio stations, or television channels looking for work. Now was the time to hide, to save her skin, to not let anyone know where she was. Until things calmed down and returned to normal. Where, damn it, where could she hide?

And then, at first in a confused, remote way, but then gradually taking shape, consistency, reality, the idea came to her. It was risky, no doubt about it. But wasn't that something her teacher had taught her, something he had often practiced in his life, that great ills require great remedies? And what could be worse than feeling threatened in the practice of her vocation? That was the wager that had finished off Rolando Garro, wasn't it, Shorty? He had lost his life, in such an awful way, for practicing investigative journalism and bringing to light the obscenities that the wealthy in this country without laws or morality could allow themselves.

It was risky, of course. But if it worked out, she would not only be protected, she might also gain some professional advantage.

Suddenly, Shorty felt that her knees had stopped trembling. And she was smiling.

16

The Landowner and the Chinese Woman

"It's all over now, Quique," said Luciano, patting his friend on the knee. "You have to forget about that subject and fatten yourself up. You're as thin as a fishbone."

"Do you think it's all over because they killed that scoundrel and *Exposed* disappeared?" Enrique made a mocking face. "No, Luciano. It'll pursue me till the end of my days. Shall I tell you what torments me most about all this? It isn't even the physical and mental harm it has done to my poor mother, or that my name has been dragged through the mud. No, no. What has become a torture are the vulgar little jokes of my friends, my partners, even at meetings of the board of directors. 'Great orgy, brother,' 'Why didn't you invite us to that roll in the hay, compadre,' 'Can you tell me how many you fucked at that party, old man?' I can't bear any more of their stupidity, the winks from so many imbeciles. I'd prefer them to insult me or refuse to greet me, as some people have done. That's why Marisa and I are thinking about taking a little trip."

"A second honeymoon? The famous little trip around the Greek islands we talked about years ago?" Luciano laughed, but immediately became serious again: "Speaking of Marisa.

I can't tell you how glad I am that you've made up and she's forgiven you. The truth is I see you both finally reconciled."

"It's true," Quique agreed, lowering his voice and glancing toward the interior of Luciano's house in case Marisa and Chabela, who had gone to see whether the Casasbellas's little girls were already asleep, had returned. "At least it's the only good thing to come out of all this melodrama. Not only are we friends again; our marriage is better now than before. The scandal and that brief separation have brought us closer than ever, old man."

They'd had Chinese food, which they had ordered from Lung Fung, and since it was well before curfew, they sat on Luciano's terrace to have a drink and chat. The two little girls had been with them for a while, but Nicasia had taken them to their rooms. The garden and tiled pool were lit, and they could see the two Great Danes playing among the trees. The butler had brought the whiskey, ice, and mineral water. It was a quiet night, with no wind and, so far at least, no gunshots or blackouts. Marisa and Chabela were returning, arm in arm and laughing.

"Share the joke, don't be so selfish," Luciano greeted them. "So the four of us can laugh."

"Not a chance, my dear husband," Chabela exaggerated, opening her eyes wide and pretending to be horrified. "It's a piece of gossip about cheatings and beatings that would make you pass out, you're such a saint."

"Don't trust the saints," said Marisa, sitting next to Quique and taking hold of his face as if she were going to scold him. "This one seems so devout, and just look at the stupidities he was capable of."

She laughed aloud, Luciano and Chabela joined in, but Quique turned pale and made a strange movement with both hands.

"I'm sorry, I'm sorry, I know you don't want people to

make jokes about it, darling." Marisa put her arms around his neck and kissed him on the cheek. "You're blushing, I can't tell you how red you are, my love."

"That's the worst thing," Quique responded to her joke. "They've turned me into a wanton profligate, me, and I've always been so well behaved."

"I have photographs that say the opposite. Come now, don't play the good little boy, Quique," Chabela chimed in, provoking general laughter.

"A toast," said Luciano, raising his glass of whiskey. "To our friendship. Every day I'm more and more convinced that friendship is the only thing that matters in this life."

"The four of us have to finally take that cruise through the Greek islands that we've talked about so often," said Quique. "Before we're too old. Two whole weeks in the sea of Ulysses, not reading any news about Peru. Two weeks without blackouts, terrorism, or the yellow press."

"What you said about love and saints has reminded me of my maternal grandfather," said Luciano suddenly, with a nostalgic smile. "Have I ever told you about him?"

"You haven't told me, at least," said his wife in surprise. "I don't think you've even told me anything about your parents. Ten years of marriage and I don't know anything about you."

"The story gave rise to all kinds of rumors, I imagine," Luciano added. "The kind that Limeños love. They're the most gossiping gossips in the world."

"Tell me all about it," Quique was moved to joke. "Because I've recently received my doctorate in gossip-mongering."

"My mother's father was one of the most arrogant land-owners in Ica, the owner of several ranches that General Velasco's Agrarian Reform took away from us," Luciano continued. "And the most pious man ever seen in this valley of the Lord. I remember him very well when I was a little boy.

Don Casimiro. He wore a black suit and a vest with a watch chain to go to church. He attended daily Mass in the little chapel in the ranch house, as well as processions, baptisms, adorations, rogations, et cetera, in the small village church. At lunch and dinner, he would bless the table when we were all seated."

Luciano stopped speaking. His expression had suddenly become melancholy; the memories of his childhood in Ica seemed to have made him sad; it was curious because the things he usually recounted about life on his grandfather's ranch couldn't have been happier: horseback riding, hunting trips, barbeques, the traps that he and his brothers set for foxes where iguanas were sometimes caught, Sunday excursions to go swimming in the ocean, and his grandfather reading aloud, pious readings, books of adventures, Salgari, Verne, Dumas, to him and his brothers, in his study with the Virgins from Cusco and old bookcases filled with dusty volumes.

"What I don't understand, Luciano," said Quique, taking advantage of a pause in his friend's account, "is why telling such nice things about your childhood makes you so sad."

There was a brief silence. Not only Quique but Chabela and Marisa were looking at Luciano, waiting for his answer.

"What makes me sad is not remembering my grandfather Casimiro but my grandmother Laura," said Luciano at last, in a changed voice. He had become very serious. Before continuing, he looked at the other three in a strange way, part ironic and part mocking. "Do you know why? Because my maternal grandmother was not really named Laura. And she was Chinese."

Marisa and Quique smiled, but Chabela opened her eyes in astonishment.

"Chinese?" she asked. "A Chinese Chinese? Seriously, Luciano?"

"Very seriously, my love," Luciano agreed. "You never knew because it was always taboo, the family's great secret."

"Well, well, the things I discover after ten years of marriage," Chabela said with a laugh. "So your grandmother was Chinese."

"Well, maybe she was American Chinese," Luciano explained, "but I think she was a Chinese Chinese. Now comes the serious part. Her father was the grocer in the ranch's little village."

"And do you want to tell me, Luciano, how it is that a great landowner from Ica like Don Casimiro, who surely thought himself a blue-blooded aristocrat, married the daughter of the grocer on his ranch?"

Marisa had leaned her head on her husband's shoulder, and he embraced her and, from time to time, caressed her hair.

"The explanation is love," said Marisa. "What else could it be? The landowner fell in love with the Chinese girl, end of story. Don't they say that Asian women are wild in bed?"

"Yes, my grandfather must have fallen head over heels for the Chinese girl," Luciano agreed. "She must have been good-looking, attractive, for a landowner loaded down with prejudices, no doubt a racist and a despot like all the people of his class, to take that incredible step: to marry in church the daughter of a grocer who, perhaps, was illiterate and had never worn shoes in his life."

There was a long pause and the sadness on his face was transformed into a smile.

"They married according to God's law in the church on the ranch, no less," he added. "There are photos of the wedding, which the family tried to destroy, but I've managed to rescue a few. Many guests came from Lima, of course, who would have been horrified by the landowner's madness. It must have been the scandal of the century, not only in Ica but also in the rest of Peru. In the photographs you can't see my grandmother's face very well, only that she was small and thin. But I'd bet she was pretty, too. What's certain is that she had a formidable character. A real matriarch."

"He probably got her pregnant, and since he was so pious, he felt the obligation to marry her." Chabela leaned toward her husband, as if examining him: "Now I understand why your eyes are a little slanted, Luciano."

"From now on we'll call you the Chinaman," Marisa added, laughing.

"Be quiet, be quiet, that's what they call Fujimori," Luciano interrupted, laughing as well. "I'd prefer half-breed."

"If they begin to call you half-breed, I'm getting a divorce," said Chabela, turning up her nose.

"Go on, Luciano," Quique urged him. "The truth is that I find the story of Don Casimiro fascinating."

"What follows is even better than the marriage of the landowner and the little Chinese girl," said Luciano. And he looked at his watch. "I still have time to get to the end of the story before curfew."

He resumed the account of his maternal grandparents, explaining that he had never been able to find out the original name of his Chinese grandmother, because before they married, his grandfather rebaptized her with the name Laura, which is what the family called her from then on. As soon as she had married, the Chinese girl began to have children—"my mother and three uncles, two of them died as children"—and gradually she began to take on authority. Not content with running only the house, she began to help her husband manage the ranch.

"When I was little, the old peons on the ranch still remembered her," said Luciano. "Wearing trousers, riding boots, a straw hat, carrying a whip and riding through the fields, watching the irrigation, the sowing, the harvests, giving orders, coming out with a curse and even a lash of the whip for peons who were lazy or intractable."

But what impressed Luciano most was that his grandmother Laura, at the traditional celebration of the National Holiday, July 28, in the middle of the party that his grandparents held for all the employees and peons, with bands and ballerinas and tap dancers brought in from Chincha and El Carmen, took off her shoes and, barefoot like the mestizas on the ranch, danced a *marinera* with one of the peons, generally a mixed-breed Indian and black, or a full black, who were always the best *marinera* dancers. Something extraordinary, in any case, for the mistress of the house, the wife of the big owner, to dance a *marinera* with a peon, applauded and urged on by dozens of peons—peasants, tenant farmers, chauffeurs, tractor drivers, and domestic workers. It was something that made them all frenetic, apparently. They applauded her wildly because, it seems, Grandmother Laura was a great *marinera* dancer. That annual dance, that *marinera* on the bare earth, as it's danced in the most mestizo towns, was something that the entire ranch waited for, the event of the year.

"I would like to have known your grandmother," said Quique, looking at his watch. "Yes, there's still time before curfew, at this time of night the traffic moves quickly and we'll reach my house in fifteen minutes at the most. Doña Laura must have been an unusual woman."

"She died very young, giving birth to the last of my uncles," said Luciano. "I'll show you some photos of her, it's enough to see her to know she had an awe-inspiring personality. It's just that . . ."

Luciano stopped smiling and became serious.

"It's just what?" Chabela encouraged him to continue with the story. "Don't leave it like that, stammering."

"The fact is that the romantic story of the landowner who

falls in love with the grocer's daughter," Luciano added, with a shrug, "has a part that's pretty cruel."

"What is it?" Marisa asked, extending her head. "It must be the most interesting."

"Once a year, Grandmother Laura took a mysterious trip. She would go alone, and be away for several days," Luciano recounted, slowly, with pauses, keeping his audience of three in suspense.

"And where did she go?" Chabela asked. "Ay, Luciano, we have to dig things out of you with a serving spoon."

"That's the question that's impossible to answer," said Luciano. "The official version is that she went to see her family. Because, when my grandmother married, her entire family, beginning with her father the grocer and, I imagine, her mother and brothers and sisters, if she had any, disappeared from the ranch. Yes, yes, from this point on everything I'm telling you is supposition. I imagine that my grandfather's family, or he himself, drove them off. He didn't care about marrying the Chinese girl. But the grocer and his family staying on and rubbing elbows with their in-laws must have been too much for Don Casimiro. They were sent into exile so there would be no trace of them. Perhaps they negotiated it. My grandfather might have given them money so they would settle as far as possible from Ica. That annual trip by Grandmother Laura was to visit her exiled family. Where? I've never known. I imagine they would have been sent to the other end of the country. To the mountains, or the jungle, who knows? In other words, perhaps I have cousins in some godforsaken little town in Loreto or Chachapoyas."

"If we're going to imagine things," Quique joked, "perhaps your grandfather or his family had them all killed. Something fast so there'd be no trace left of that familial shame. Your grandmother Laura, on her annual trip, probably went to place flowers on the graves of all her relatives."

Marisa and Chabela laughed, but not Luciano.

"You say it as a joke, but I've thought that something like that wasn't impossible back then. Half a century ago, what value could the lives of some wretched Chinese have had? Perhaps they did have them killed, yes. Those people were quite capable of it."

"I suppose you're joking, Luciano," Chabela protested. "I suppose you're not seriously saying something so monstrously stupid."

"It's a harsh ending to a story that's so romantic," Marisa said with a sigh. "I think we ought to go, Quique. I don't want us to be late and have some patrol stop us. We've had enough problems, haven't we?"

"Yes, yes, leave now," said Chabela. "One of those patrols stopped a friend of mine after curfew and the police were so brash they got a pile of money from her."

"The damn curfew," said Quique, standing up, still holding his wife's hand. "The truth is, I'd stay all night listening to you tell the story of the Chinese girl."

"It did me good to tell you about it," said Luciano, accompanying them across the huge garden to the exit. "The great shame of my maternal family burned inside. I feel as if I've made amends to my grandmother Laura, and all her kin."

At the street door there was a booth with an armed guard, who said good night to them. Quique and Marisa said goodbye to Luciano and Chabela, got into their car, and left.

"Listen, listen," said Quique in a suggestive way. "When you and Chabela said goodbye you almost kissed each other on the mouth."

"Did it make you jealous?" Marisa asked with a laugh. But when she saw that Quique had slammed on the brakes, she became alarmed. "Why are you stopping?"

"It didn't make me jealous, it made me envious, Blondie," he said. "I stopped to kiss you. Give me your mouth, darling."

He kissed her hard, putting his tongue in her mouth, swallowing her saliva.

"That's enough, Quique," she said, pushing him away. "It's dangerous, we can be mugged. It's very dark here, keep driving."

"I'm more in love with you every day," he said, starting to drive again. "This damn scandal was good for this, at least. To know that I'm crazy about you. That I'm lucky enough to have married the most beautiful woman in the world. And the most delicious in bed, too."

"Don't look at me, look at the road, Quique, we'll have an accident. And please don't drive so fast."

"I want to get home fast so I can undress you myself," he said. "And kiss you from your hair down to your feet, millimeter by millimeter, yes, yes, from your head to your feet. And tonight, no turning out the light. I'll turn them all on, not just the one on the night table."

"Go on, I don't recognize you. You're not like this, Quique. What's happened to you, if you don't mind my asking."

"I've discovered that you're the most sensual and exciting woman in the world, my love."

"Coming from an expert in the subject, it's a great compliment, Your Majesty."

"Be careful about those jokes, or I'll stop again right now and make love to you in the car, Blondie."

"Ooh, how frightening," Marisa said with a laugh. "Don't go so fast, Quique, we'll have an accident."

He slowed down a little and they spent the rest of the drive home joking and laughing. When they reached San Isidro, across from the Golf Club, they still had ten minutes before curfew began.

"Why are there so many police?" Marisa asked in surprise.

There were two patrol cars blocking the ramp that led to

the building's garages, and both had their lights on. When they saw that Enrique's car had stopped in front of them, the doors of the patrol cars opened and several men in uniform and civilian clothes got out, approached, and surrounded the car. Quique lowered the window and an officer bent over and brought his head very close to speak to him. He carried a lit flashlight.

"Engineer Enrique Cárdenas?" he asked, raising his hand to his kepi.

"Yes, that's me," Quique agreed. "What is it, officer?"

"Good evening, Señor Cárdenas. You need to come with us. But you can park your car first. We'll wait for you, that's no problem."

"Come with you where?" Quique asked. "Why?"

"Dr. Morante, the prosecutor, will explain it to you," said the police officer, moving aside to make room for a man in civilian clothes, short, gray-haired, with a small brush mustache, who nodded to the couple.

"I'm sorry, Señor Cárdenas," he greeted him with forced amiability. "I have an order from the judge that explains our presence here. You're under arrest."

"Under arrest?" said Quique, astounded. "May I ask why?"

"For the murder of the journalist Rolando Garro," said Dr. Morante. "There is a formal charge against you, and the judge has issued an arrest warrant. Here it is, you can read it. I hope it's a misunderstanding and that everything is cleared up. I don't advise you to resist, Engineer. That could work against you."

17

Strange Operations Regarding Juan Peineta

Juan Peineta left the Hotel Mogollón very early, asking himself again where Serafín had gotten to, since he hadn't shown up for three days. Or was it four? Or more than a week? That's enough forgetting, damn it. He headed for Abancay Avenue. Just as well that Willy Rodrigo, the Ruletero, lived in Barrios Altos now. Before, when he was in Callao, going to see him was a real adventure. He had to walk to Plaza San Martín, where he took the microbus to Callao. It was the only vehicle he got into, every month or month and a half, to visit his compadre and friend, king of the *timba*. Nobody knew where his nickname, the Ruletero, came from until one day Willy told him it was from one of the mambos of Pérez Prado, the inventor of that rhythm, a kind of music that, in his youth, he would sing and dance all day. But neither he nor anyone else in Lima knew what the strange Cuban word *ruletero* meant: pimp? cabdriver? lottery ticket seller?

Why did Willy want to see him so urgently? It was a strange call he'd made the night before to the Hotel Mogollón: "I need to see you very urgently, Juanito. I can't say anything else on the phone. Shall we have lunch tomorrow? Great. Until tomorrow, then." What was it about? Why hadn't Willy given him at least a clue? Juan Peineta began to walk up

Abancay Avenue; at the Congress he would turn toward the long, winding Junín Alleyway, and at the end of that he'd be in Five Corners, where Willy lived: at least he remembered the way clearly. At times he had the feeling that more things evaporated from his memory each day, that soon he would be a phantom without a past.

He and Willy had been friends since the days when Juan Peineta practiced the noble art of declamation and the Ruletero owned a large theater in the Cantagallo district, in Rímac; he would hire Juan to recite his poems between the dance numbers and Andean songs. Willy's theater also offered evenings of wrestling, but he didn't invite Juan Peineta to these shows (he had once, and the whistling and shouts of "Queer!" and "Faggot!" from the galleries dissuaded him from serving that dish a second time). The Ruletero had sold the theater some time ago; now he managed a gambling house in Five Corners, not far from the monument to Felipe Pinglo, the great composer of old-style waltzes. Earlier, when he lived in Callao, Willy had another monument close to his house: the one to Sarita Colonia, the patron saint of thieves. Nobody was as different from Juan Peineta as Willy, the night owl in his dive where unfortunate gamblers with bad reputations came to find their luck, many of them holdup men, ex-convicts who rubbed elbows at night with drunkards, pimps, and vagrants who sometimes settled their differences with knives or kicks. Also swarming among Willy's clients were the informers and undercover cops who went there to cadge a beer and pick up information.

And yet they were joined by a friendship greater than the vast differences in their lives. For a long while, four or five times a year, Juan made the long trip from the center of Lima to that rough district around the port of Callao to spend the day with his old friend. Now, since Willy had moved to the center of colonial Lima, it was easier, he no longer had to make that endless, uncomfortable trip to the port, just this tedious walk. Willy invited him to have lunch at some noisy bar where they had fresh mussels and cold beer. As they concentrated on the feast, they recalled the old days when Juan earned his living by practicing his vocation as an artist-reciter and was happily married to Atanasia, and Willy managed his folkloric theater, which allowed him to take to bed some of the artists who filed through his tent, though Juan believed he hadn't made love to as many as he boasted about. Because Willy was also a braggart. Juan knew he exaggerated and lied but enjoyed listening to him anyway. Why had Willy called him so urgently? Why hadn't he wanted to tell him anything on the phone?

It took him almost an hour to reach the labyrinthine crossroads of Five Corners, in the heart of Barrios Altos. When Juan was young, the neighborhood was full of Peruvian-music clubs and many bohemians lived there: artists, musicians, even the white kids from Miraflores and San Isidro who were fans of Peruvian music came to hear the best singers, guitar players, and *cajón* players and to dance with mixed-race cholos and blacks. There were still traces of the golden age of Barrios Altos, the age of La Palizada, Felipe Pinglos, and all the great composers and promoters of Peruvian music.

Now the neighborhood had decayed and its streets were dangerous. But Willy was in his element here, presiding over the gambling house. He seemed to make a lot of money, though Juan Peineta was afraid Willy would be knifed one of these days. He walked slowly, enduring the pain of his swollen varicose veins, along the lengthy, serpentine, and always crowded Junín Alleyway. The city became poorer and older as he walked past the stands where they sold flowers, food, fruit, all kinds of fried food, all kinds of trinkets, past old colonial houses that seemed on the point of collapsing, past the children in rags, beggars or vagrants who slept in doorways or beneath lampposts. In addition to colonial churches, there were many associations and crosses around which a group of the devout sometimes lit candles to Holy Christ or the saints, praying on their knees and touching the image. There, after passing the Convent of Las Descalzadas and the Heeren Manor, in an unpaved alley, was Willy the Ruletero's gambling den.

Generally he found him in good humor, and Willy would welcome him with the same joke: "How nice to know you're alive and haven't kicked the bucket yet, Juanito!" But this time Willy was serious and frowning; he embraced his friend without saying anything. "I was worried about that phone call last night, old man," Juan said. "What's going on?" Willy only covered his mouth and indicated with his hand that they should leave his shop. His face was marked by moles, and he was a grizzled man, still strong for his seventy-plus years; he wore faded overalls, a gray sleeveless sweater, and worn moccasins without socks. Half embracing him, he pushed Juan Peineta, moving him away from the small building of wood and adobe, with a corrugated roof, where his gambling operation took place and where he lived alone or, as he would say, with "bargain-priced women."

"Why don't we go into your house to rest a little while, Willy?" Juan Peineta suggested. "You're acting very mysterious, compadre, and I'm exhausted by the walk."

"Let's go and talk far from here, Juanito," the Ruletero answered in a low voice, looking all around. Blinking, he added: "This place has become dangerous. Not only for me. For you, too, compadre. I'll explain soon."

Silent, scowling, with a worried air that made Juan Peineta much more upset than he already was, Willy had him walk several blocks through a myriad of narrow unpaved streets, half-built one- or two-story houses, all of which were crowded with very poor people, barefoot or in slippers, the men in undershirts and many women with handkerchiefs on their

heads, the kind that the devout of some evangelical sects tend
to wear.

Juan noticed that his friend was favoring his left foot: Was
he limping because he had stumbled?

"It seems it's rheumatism and there's nothing you can do
about it," the Ruletero replied with a bad-tempered grimace.
"A woman in the neighborhood, half a witch who cures with
herbs, is giving me baths, so far with no results. I now have an
old man's ailments, Juanito. You have a messed-up memory; I
have my messed-up legs."

What was wrong with Willy? He wasn't the man he always was, the high-spirited jokester Juan had known for more
than thirty years, the one who seemed to let everything roll
right off his back, who never lost his good humor for anything or anybody. He was edgy, suspicious, and frightened.
Juan saw that before stepping into any of the cheap taverns
where they stopped, Willy hesitated so he could sniff them out
first. At several he decided not to go in, without giving any
kind of explanation to Juan Peineta.

"It worries me to see you like this, Willy," he said finally,
as they continued their search for a place where they could sit
down quietly and talk. "What the devil's wrong, brother, why
are you so suspicious and jumpy?"

Instead of answering, Willy, very seriously, raised a finger
to his lips indicating that Juan should shut his mouth and be
quiet. There'd be time to talk later.

Willy finally found what he was looking for. A tiny bar
where, though it was daytime, a faint lightbulb burned, covered in flies, with half a dozen empty tables. They sat down
near the door and Willy ordered a really cold beer—Pilsen
Callao, of course—and two clean glasses.

"Are you finally going to tell me what the hell is going on,
Willy? Why the devil are you acting so strange, brother?"

Willy fixed his large yellowish eyes on him in a look filled with apprehension.

"They're cooking up something that I don't like at all, brother," he said, lowering his voice and glancing around with a suspicious look, something Juan didn't recognize in him either. There was a long pause before he added: "I'm going to tell you everything, because I have the feeling they've involved you in this mess, too. It's about . . ."

But he stopped talking because the barefoot man serving them approached with the beer and glasses. He filled them, with a very high head, and Willy continued speaking only when the bartender was at a distance, behind the small counter:

"It's about the reporter they killed, that one you hated so much, Juanito."

"Rolando Garro?" Juan Peineta gave a start in his chair and crossed himself. "Shall I tell you something, Willy? I was very happy they killed him, why should I lie to you. Because he ruined my life, as you know. But I'm sorry about it. You shouldn't be happy about other people's misfortunes, even when it's a guy as wicked as Garro. I went to confession and the priest really lit into me. I don't hate him anymore. I feel sorry for him instead. God in heaven knows what to do with him. It seems his death was horrible."

He fell silent because Willy the Ruletero didn't seem to be listening. When he saw that Juan Peineta wasn't talking he returned to reality from the introspection or daydream that absorbed him.

"You read that they found him dead here, in this neighborhood, didn't you?"

Juan Peineta nodded.

"Very close to the monument to Felipe Pinglo, almost at Five Corners. Yes, yes. But why are you asking me that, Willy?"

"Because it isn't true," said the Ruletero, lowering his voice even more. "They didn't find him. They brought him in a car that could only belong to the police. Or to State Security. They're the only ones who dare to come into this neighborhood at night. They took his corpse out of the car, as destroyed as it was, and left it at the door of my gambling parlor. Don't you think that's strange, Juanito? Don't you think it's a real coincidence that they chose my place to toss the corpse of the reporter? Let me ask you what exactly their intention was."

"Are you sure about what you're telling me, Willy?"

"I saw them," his friend said, nodding, giving a little bang to the table. "Cars don't drive down my street at night, brother. They're shitting with fear that they'll be held up. The ones who drove there could only be cops or soldier boys. Police or State Security. When I heard the car's engine, I watched from the window. And I saw everything with these eyes."

"But wasn't it the millionaire they arrested who gave the order to kill him, Willy?" The former reciter was surprised.

"I'm not telling you anything I didn't see," declared the Ruletero, drumming nervously on the tabletop; several flies rose into the air. "I don't know who killed him. The only thing I know is that they didn't find him dead in Five Corners, they brought him in a car when he was already dead, and threw his body in front of my shop. Who knows why? And the ones who brought him could only have been cops or soldier boys from State Security, that's something I'm sure about. The patrol cars showed up two or three hours later. I didn't let them know, of course. The only thing I did was get all the gamblers out by the false door, turn out the lights, get into bed, and pretend I was asleep. What I'm telling you I haven't told anyone else. You must understand that it's something to worry about, isn't it, Juanito?"

"But why, brother?" Juan Peineta tried to reassure him. "Why would you worry about something that doesn't concern you?"

"Why do you think they decided to leave Garro's body at the door of my parlor? Coincidence? Coincidences don't exist, brother. Everything that happens has its reason, even more so when there's a murder involved."

"In other words, you think they did it on purpose to involve you in his death. Don't be so afraid, Willy. For sure they left it there for no reason, just because, just how they would have left it anywhere else."

"Wait till I finish the story, brother," said Willy, giving him a pitying look. "This is just the beginning. I'm telling you they left it there for a reason that has to do with me. And with you, too, Juanito. With you, yes, just what I said. I thought I might have been wrong when they arrested the miner, that Enrique Cárdenas, accusing him of planning the crime, because Garro was blackmailing him with the photos of his orgy in Chosica. But, but . . ."

He stopped speaking and looked at Juanito for a long time as if he were at his wake and was contemplating his corpse. Juanito became alarmed.

"What is it, Willy?" he asked. "Why did you suddenly stop talking and why are you looking at me that way?"

"Because it seems this whole business has much more to do with you than with me, brother. I'm sorry I have to give you this bad news. It's the truth. With you, not with me. I'm in on this just in passing, as they say. Just because I'm your friend."

It seemed to Juan Peineta that the chair he sat in suddenly rose up and fell to the floor, shaking all his bones. His head began to hurt, a shiver ran down his spine. What did all this mean? He didn't understand anything. Had he forgotten something important? He searched his memory without finding anything.

"What are you saying, Willy?" he murmured. "With me?"

"That's why I called last night and asked you so urgently

to come and see me," Willy whispered, bringing his face very close to his friend. "You can't talk about these things on the phone. The good news is that they don't even know that you live in the Hotel Mogollón. Isn't it incredible? Well, it's the truth: they don't know."

"Who?" stammered Juan Peineta. "Who is it you're talking about?"

"Who would it be, Juanito," Willy said mockingly. "The cops or the soldier boys of State Security. They're the only ones, I already told you that."

They had shown up three or four days after the mysterious car came in the night and left the destroyed corpse of Rolando Garro in front of Willy the Ruletero's gambling parlor. They were in civilian clothes and had crew cuts, and so, as soon as he saw them, Willy knew right away they were military. They shook his hand and smiled with that slightly false smile of police and security agents when they're on duty. They showed him credentials encased in plastic where Willy could make out seals, a Peruvian flag, and minuscule, undetectable photographs.

"This is an informal visit, Willy," said the one who seemed the older of the two visitors. "I'm Captain Félix Madueño. I don't exist, by the way. I mean, we haven't come, we're not here. You're intelligent and understand me, don't you?"

Willy only smiled as he filled with apprehension. This was beginning badly. Had they come to shake him down or what?

"This looks like a gambling parlor for the starving," remarked the other one, pointing at the chipped walls, the dirty windows, the cobwebs hanging from the ceiling, the rickety tables, the tamped-down dirt floor. "And yet, Willy, we know that millions of soles are gambled here every night."

"I wouldn't say it's that much," a smiling Willy said very prudently. "In any case, there's no limit on bets as long as the play is honest. That's the house rule."

"Don't look so worried, Willy," said the one who had spoken first. "We didn't come to ask you about your business or your clients, the gamblers who spend everything they have here."

"And what they don't have, too," said the other one.

"We're interested in your friend Juan Peineta."

"Really, Willy?" the former reciter asked, more and more surprised and frightened. He didn't believe what he was hearing, it seemed to him that any moment now Willy would burst into laughter and say: "It was a joke, brother, to see if you'd shit your pants." "They knew my name? They came to talk to you about me?"

"Yes, nobody but him," the older one had said, nodding, the one who had said his name was Captain Félix Madueño. "We know that you're very good friends, aren't you?"

"Of course he's my friend," Willy had agreed. "When I had the theater, in Cantagallo, Juanito would recite his poems between the performances of folkloric music. He did it very well. He was an artist."

"And he also comes to visit you here and you have lunch together from time to time, isn't that so?" the other one declared.

"Yes, from time to time he comes around here to remember the old days," said Willy. "I haven't seen him for a long while, wherever he is. I hope he hasn't died."

"We need his address and telephone number," said the one who had spoken first, in a somewhat acid tone. "Would you do us the favor, Ruletero?"

"Do you know what surprised me most, Juanito?" said Willy in answer to the stupefied expression of the former declaimer. "That the agents of State Security, who knew so many things, that we were friends, that you came from time to time to have lunch with me, didn't have the slightest idea that you've been living for years in the Hotel Mogollón. Don't you think that's incredible?"

"No, I don't," replied Juan Peineta, speaking with difficulty, as if something were caught in his throat. "That's underdevelopment, Willy. And you, what did you tell them?"

"I don't think he has a fixed residence, he lives here and there, where his friends put him up, I suppose, or in those charity shelters that some convents have. I'd be surprised if he had a phone."

"Do you want to fuck around with us, Willy?" said the younger man in an aggressive tone, but still smiling. "Do we look like assholes to you, the king of the gambling parlors?"

"Of course not, chief." Willy swore with his fingers forming a cross. "If Juanito had a fixed address, I'd give it to you, of course I would. But I doubt he's ever had one. Not to mention a phone. Juan Peineta's on his last legs, he doesn't have a place to lay his head, didn't you know that? He's like a stray dog. Ever since he stopped being one of the Three Jokers, his life has been going downhill. He reached bottom a while ago. He lives on charity, just in case you didn't know. Besides, he's losing his memory, sometimes he doesn't even know who he is."

"Poor Juan Peineta," said the older one sardonically, handing him a piece of paper. "Do us a favor, Willy. Find out his address for me and call me at this number. Ask for Captain Félix Madueño or for Sergeant Major Arnilla."

"Keep this our secret, Willy," said the younger man. "And, of course, now that we're leaving, you won't be dumb enough to go and tell your friend we're looking for him."

"I'd never do that," Willy protested, banging the table with his fist. "I've always gotten along very well with the law."

"Of course you have, Willy, you're an exemplary citizen and everybody knows it," said Sergeant Major Arnilla, holding out his hand. "Until the next time, compadre. Don't forget, find that address for us. As soon as you can."

"And they left," said Willy. "Of course, I ran to call you at the Hotel Mogollón. Now you understand why I couldn't leave any message: I had to tell you in person."

Juan Peineta had the strange sensation this wasn't happening, that it was a nightmare and at any moment he'd wake up and laugh at the fear he'd felt over what hadn't happened and wasn't going to happen. But there was his friend, Willy the Ruletero, looking at him sorrowfully. The man at the bar came over to ask whether they wanted him to prepare a corvina ceviche for them.

"Is it fresh?" Willy asked.

"They brought it in early this morning from Callao, right after it was caught."

"Two nice corvina ceviches, then. And another beer, but nice and icy."

"I don't understand anything, Willy," Juan stammered when the bartender walked away. "Why are these people from the police or the army looking for me?"

Willy pressed his hand, caught him by the arm, and squeezed it in a gesture of solidarity.

"I have no idea, brother," he said, sadly. "But this doesn't smell good to me, Juanito. I suspect somebody has involved you or else wants to involve you in some ugly business. Especially because they came to see you only a few days after those guys left the body of that reporter who fucked up your life in the doorway of my parlor. Everybody knows you hated him, that you've been sending letters to the papers denouncing him for years. Don't you see the connection there might be among all these things?"

"What do you mean, Willy? What things are connected? It doesn't make sense. What that bastard Garro did to me happened ten or twelve years ago. Maybe not so long ago, but more than five years, at least."

"I know, Juanito," said Willy; he wanted to reassure him, but everything he told Juan alarmed him even more. "The things the police do don't follow any logic. But one thing is very clear. They're cooking up something very ugly against you. I don't know what it is, but it's certain that if those guys get their hands on you, something bad will happen. It's lucky they don't know where you are. You have to get away and disappear for a while, brother."

"Get away, Willy?" Juan was openmouthed. "Where? And with what? I don't have a red cent, brother. Where would I get away to?"

Willy nodded and gave him another fraternal pat on the arm.

"As much as I'd like to, I couldn't put you up, Juanito. They'd find you right away at my place. Look, think, turn it around a little, and something will occur to you. But please, don't tell me where you're going to hide, if you find a hiding place. I wouldn't want to know so I won't have to lie again to those cops, or whatever they are, if they question me about where you are."

Juan Peineta kept looking at his friend without knowing what to say. Was this happening to him? Was he really awake? A person whose life had been reduced to living in a miserable hole, who received a ridiculous pension, who had to go to the dining room of the Barefoot Carmelites so he wouldn't become tubercular. Could it get even worse? Hunted by the police or State Security, him, Juan Peineta? It was so absurd, so illogical, that he didn't know what to say or do.

"I have nothing to hide, Willy," he finally said. "The best thing would be for me to meet with these guys who came to see you and ask them why they're looking for me, what they want with me. It can only be some confusion, a misunderstanding. Don't you think so, brother?"

"I would advise you not to be so stupid, Juanito," said Willy, looking at him sadly. "If they're looking for you, it's dangerous for you. If there's some confusion or a misunderstanding, for you or for me, or for anybody who isn't a big fish, things can turn out very badly. Well, you must know what you're doing. I've told you this because I respect you, you're an old friend, and I don't have many left. I think you're the last one. I wouldn't like them to get you involved in something ugly, or even make you disappear. You know very well they disappear people here and nothing happens because the terrorists are to blame for everything. You'll see what you'll do. The only thing I ask is that if they detain you, you won't tell them that I called and told you what I told you."

"Of course I won't, Willy," said Juan Peineta. "You don't know how grateful I am that you alerted me. Of course I'd never tell them that you called to warn me. If they ask me, I'll say I haven't seen you for a long time."

"That's it, that's right," said Willy the Ruletero. "And given how things are, it would be better if we stopped seeing each other for a little while. Don't you think so?"

"Of course," said Juan, his face contorted by worry. "You're absolutely right, brother."

18

Engineer Cárdenas's Longest Night

When his eyes grew accustomed to the darkness in the room and the silent figures that filled it, he made out a chalk inscription in large letters on one of the badly painted walls, which said:

> *And when he hoped for the good,*
> *Evil suddenly occurred;*
> *When he hoped for the light,*
> *Darkness came.*

Was it biblical? He was overwhelmed by terror but very aware that the place was saturated with a stink that made him dizzy—it smelled of many things, but especially excrement, sweat, and urine—and was teeming with men, some half-naked, some sitting on a rough cement bench, and others squatting or lying on the ground. No one spoke, but Quique sensed that from the shadows surrounding him, dozens of eyes were fixed on him, the most recent arrival in this cellar, jail, torture chamber, or whatever it was. He thought he was having an incomprehensible nightmare that couldn't be happening to him, and although all of this was due to a monstrous confusion, there was no longer time for it to be cleared up. He would probably die or, even worse, spend the rest of his life in this prison. His eyes were filled with tears; he felt an enormous sadness and began to sink into demoralization. Then he noticed that one of those faceless figures, naked from the waist up, moved on the floor very close to his feet, heaved himself up, and putting his face very close to his, whispered: "Want me to suck you off? Five soles." In the darkness he felt the man's hand exploring his fly.

"Let me go, let me go, what's wrong with you!" he shouted, standing up and hitting away the man's hand.

There was a sudden agitation around him, bodies that moved and calmed down again almost instantly.

"Worse for you, whitey," said a voice at his side, soiled by foul breath. "If you don't like being sucked, you must like sucking. Kneel down between my legs, open your mouth wide, and start to suck. It's dead now but it'll get hard in no time if you do it with love."

Stumbling among the bodies stretched out on the floor, he made his way to the door. He pounded on it with his fists, desperate, shouting: "Guard, guard!" He heard mocking laughter behind him. No one moved, and no guard came to help him.

Then he felt next to him, very close, a large, strong body that with assurance held him around the waist and whispered in his ear: "Don't be afraid, white boy, I'll look out for you." He felt the man's thick breath burning his face.

"I don't have money," he murmured. "They took my wallet at the station."

Curiously, the person who was holding him around the waist gave him a certain security and lessened the fear that overwhelmed him. "It doesn't matter, you'll pay me later, I trust you, white boy. I'll give you credit." Quique felt his legs trembling and was sure that if the man let him go, he'd collapse on the floor like a sack of potatoes. "Come, let's sit over there," the strong man said in his ear. Quique found himself being pushed slowly, and he moved forward in the darkness, feeling his feet brushing against bodies stretched on the floor, some snoring, others babbling incoherently. He kept repeating to himself like a mantra that this wasn't happening, reproaching God for punishing him this way, wondering what could have happened in the world that he, a professional from a good family, respected and successful, was here, in a filthy police holding cell, among criminals, degenerates, and madmen. At times he bumped into the stone bench built into the wall; the strong man holding him gave a curt order to make a space so they could sit down. He must have been one of the bosses, because he was obeyed immediately. He made Quique sit down and sat beside him, very close, always holding him around the waist. Quique felt the man's body against his and knew he was very strong. The awful fear that crushed him began to subside. "Good, thank you," he murmured very softly. "Help me, please, with these guys. I'll pay you later, whatever you want."

There was a pause and Quique felt that the strong man brought his face up to his—it seemed that his fetid breath came into his nose and mouth, making him dizzy—and said very quietly, in a whisper: "You were lucky, white boy, that I came forward. If those blacks over there get you and take you to their corner, they'll pull down your trousers, put a little Vaseline in your asshole, and line up to fuck you for as long as they want. And that wouldn't be the worst, because at least one of them has AIDS. But don't worry, as long as I protect you, nobody'll touch you. I'm the law here, white boy."

Quique's heart skipped a beat when he noted that one of the strong man's hands had moved away from his waist, but it wasn't to make him more comfortable but to take his right hand and pull it to his fly. With horror he felt that it was open, and that his fingers were touching a penis as hard as rock. He made a movement to pull away, but the strong man stopped him brutally, flattening him against the wall, helped by his own weight. Now the tone of his voice had changed, it was threatening: "Jerk me off, white boy. I don't want to hurt you, but if you don't do what I say, I will. I'll protect you, I promise. Now jerk me off, I'm horny." Repulsed, frightened, trembling, Quique obeyed. Seconds later he felt the strong man ejaculate. He had his semen on his hand and surely on his trousers as well. At some point he had started to cry. The tears ran down his cheeks; he felt an awful shame and disgust with himself. "Forgive me, forgive me for being such a coward," he thought and didn't even know whose forgiveness he was asking for, because he no longer believed in God or anything else, maybe only the devil. Anything was better than what he was going through now, even their killing him, even killing himself.

He closed his eyes and tried to sleep, but he was too tense and frightened to let himself drift off. He tried to calm down. There was some confusion, a misunderstanding. He, Enrique Cárdenas, couldn't be abused like the indecent fauna of pickpockets, pimps, bums, and faggots that crowded this pestilential place of degenerates and monsters. He was too well known and important to be mistreated this way. Marisa would have called Luciano and between them alerted all his influential friends, and not only in Peru, his mining partners, the institutions he belonged to, they would have awakened ministers, deputies, judges, the Doctor, President Fujimori, filed complaints and sought redress. That's it, that's right. There would be a great mobilization of people, night and day, becoming interested in his case, taking action. They'd come and get him out of here, begging his pardon. He would tell them it was all right. He forgave, he pardoned, he forgot. But in his heart and in his head he would never forgive the pigs who had made him suffer this great humiliation, made him live these revolting days and nights among repulsive people, who had offended, degraded, and mocked him, and made him suffer the worst fear and most terrible shame of his life. The hand into which the son of a bitch beside him had come was sticky— he seemed to have fallen asleep—and he didn't dare take out his handkerchief and wipe away the dried semen in case the guy awoke and demanded something even worse than being masturbated. He felt an unchecked desire for revenge, to make Fujimori and the Doctor pay for this night of horror. Because it was them, of course it was, no one but them who'd had him imprisoned.

And then he detected a ray of light at the only window in the room. Was day breaking? Between the bars, that whitish gray light cheered him, lessening his despair. His head was itching and he thought it must be crawling with lice from this hellhole. When he got out he'd have to shave his head and rub his skull with alcohol; he'd heard that this was how they de-loused recruits in the barracks. Was it possible this was hap-pening to him? He felt all his muscles softening. "I'm not falling asleep," he thought before he lost consciousness. "I'm passing out." Asleep or passed out, he had nightmares that he couldn't precisely remember afterward, only that all around him it was the dead of night, a world of darkness, his feet sinking into a gelatinous mud and invisible creatures biting his ankles, the way they did during that trip to the Amazon when he was a student, when gnats had pierced the leather of his boots and covered his ankles with bites. He smelled the odor of semen and retched but couldn't vomit.

When he opened his eyes, light was coming in through the grated window of the long room and he thought he was watching an impressionist movie, because the twenty or so men—old and young—crowded into the place were like human caricatures. Shaggy, covered with scars, with tattoos, some half-naked and barefoot, others in flip-flops, lying on the floor or huddled on the cement bench, sleeping openmouthed, one-eyed, toothless, short Indians who looked around in fear, husky black-Indian mixed breeds without shoes and in torn overalls. The strong man he had masturbated was no longer beside him. Which of these poor devils could he be? He noticed that nobody seemed to look at him or pay him any attention. His bones ached because of his uncomfortable position. He had an awful thirst and his tongue was like sandpaper rasping against his gums. He thought that with a cup of tea or coffee he would feel much better. Or if he could take a bath! What would happen to him now?

In the police station they had taken not only his wallet and watch but his wedding ring, too. What time could it be? How many hours had he been in this hellhole? How much longer would he be here? He thought he wouldn't spend another night in this den, exposed to the aberrations of these degenerates. At least for the first two days, while they were interrogating him, they had kept him by himself in a small room, with a chair. He would bang his head against the wall until he split it open and bled to death. He would put an end to this even if he had to commit suicide. And then he felt someone shaking his arm to wake him. He had fallen asleep or passed out again.

He saw the face of an old man with a tangled beard who seemed to be chewing coca. He heard him say in a well-masticated Spanish: "They're calling you, Don." And he pointed at the door.

It was very difficult for him to stand and even more difficult to start to walk, sidestepping the bodies on the floor that were in his way. The door was closed but as soon as he knocked on it with his knuckles, it opened with a metallic sound. He saw the face of a guard in a helmet and armed with a submachine gun.

"Engineer Enrique Cárdenas?" the guard asked.

"Yes, that's me."

"Follow me with everything," said the guard.

"What do you mean 'everything'?" he asked.

"Your things."

"My things are what I'm wearing."

"Fine."

It was a great effort for him to climb the stairs that he didn't remember coming down the night before, when they put him in the cell. He had to stop several times, climbing the ten or fifteen steps while leaning against the wall. At the top of the stairs was another door and then a corridor where he saw several guards smoking and talking. He felt a fatigue so great he couldn't lift his feet but had to drag them. His heart was pounding and he felt dizzy. "I have to fight it, I can't pass out again."

At last a door was opened and the strong light of a sunny day came in. Through the mist over his eyes he saw Marisa's silhouette, so beautiful, and Luciano, as elegant as always, and he attempted to smile at them but his legs weakened and things went black. "He's fainted," he heard someone say. "Call the medic, hurry."

19

Shorty and Power

Shorty knew this could happen. But she never imagined it would happen like this, and especially with whom. Since making the accusation that her boss, Rolando Garro, the director of *Exposed*, had probably been killed by order of the miner Enrique Cárdenas, whose photographs in an orgy with prostitutes Garro had published in his magazine, she had been the center of the news: photos, interviews on the radio, in newspapers, and on television, and endless interrogations by the police, the prosecutor, and the examining magistrate. Thanks to her audacity and the huge publicity generated by her accusation, she now felt safe. She had repeated it endlessly in every interview: "If I'm hit by a car or a drunkard smashes my head against the pavement, you'll know who is behind my death: the same person who paid the assassin who so cruelly murdered my boss, my teacher, and my friend, Rolando Garro."

Was her life really safe now with the publicity that surrounded her? For the moment, no doubt about it. Which did not prevent the fact that at night, when she got into bed in her little house on Teniente Arancibia Alleyway, in Five Corners, she suddenly had one of those attacks of terror that made her feel ice in her spine. How long would she remain safe thanks to the accusation? When she stopped appearing in the papers, the danger would start up again. Especially now that Engineer Enrique Cárdenas, after being held a few days for interrogation, had been freed provisionally by the judge, though with the order not to leave the country.

This time the car came not at night but at dawn. There was already a crack of light at her small bedroom window when Shorty woke to the sound of a car braking on the street facing the alleyway where her house stood. A short time later she heard knocking at her door. There were three men, all in civilian clothes.

"You have to come with us, Señorita Leguizamón," said the oldest one, a pudgy mixed-breed with a gold tooth, wearing a scarf and a leather jacket; when he spoke he showed the red tip of his tongue, like a lizard.

"Where?" she asked.

"You'll see," the man replied with a smile that attempted to be reassuring. "Don't worry. Someone important is expecting you. I suppose you're too intelligent to turn down this invitation, aren't you? If you'd like to wash and fix yourself up a little, there's no problem. We'll wait for you here."

She washed her face and brushed her teeth, and threw on some clothes. Coarse linen trousers, sandals, a blue blouse, and the handbag with her papers and pencil holders. An important visit? A trick, of course. On her cell phone she wrote: "Three men have come for me. I don't know where they're taking me. Reporters, my friends, pay attention, anything might happen to me." She tried to control herself and hide the fear she felt. Something told her that this was one of those decisive moments that change a life or end it. Had she wagered correctly, making that accusation, or had she put a rope around her neck? Now you'll find out, Shorty. "I'm not afraid of death," she said to herself, trembling from head to foot. But she was afraid they'd make her suffer. Would they torture her? She

remembered reading somewhere that the Doctor had ordered
some military men who had conspired against Fujimori to be
injected with the AIDS virus. She felt a few drops of piss stain
her trousers.

The car didn't go toward the center of Lima; it turned at
the Plaza Italia, drove down the Huanta Concourse to Grau
Avenue, and then, to her surprise, took the Panamericana,
toward the beaches. As soon as they had entered the Panamericana Sur Highway, one of the men between whom she
was sitting took out a hood of unbleached linen and told her
she had to cover her head. He helped her to put on the hood
with the greatest delicacy. They didn't handcuff her or tie her
hands. The hood was padded, it didn't scratch her face, it was
a gentle sensation, almost a caress. She saw nothing but black.
It seemed they were making a lot of turns; finally she heard
voices and, after a long time, the car stopped. They helped
her get out, and taking her by both arms, had her go up some
steps and walk down what must have been a long hallway.
She noted that they treated her with consideration, taking
care that she didn't trip or bump into anything. Finally she
heard them open and close a door.

"You can take that rag off your head now," said a man's
voice.

She did, and the person in front of her was exactly who
she thought it was from his voice. Him, it was him. Her surprise was so great that now Shorty's knees trembled more
than before. Was it really him? She clenched her teeth so that
fear wouldn't make them chatter. They were in a windowless
room, the lights were on, there were several paintings in strident colors on the walls, chairs and sofas, end tables with
miniature ornaments, a thick rug that muffled footsteps. Not
very far away one could hear the murmur of a rough ocean.
Was this his famous secret refuge at Arica Beach? Shorty was
still astonished. It was him, no doubt about it, and he was

observing her, intrigued, examining her openly, as if she weren't a human being but an object or an animal. Those watery, slightly protruding gray eyes from which a glacial look emanated. She had seen him in hundreds of photographs, but now he looked different: older, rather short, hair beginning to thin, exposing parts of his skull, full cheeks, a mouth open in a grimace of boredom or displeasure, a body that showed signs of obesity in breasts and belly. So this was the lord and master of Peru. He wasn't in uniform but wore civilian clothes, dark brown trousers, moccasins with no socks, and a slightly wrinkled yellow shirt printed with stars. He was holding a cup of coffee that he raised to his mouth from time to time, taking a sip, without halting the detailed ocular inspection he was subjecting her to.

"Julieta Leguizamón," he murmured suddenly in a thick voice, as if he were recovering from a cold or had just caught one. "The famous Shorty about whom Garro told me so much. All of it good, of course."

He indicated a table with cups, plates, pitchers of juice, and coffeepots.

"Some fruit juice, coffee, toast and marmalade?" he added drily. "This is my breakfast. But if you prefer something else, boiled eggs, for example, they'll prepare it right now. You are my guest and this is your home, Shorty."

She didn't say anything; she had calmed down a little and now waited in fear for the famous Doctor to tell her why he had brought her here. But he continued to drink his coffee and chew on his toast and marmalade as if she weren't there. This was his famous refuge, the bunker he had built on one of the southern beaches. Rumor had it that great orgies were held here.

What did she know about him? Not much more than other Peruvians, aside from this. That he had been a cadet and an obscure army officer until the military coup of October 3, 1968, by General Velasco Alvarado, when he became an aide to General Mercado Jarrín, in charge of foreign affairs for the de facto government. He held that position when the army discovered he was spying for and passing secrets to the CIA. The Velasco regime, which claimed to be socialist, had established a closer relationship with the USSR, which during those years had become the major supplier of weapons to Peru. Then an artillery captain, he was arrested, tried, found guilty, discharged from the army, and sent to a military prison. While serving his sentence, he studied law and became an attorney. This was when people gave him the nickname "the Doctor." When he was pardoned and released from prison, he achieved some notoriety as a lawyer for drug dealers, getting them out of prison or reducing their sentences by corrupting or intimidating judges and prosecutors. It was said that he had been Pablo Escobar's man in Peru. Apparently he came to know the judicial underworld like the palm of his hand and used the disorder and corruption in the courts for his own benefit—and the benefit of his clients.

But his real fortune, according to the legend that surrounded his figure, came in the elections of 1990, won by Engineer Alberto Fujimori. Between the first and second stages of that election, the navy discovered that Fujimori wasn't Peruvian but Japanese. He had come to Peru with his immigrant family, and they, to assure his future, like many Asian families who wanted to provide security to their descendants, had falsified (or bought) a birth certificate for him, indicating that he was born on July 28, the date of the National Holiday. They had also arranged a baptism for him that apparently confirmed his Peruvian nationality. When it began to appear in the press, between the two elections, that the navy would soon make its discovery public, Fujimori became terrified. His being Japanese automatically nullified his candidacy; the constitution was unequivocal in that regard. At that moment, it seems, contact between the aforementioned Doctor and the cornered candidate emerged. The Doctor was fast and clever. In a few days, all indications of the falsification had disappeared, and the naval officers who discovered it had been bribed or intimidated to be silent and destroy the evidence, which never came to light. The baptismal certificate was mysteriously torn out of the parish registry and disappeared forever. From that time on, the Doctor had been Fujimori's right arm and, as head of the Intelligence Service, the presumed author of the worst villainies—trafficking, robberies, and political crimes—committed in Peru for the past ten years. It was said that the fortune he and Fujimori had overseas was dizzying. What could this devil want with a poor show-business journalist, a reporter for a minor publication that, to top it all off, had just tragically lost its director?

"Juice and coffee are fine, Doctor," Shorty articulated, almost without a voice. No longer frightened, she was stupefied. Why had he brought her here? Why was she standing before the most powerful and mysterious man in Peru? Why was the head of the Intelligence Service treating her with so much familiarity and talking about Rolando Garro as if the two of them had been the best of friends? Her boss had never even mentioned that he knew this personage, though he sometimes spoke of him with undisguised admiration: "Fujimori may be the president, but the man who gives the orders, the one who makes and breaks, is the Doctor." It turns out they knew each other. Why hadn't Rolando ever told her?

"I haven't gone to bed yet, Shorty," he said, yawning, and she understood that the Doctor's sunken, reddened eyes were due to lack of sleep. "Too much work. Only at night can I concentrate on what matters without being interrupted by all kinds of foolishness."

He stopped speaking and looked her over slowly, from head to foot, delving into her again as if wanting to verify the most secret things she kept in her memory and in her heart.

"Do you know why I'm looking at you this way, Shorty?" the Doctor said, guessing what she was thinking. He spoke with an accent that occasionally revealed the singsong of Arequipa. Now he smiled at her amiably, to reassure her. "Because I can't believe a woman as small as you can have such big balls. Such big ovaries, I mean, excuse me. And please excuse my frankness, too."

He celebrated his witticism with a little laugh that wrinkled his face, but she didn't laugh. She had fastened her large, unmoving eyes on that powerful person and she didn't thank him for the unexpected praise she had just received. She recalled what Rolando Garro had once said to her: "He must be the richest man in Peru by now, and besides, he gives the order to kill people without a tremor in his voice or hand."

"Accusing the engineer Enrique Cárdenas of murder!" he exclaimed, slowly savoring what he was saying, in a tone that tried to show respect and admiration for her. "You know he's one of the most powerful men in Peru, don't you, Shorty? Because of the harm you've done to him, he could disappear you in the blink of an eye?"

"I did it so he wouldn't have me killed too, the way he had Rolando Garro killed," she said, speaking slowly, with no tremor in her voice. "After my accusation, he couldn't do anything to me; it would look as if he'd signed off on my death."

"I see, I see," he said, taking another swallow of coffee and handing her the cup in which he had just poured American coffee with a splash of cream. "You know what you're doing and have plenty of courage and brains, Shorty. This time you were wrong, but it doesn't matter. Shall I tell you something that will surprise you? I've been keeping track of you for some time, and you're just as I imagined. Even better. Do you know why I sent for you?"

"So that I'll withdraw my accusation against Engineer Cárdenas," she responded immediately, with absolute certainty.

She saw that after a moment of confusion, the Doctor began to laugh with a free, open laugh that reassured her again. She felt she was no longer in danger, in spite of being here with a man like him. She recalled that Rolando Garro had also told her once: "They say he's cruel, but generous to those who help him kill and steal: he makes them rich too."

"The truth is I like you, Shorty," the Doctor said, becoming serious, and scrutinizing her with the yellowish look, inquisitive but without light, of tired eyes. "I suspected it because of what Rolando had told me about you, but now I'm sure: we're made to understand each other. And that's the truth, my dear Julieta Leguizamón."

"That isn't why you sent for me, is it?" she asked.

"No," he replied immediately, shaking his head. "But the truth is, by the way, that it would be to the benefit of both of us if you withdrew that accusation right away. Let that poor millionaire enjoy his mines and his millions in peace. There won't be any problem. It's a simple procedure. You'll tell the judge that you felt confused after the death of your boss and great friend, the editor of your magazine. That you weren't in your right mind when you made that absurd accusation. Don't worry, the engineer won't do anything to you. I'll get you a good lawyer who'll help you through all the steps. Of course, it won't cost you a cent. I'll take care of that, too. It would be better for us if you withdraw it, Shorty. Yes, just what I said: better for you and for me. Besides, in this way we'll have begun to work together. But, in any case, that isn't why you're here."

Then he was silent, observing her while he took small sips of a second cup of coffee. Shorty heard the sound of the ocean; it seemed to come closer, it seemed as if it would burst into the room, and then it withdrew and grew faint.

"If that wasn't the reason, to what do I owe the honor of being here with you, Doctor, in nothing less than your secret beach refuge that people talk about so much?"

He nodded, serious now, hiding another yawn with his hand. Shorty noticed that a little yellow light was shining in his eyes and that his voice was different: he was giving orders and there wasn't a trace of amiability in his words.

"As you can imagine, I can't waste time listening to you tell lies, Shorty. So, I beg of you, talk to me with complete frankness, limiting yourself to concrete facts. Understood?"

Shorty nodded. When she heard the Doctor's intonation changing, she became alarmed again. But deep in her heart, something was telling her she wasn't in danger; that, on the contrary, this visit was mysteriously opening for her opportunities that she shouldn't squander. Her life could change for the better if she took advantage of the opportunity.

"That story about the photos that Garro published in *Exposed*," said the Doctor. "The ones of Engineer Cárdenas, naked and enjoying himself with prostitutes in Chosica. Tell me about that story."

"I can only tell you what I know, Doctor," she said, taking her time.

"Plenty of details, with no digressions," he specified, very seriously. "I repeat: concrete facts and no conjectures."

Shorty knew immediately that she had no alternative. And then, with all kinds of details, she told him the absolute truth. Ever since, a couple of months ago, Ceferino Argüello, the photographer for *Exposed*, with an air of great mystery had approached her desk in the editorial office of the magazine. He wanted to talk to her alone: it was a confidential matter, nobody else on the weekly could know. She never imagined that poor little Ceferino Argüello, so insignificant, so respectful, so timid, so long-suffering that not only the editor but any reporter on the magazine could treat him like dirt, yell at him, quarrel with him about anything, would ever have anything so explosive in his hands.

At about five in the afternoon, Shorty and Ceferino went to have lunch at Señora Mendieta's Peruvian Delight, on the corner of Calle Irribarren, not far from the Surquillo police station. They ordered two cafés con leche and two crisp pork rind sandwiches with onion and chili peppers. Shorty, amused, saw that before he spoke, the photographer wrung his hands, grew pale, opened and closed his mouth without the courage to say a word.

"If you have so many doubts, it's better you don't tell me anything, Ceferino," she murmured. "We'll have lunch, we'll forget about the matter, and we'll still be the friends we always were."

"I want you to take a look at these photographs, Shorty," Ceferino stammered, looking around suspiciously. He handed her a portfolio, closed with two yellow bands. "Careful, nobody else can see them."

"Were they the photos Garro published in *Exposed*?" the Doctor interrupted her.

Shorty nodded.

"And how did this Ceferino get hold of them?" he asked. He was very focused, and now his glance seemed to go right through her.

"He's the one who took them," said Shorty. "The guy who organized that orgy hired him. A foreigner, apparently."

"Señor Kosut," murmured Ceferino Argüello, so quietly that Julieta had to move a little closer to hear what he was saying. Her face was still burning from the impression those photos had made on her. "I had already done some other dirty little jobs for him. He liked to be photographed in bed with women. And he wanted a lot of pictures of this one without the guy being aware of it. A gent, important, with some money, he said. He took me to the house in Chosica to get everything ready. That is, the hiding places for taking photographs. We even saw the best way to light the place. I spent I don't know how much on rolls of film. We had agreed that he'd pay for all the materials and five hundred dollars for my work. But he stiffed me. He was living at the Hotel Sheraton. And suddenly he disappeared. Vanished into thin air, yes. He left the hotel and was gone. Never heard anything more about him. Until now."

"How long ago?" the Doctor asked.

"Two years now, Shorty," said Ceferino. "Two years, imagine. I'm really short of cash. I thought Señor Kosut would come back, but he never showed up again. Maybe he died, who knows what could have happened to him. I have a wife and three children, Julieta. Do you think something could be done with these photographs? For me to earn a few bucks, I mean. And at least get back what I invested."

"This is really a very ugly business, Ceferino," said an uneasy Shorty, lowering her voice. "Don't you know who the man was that you photographed doing those dirty things?"

"I know very well, Shorty," said Ceferino, in an almost inaudible whisper. "That's why I'm asking you. A guy that important, couldn't he maybe pay me a lot to get the photographs that make him look so bad?"

"You want to blackmail that fat cat?" Shorty laughed, astonished. "You, Ceferino? Would you really dare to do it? Do you know the risk you run, blackmailing somebody so influential with something like this?"

"I'd dare to do it if you helped me, Shorty," Ceferino stammered. "I don't have much character, it's true. But you do, you have more than enough. Between the two of us maybe we could earn a few bucks. Wouldn't you like that?"

"Thanks very much, Ceferino, but the answer is no," said Shorty in a definitive way. "I'm a reporter, not a blackmailer. Besides, I know my limits. I know who you can get mixed up with and who you can't. I'm temperamental, that's true, but I'm not a masochist or suicidal."

She held one of the photos of the orgy in her hand and looked at it with displeasure and, at the same time, with a strange sensation. Could what she was feeling be envy? She was sure she'd never be with a man doing the things that whore was doing, that she'd never take part in an encounter like that where different men would fuck her in all different places. Was she sorry? No: it made her sick, made her feel like vomiting.

"In any case, Ceferino, if you want some advice, the best thing would be for you to consult the boss. Talk to him, tell him the story of this Kosut. He knows more about these things than you or I do. Maybe he'll help you earn those soles you need."

"And then you and Ceferino went to take Rolando Garro the photos and tell him the story of Chosica," the Doctor continued, very certain of what he was saying. "And Garro got the idea of blackmailing Engineer Enrique Cárdenas without asking my permission or telling me about the matter. Do you know how much he asked for?"

Shorty swallowed saliva before she answered. Why did Rolando Garro have to ask permission of the head of the Intelligence Service to do what he had done? Was Rolando working for this individual? What she had always thought a rumor spread by her boss's enemies, was it true then? That one worked for the other, that he was one of his journalistic hunting dogs?

"In fact, it wasn't blackmail, Doctor," Shorty suggested, choosing her words carefully, thinking that saying something she shouldn't could place her in a difficult situation. "He took him the photos to encourage him to invest in the magazine. It was Rolando's dream, if you knew him you must know that. To transform *Exposed* into a great weekly, better known and better selling than *Oiga* or *Caretas*. Rolando thought that if Engineer Cárdenas became an investor, or even better, president of the board of directors of *Exposed*, all the publicity companies would begin to take out ads with us because the magazine's image would become prestigious."

"It doesn't cost anything to dream," the Doctor murmured between his teeth. "Which shows that Rolando Garro was much less intelligent than people thought. But you haven't answered my question. How much did he ask him for?"

"One hundred thousand dollars to begin with," said Shorty. "Like a first investment. Then, when the engineer saw that things were going well, he'd ask him to put in more. He told him, so he could see that the game was clean, that he could name his own manager or auditor to watch over how this new infusion of capital was spent."

"It was Garro's stupidity," said the Doctor, filled with sorrow. "Not to want to blackmail him but to ask for that ridiculous sum. If instead of a hundred thousand he'd asked for half a million, maybe he'd be alive. The smallness of his ambitions was his downfall. And then the miner, instead of going along with him, threw him out of his office?"

"He treated him very badly," Shorty agreed; she didn't really understand the background of what the Doctor was saying, but she was sure now that between her boss and this man there'd been a complicity greater than she had ever suspected. And not only journalistic, but something dirtier, too. "He insulted him, he said he'd never put a cent into that disgusting rag. He threw him out of his office, threatening to kick him if he didn't get out as fast as a polka."

"Chagrined and humiliated, the imbecile published the photographs of the orgy," the Doctor concluded, yawning again with a bored expression. "He let anger get the better of him and did the stupidest thing of his life. And paid dearly for it, as you saw. And to think that I warned him about that."

He looked at Shorty for a long time in silence; she didn't blink or close her eyes. Why was the Doctor saying these things to her? What was it exactly that he wanted her to know? What kind of threat or warning was he aiming at her with what he said and the secrets he revealed? She had started to tremble again. Hearing what she was hearing brought her back to the danger of her situation.

"I don't know what you mean, Doctor," she murmured. "I don't want to know anything else, I beg you. I'm only a journalist who would like to live and work in peace. Don't tell me anything that will put my life in danger, please."

"Rolando did things he never should have done," said the Doctor, not taking his eyes off her, as if he hadn't heard her. He spoke in a philosophical manner as he took another swallow of his coffee. "In the first place, trying to blackmail that millionaire for a paltry sum like a hundred thousand dollars. In the second, publishing those photos in a stupid fit of pique. And, above all, behaving irresponsibly without letting me know what he intended to do. If he had acted with more loyalty toward me, with greater calm, as these things should be done, he'd be alive and might even have made a nice profit."

"I beg you not to tell me anything else, Doctor," Shorty entreated. "I beg you, I don't want to know another word about this matter."

The Doctor made a curious face without looking away, and it seemed to Shorty that all of a sudden, he was doubtful.

"Since you're going to work for me, you have to learn about certain subjects," he murmured, shrugging, not attributing much importance to the matter. "You have to become involved. I trust in your discretion. For your own sake, it's a good idea that everything you learn here you keep secret, as silent as a tomb."

"Of course, Doctor," Shorty agreed. And, almost without transition, knowing very well that she should ask the question, she added: "Do you believe that Enrique Cárdenas ordered Rolando killed?

The Doctor shook his head no.

"He doesn't have the guts to kill anybody, he's a weakling, a rich kid," he affirmed, shrugging his shoulders again with a contemptuous look. "At this point knowing who killed him is irrelevant, Shorty. Rolando acted badly and paid for it. Well, let's not waste time; we'll get right to the point. What's going to happen to *Exposed*?"

"It'll disappear," she said. "What else could happen to the magazine without Rolando?"

"Reappear with you as editor, for example," said the Doctor immediately, looking at her with a mocking gleam in his eyes. "Can you do it? Rolando thought so. I'm going to take his good opinion of you seriously. I'm prepared to help you and to keep *Exposed* alive. You decide how much you want to earn as editor. We won't see each other very often. I want approval of the finished issue before it goes to press, and sometimes I'll give you the headlines. I'm a good headline writer, though you may not believe it. We'll see each other only under exceptional circumstances. But we'll maintain weekly communication by telephone, or if the matter is delicate, by messenger. Captain Félix Madueño, remember that name. I'll tell you who has to be investigated, who has to be defended, and above all, who has to be fucked over. Once again I ask you to excuse the language. But I repeat it because it will be the most important part of your obligations to me: to fuck over those who need to be fucked over. Fuck them over the way Rolando Garro knew how to do it. That's all, for now. You know already, from now on things will go very well for you. But don't forget the lesson: I forgive everything except traitors. I demand absolute loyalty from my collaborators. Understood, Shorty? See you later, then, and good luck."

This time, instead of shaking her hand, the Doctor said

goodbye with a kiss on her cheek. Hooded once again, Shorty felt her heart pounding as she retraced her steps in the hallway and on the stairs and got into the car. She was frightened and excited, horrified and filled with hope. Contradictory ideas and impulses whirled around her head. For example, to call a press conference, and in a room filled with reporters, stirred by the flashing cameras, to publicly beg the pardon of Engineer Enrique Cárdenas and state that the real killer of Rolando Garro was the Doctor, that genius of evil. A second later, she saw herself occupying the chair of the deceased editor of the weekly, calling the reporters to prepare the week's issue, and thinking about when she would move, into which neighborhood, and how good it would be to know that never again—never again—would she set foot in the shabby alleys of Five Corners.

20

A Whirlpool

"Relax, Quique, for God's sake," said Luciano, giving his friend an affectionate pat. "I can't stand seeing you with that face of a beaten dog."

"You're hurting me." Marisa tried to turn her face away from her friend, but Chabela, who was stronger, didn't stop and kept biting her lips and crushing her with the weight of her entire body. "What's wrong, you madwoman, what's going on?"

"The only thing I ask of my collaborators is loyalty," the Doctor repeated for the tenth time, hitting the table with the palm of his hand. "A doglike fidelity, I've already told you, and I'll repeat it as often as I have to, Shorty."

"I'm relaxed, I'm calm, Luciano, I assure you," Quique said. But the bitterness on his face, the grimace of his mouth, the tone of his voice contradicted him. "I don't feel like dancing with joy or shouting hurrah, of course. But now that the worst has happened, I'm getting better. I swear to God I am, Luciano."

"What's wrong?" Chabela finally freed herself from her friend's mouth and reproached her with her eyes. "Do you really want to know? I'm jealous, Marisa, that's what's wrong. Because suddenly you've become Quique's geisha. Your husband's little whore. At this rate, at any moment you'll dismiss me the way you dismiss a servant."

"I don't know why you say that, Doctor," Shorty murmured in surprise. "I believe I'm fulfilling my obligations to you very well. It's what matters most to me, I assure you. That you're happy with my work."

"I say it because I would never want what happened to Rolando Garro to happen to you," the Doctor sweetened his bad temper. "It's a warning, not a reprimand."

Marisa laughed and threw her arms around Chabela's neck, obliged her to lower her head, and kissed her with an open mouth, swallowing her saliva with pleasure. Then she moved her away and, still holding her by the neck, murmured with a smile:

"It's the first time you've made a jealous scene with me. You don't know how those jet-black eyes of yours are flashing right now. Black, deep black, and at the back a little blue flash. I love them!"

"Are you trying to buy me off with all that flattery, you wretch?" Chabela stammered, kissing her, too.

They were both naked, Chabela mounted on top of Marisa, each of them sweating from head to toe. The sauna was burning. The wood in the small space, dampened by the heat, emitted an aroma of eucalyptus, and a breath between human and vegetal hung in the air.

"Let us drink to happiness, my friends," said Señor Kosut, raising his glass. "Bottoms up! Here you say *seco y volteado*, I've learned that already! So, *seco y volteado*!"

"It isn't true, Quique," Luciano corrected him, smiling affectionately. "It's been a terrible experience for you, of course, but you have to overcome it psychologically, uproot it from your spirit. The important thing is that it's over. It's behind you, brother. Who's talking now about the scandal, or the Chosica photographs? Everybody's forgotten them, there are other things, other scandals that have buried what happened to you. No strings attached to you. Somebody stopped saying hello? Barely two or three imbeciles, and it's just as well you're rid of them. You don't have the same friends you always had? And Rolando Garro's dead and buried. What else do you want?"

"He may be dead and buried," Quique interrupted, "but *Exposed* is out again, with better paper and twice the photographs it had before. And the editor is none other than Julieta Leguizamón, Garro's pal and disciple when they were covering me with shit and slander. The same woman who accused me of having had Garro killed by a hired assassin! You think that's nothing? You think that with all this I can be calm and happy, Luciano?"

"You'll never be mentioned again in that rag, Quique. The Doctor committed to that and he's keeping his word. That little woman published a retraction and begged your pardon in the same issue. The case has been stayed indefinitely. After a while we'll make it disappear and there won't be a trace of this matter in the judicial archives. It will all be buried. Forget about it. Pay attention to your work, to your family. That's all that should matter to you now, old man."

"The truth, plain and simple, is that Rolando Garro behaved badly, he was disloyal, he disobeyed me," said the Doctor, becoming excited again. He looked at Shorty as if he wanted to make her disappear with his dark, watery eyes. "I expressly forbade him to publish photos of that rich guy's orgy in *Exposed*. I know how to choose my enemies. You shouldn't challenge those who are more powerful than you. Rolando deceived me, he told me he had torn them up, and then suddenly he published them. He could have gotten me involved in a goddamn mess. Do you understand what I'm telling you, Shorty?"

"Ladies, take off those uncomfortable clothes and show

us your secrets," said Señor Kosut, refilling the empty champagne glasses himself. He spoke good Spanish, with a pure accent.

"Let me kiss you where you like it, my love," Marisa whispered into Chabela's ear. "I love your jealous scene, it proves you really love me. I want to give you pleasure, swallow your juices, hear you panting when I make you come."

Chabela agreed without answering her. She helped her to slip under her body, to the lower platform in the sauna, to sink her head between her thighs while she, at the same time, leaned on her side and spread her legs. Marisa, sitting backward on the lower platform, sank her head, put out her tongue, and began to lick the lips of Chabela's sex; she did it slowly, persistently, longingly, with love, taking her time to reach the clitoris.

"I felt jealous, yes, Marisita," Chabela said as she felt the heat rise through her body and a little tremor ran along her thighs, her belly, and up to her head. "I see you being more affectionate than ever with Quique. You lean into him, keep kissing him in front of Luciano and me, the two of you are always holding hands. You're making me move from love to hate, I'm warning you. Slower, please. I'm enjoying this, darling, don't make me come yet."

"You, señorita, sit on my phallus, penis, or prick, as the natives say," Señor Kosut asked and ordered with elaborate courtesy. "And you, come over here, Blondie, kneel down and offer me your sex. It doesn't matter if it isn't very clean, that kind of detail doesn't worry me. If it smells of Parmesan cheese, even better, ha-ha. I'll tell you ahead of time I'll do what the French call *minette* and the Spaniards, always so vulgar, call sucking, I believe. And my dear Peruvians, what do you call it?"

"A little lick," Licia or Ligia said with a laugh. "The little horn is upside down."

The champagne had begun to affect Enrique Cárdenas. He didn't drink very much; he didn't like it and had never held it very well. Besides, he was stunned by what he was seeing. But something different had begun to suggest itself to him. Until that moment he had been disconcerted, confused, dumbfounded, not knowing how to respond to what was happening around him. Now he felt an excited tickle in his fly. "Do you want me to help you take off your clothes, honey?" said one of the fat women among whom he was sitting.

"I don't know what you mean, Doctor," murmured Shorty, pretending to maintain her usual sangfroid. But she was uneasy. None of this seemed normal. What mistake had she made? What was the point of the Doctor's rash confidences? Had he ordered Rolando's death? If so, she was in danger again. Those confidences meant she was an accomplice. She had made every effort in the world to follow the Doctor's instructions, and until now, he had always congratulated her. "I try to follow your orders to the letter, Doctor."

"I mean that I consider you a magnificent collaborator." The Doctor's tired face smiled at her, and his smile exaggerated his plump cheeks. "I'd never want to do without your services, Shorty, much less have to punish you as a traitor, as disloyal. Yes, yes, I know what you're thinking. In effect, I'd never want what happened to Rolando Garro to happen to you."

Shorty felt as if her heart had stopped beating. He'd given the order, he'd had him killed. She knew she had turned very pale and that her teeth were chattering. Her large, unmoving eyes were fixed on the Doctor. He put on an afflicted face.

"I shouldn't have said anything to you, I knew it would cause you grief, but it was indispensable for you to know what's at stake, Shorty," he said, slowly and very seriously. "Something bigger than you and me. Power. You don't fool around with power, my friend. In the end, things are always a matter of life or death when power is at stake. Doing what I had forbidden, blackmailing that millionaire, compromised me. He saw the twig, not the forest. He could have brought down everything I've built, ruined me, finished me. Do you see? I had to do it, with pain in my soul."

"Kill him so savagely?" Shorty rasped, as if there were a sudden obstruction in her throat. "Hurt him like that? Just because he disobeyed you?"

"The men were excessive, that's true, and that was bad, I reproved them and fined them," the Doctor acknowledged. "The men who perform these necessary tasks are not normal people like you and me. They're savages accustomed to killing, heartless beasts. Sometimes they go too far. They went too far with Rolando. I was very sorry about that, believe me."

"I don't know why you tell me these things, Doctor. The truth is they frighten me."

"I say these things to you because I trust you and because you're now my star collaborator, Shorty. That's why you're earning more money now than you ever have in your life, and people fear and respect you." The Doctor's voice softened. "That's why you could leave your hovel in Five Corners and move to Miraflores. And buy clothes and furniture. So things between us should be very clear. We're friends and accomplices. If one goes down so does the other. If I go up, so do you. And so, you know, total fidelity, that's what I expect of you. And now, let's get to work. How are things going in the matter of Deputy Arrieta Salomón? He's our first priority."

"I don't give a damn what it's cost me to wipe away all this filth, Luciano," said Quique. "But the wounds left in my memory and emotions will never be erased, brother. I swear by my poor mother, may she rest in peace. My siblings think the sorrow and bitterness this scandal caused her are what killed her. They're right, of course. Which means I'm the one who killed my poor old mother, Luciano. Do you think I'll ever be able to forgive myself for her death?"

"There, that's it," panted Chabela with the half voice she had now. "I'm coming, Blondie."

And a little while later she felt Marisa get up, still embracing her, and search for her mouth and pass her the mouthful of saliva she had kept for her. "Swallow these delicious juices I get from you when I suck you," she commanded. And an obedient Chabela swallowed them. They embraced and kissed each other again, and then Marisa spoke into her ear in that thick voice she had when she was excited:

"You shouldn't be jealous, Chabelita, because when Quique and I make love you're always there between us."

"What are you saying, you fool!" Chabela in alarm took Marisa's head in both hands and moved it a few centimeters from her own face. "You haven't told Quique that . . ."

Marisa threw her arms around her neck and spoke, placing her mouth on Chabela's and saying the words between her teeth:

"Yes, I've told him everything. He becomes more excited than a madman, and that's why every time we make love you're always there, doing dirty little things with us."

"I'll kill you, I swear I'll kill you, Marisa," her friend exclaimed, not knowing whether or not to believe her, with one hand raised that, suddenly, she let fall. But instead of hitting her, she put it between her friend's legs, caught at her sex, and squeezed it.

"Easy, you're hurting me," Marisa protested, purring.

"Put a pinch of coke on your penis and a little more up your nose," said Señor Kosut, like a physician prescribing for a patient. "You'll be like new, able to fuck those young ladies who are all over you in the ass, the sex, and the mouth, my lord."

"Are these ladies going to spend the whole morning in the sauna?" Luciano wondered, checking his watch. "The truth is I'm hungry. What about you, old man?"

"Let them enjoy themselves," Quique replied. "I wish I were like them. All this rolls right off them, they're concerned for a moment and then they're back to clothes, gossip, shopping, whatever. How lucky to be so frivolous."

"Don't believe it, old man," replied Luciano. "This terrorism business doesn't let Chabela sleep. She's obsessed by the idea that those villains will kidnap me, like Cachito, or even worse, our daughters. The poor thing has to take pills now so she won't be awake all night."

"Shall I tell you what keeps me awake, Luciano?" said Quique. And he added, lowering his voice, as if someone else could hear them in the huge, deserted garden where the two Great Danes played in the distance. "Too many things in this matter are not at all clear. First, the idea that this poor devil, this sclerotic old man, Juan Peineta, could be the killer of Rolando Garro. Have you swallowed that story? Well, I haven't."

"He himself said he was guilty," replied Luciano after hesitating for a moment. "Wasn't he a guy who spent his life sending insults and threats to Rolando Garro? Dozens of those letters were shown at the trial, weren't they? Don't be more Catholic than the pope, Quique."

"Nobody believed that confession, Luciano. Who would believe that a human ruin like that poor reciter could commit so horrible a murder?"

"Be that as it may, we have to be realistic. What matters are the results. It's to your advantage more than anyone else's that they find the reporter's killer and leave you in peace once and for all," said Luciano. "True, it's not impossible that all this was planned by the Doctor. Probably there's something dirty behind what we know. But, man, how can that matter to you?"

"I don't even remember who this Don Rolando Garro is, gentlemen," Juan Peineta stated. "Although it's true, his name sounds familiar. Don't think that hitting me will bring back my memory. I should be so lucky. My head has been mush for a long time now, you know. Now I beg you, for God's sake: leave me in peace, don't hit me again."

"What the judge is offering is to get you out of the lottery, asshole," the inspector insisted. "You confess that it was you, the judge orders the psychiatric exam, and the doctors' diagnosis is that you're not responsible due to your dementia praecox."

"Dementia praecox," the prosecutor repeated. "Instead of Lurigancho Prison, a rest home. Imagine. Nurses, good food, medical attention, free visits, daily television, and movies once a week."

"All that instead of an awful hole full of rats in the Hotel Mogollón, which is going to collapse any day now, crushing all the tenants," the inspector explained. "You'd have to have shit for brains to refuse a splendid offer like this one."

"Can I take Serafín to that rest home?" the reciter asked, suddenly interested. He added: "That's my cat's name, I gave him that nice name. The poor thing lives in terror, afraid those half-breeds who make pussy-cat stews will catch him. I'd be very grateful if you'd stop hitting me. I'm losing my sight from being hit so much in my head. A little Christian charity, gentlemen."

"It's just that blows leave no marks on your head, Juan Peineta," the inspector said with a laugh. The other individuals who were there laughed too. Juan Peineta thought it was a courtesy and tried to imitate them. In spite of another blow he received at the back of his neck with the rubber truncheon

that left him a little dazed, he laughed too, just like his tor-
turers.

"You can take your cat Serafín, your dog, and even your
whore if you have one, reciter," the inspector repeated.

"Sign here and write clearly," the prosecutor said, pointing to the exact spot at the bottom of the paper. "And don't
ever open your mouth again, reciter. The truth is, you're a lucky
man, Juan Peineta."

"There's just one little problem, Señor Prosecutor," the
reciter stammered in an anguished voice. "And it's that this
gentleman, whose name I've already forgotten, I didn't kill
him. I don't even remember if I know him, or what he does in
life, or who he is."

"We'd better get going, Chabelita," said Marisa. "They'll
think it's strange that we're taking so long in the sauna. And
besides, with the dark circles under your eyes, I don't know
what Quique and Luciano will think of you."

"When they see yours they'll know you've committed several mortal sins," Chabela said with a laugh. "All right, let's
go. But first you'll tell me if it's true that you've told Quique
about us. And if it's true that your sweet husband gets excited
thinking that you and I make love."

"Of course I told him." Marisa laughed. "But not as if it
were true, just as a fantasy so that he'll perk up and be in shape.
There's nothing that excites him as much, I swear. Does it get
you very excited to imagine Chabela and me this way, Quique?"

"Yes, yes, my love," Quique agreed, embracing his wife,
caressing her, reckless. "Tell me the rest, tell me that it's true,
tell me that it really happened, that it's happening now, that it
will happen today, and happen again tomorrow."

"And now, when I'm satiated," said Señor Kosut, yawning, "as always, I'm sleepy. I suppose you won't care if I take a
little nap, will you? Keep on enjoying yourselves and forget
about me."

"Do you know something? The idea excites me, too." Was Chabela joking? "Would you care if I fucked your husband, Marisa?"

"Let me think about it." Was Marisa joking? "Would you care if I masturbated watching you make love?"

"Is Quique a good screw?" Chabela asked.

"Please don't use that word, Chabela," Marisa protested, making a face. "I think it's the most vulgar thing in the world and it makes me allergic. Say *make love, fuck, fornicate*, whatever. But never *screw*: it seems as dirty as saying *shit* and it makes me allergic. To answer your question: yes, he's a terrific fuck. Especially recently."

"If you want, I'll lend you Luciano so you can fuck him." Was Chabela joking? "The poor thing is so pure he probably doesn't know those things exist in life."

"I'm convinced they forced Juan Peineta to say he was guilty, for money or out of fear," Quique declared. "But if it wasn't him and it wasn't me, Luciano, who the hell killed that son of a bitch Rolando Garro?"

"I don't know and I don't want to know," said Luciano immediately. "And it shouldn't matter to you either, Quique. Better not stick your nose into those stinking mysteries of power where Fujimori and the Doctor rule. That's where the matter lies, no doubt about it. It isn't our affair, happily. Think about that, Quique. Whoever he was, he's good and dead. He was looking for it, wasn't he?"

"Is something wrong, señor?" asked the woman who said her name was Licia or Ligia. "You've turned so pale."

"Don't you feel well, Engineer?" asked Señor Kosut, opening his eyes and sitting up on the sofa where he had stretched out.

"I think I had more to drink than usual," stammered Engineer Cárdenas. He tried to get up, but Licia's or Ligia's body, perched on top of his, prevented him from doing so. "Would you mind letting me up? Is your name Licia or Ligia? I think I'm going to vomit. Is there a WC around here?"

"I'm really afraid I've pissed in my pants," Juan Peineta finally confessed. "I'm soaked from head to toe and can catch cold. I'm very sorry, gentlemen."

"We'll get you clean trousers and underwear," said the one who seemed to be in charge. "Sign here, too, please."

"I'll sign wherever you like," said Juan Peineta, and his hand trembled as if he suffered from Parkinson's. "But I want to make it clear that I haven't killed anybody. Much less that poet, he was called Rolando Garro, wasn't he? I never even killed a fly, if my memory doesn't deceive me. But recently, the truth is that my memory has played some bad tricks on me. I forget things and names all the time."

"I have to go," Engineer Cárdenas announced, leaning against a wall to keep from falling to the ground. "It's late and I don't feel very well."

"Lots of hits of coca, *papacito*," said Licia or Ligia, laughing.

"I'd be grateful if you'd call me a taxi," said Engineer Cárdenas, still leaning against the wall. "I don't think I'm in any shape to drive."

"You have lipstick all over your face and shirt, honey," said Licia or Ligia, shaking out his jacket. "Better wash your face before you go home if you don't want to make your wife really angry."

"I'll take you myself, Engineer," offered the amiable Señor Kosut. "The car and driver I've hired is waiting for us at the door. You're very smart not to drive in this state."

"I don't know why you're still here at the magazine, Ceferino Argüello," said Shorty, casting a profoundly disparaging glance at the photographer for *Exposed*. She held the photos in her hand and looked at them with the same contempt she showed the distressed Ceferino. I told you: you have to destroy Arrieta Salomón with the ridiculous. And instead of discrediting him, your photographs present him as the most normal and ordinary man in the world. Even better than what he really is."

"But you can see that he's drunk, Julieta," Ceferino said in his own defense. "His eyes are glassy, and in the laboratory I can make them look worse if necessary."

"Do that, at least, retouch it so it looks like he's vomiting down his shirt front. Make him ugly, degrade him. Use your imagination, Ceferino. Make it look like there's vomit on the floor. Do you understand what I'm telling you?"

"I can't perform miracles, Shorty," Ceferino Argüello begged, his voice breaking. "I make an effort to do everything you ask of me. And every day you treat me worse. Even worse than Señor Garro treated me. It doesn't seem as if we're friends anymore."

"Here we're not," declared Shorty, very energetically. "Here, at the magazine, I'm the editor and you're an employee. We're friends outside, when we have coffee. But here I give the orders and you carry them out. It's a good idea for you to be very clear about that, for your own good, Ceferino. Go on, retouch the photos and do a lot more damage to that dumb bastard. This week we have to devote the bulk of the magazine to him, and he should be left nicely fucked over. Orders are orders, Ceferino."

"We'd have to take a little trip to Miami again," said Chabela, talking from the shower. "Would you like that?"

"I'd love it," answered Marisa, who was using the hair dryer. "A weekend of being calm and happy. Without blackouts, or bombs, or curfews. Dedicating ourselves to shopping and swimming in the ocean."

"And doing a few crazy little things, too," said Chabela; the stream of water from the shower barely let her speak.

"And?" asked the Doctor.

"Full speed ahead," said Julieta Leguizamón. "Deputy Arrieta Salomón could be accused of sexual harassment by his driver or a female employee."

"Why not both?" asked the equitable Doctor. "That would show that he's sexually depraved with no extenuating circumstances, wouldn't it?"

"There's no reason not to," the editor of *Exposed* agreed. "The thing would be a little baroque, that's true. He'd harass his driver so the man fucks him, and the girl so he could fuck her. That's it, isn't it?"

"I like people who understand things right away with no need to repeat them, Shorty. How much will the joke cost?"

"It'll be enough to put a little fear in them, to soften them up," she said. "And then they'll be happy with some nice tips."

"Get it started," said the Doctor. "A faggot and a rapist at the same time. Excellent! He'll be worse than a consumptive's spit. Let's see if he understands the warning and stops fucking around."

"You look a little pale, Doctor," said Shorty, changing the subject. "Aren't you getting enough sleep?"

"I forgot what sleeping was a long time ago, Julieta," said the Doctor. "If I weren't so busy, I'd go to one of those clinics where they hypnotize you and put you to sleep for a week. It seems you wake up like new. Okay, see you later, Shorty, take care of yourself. And by all means, in this issue make Deputy Arrieta Salomón swallow rivers of shit."

" 'Dark swallows will return to your balcony to hang their nests,' " said Juan Peineta, his eyes filled with uncertainty. And after hesitating for a moment, he asked: "What's the music to that Creole waltz?"

"I don't think it's a waltz; it's a poem by Gustavo Adolfo Bécquer," interjected the female nurse with a mustache.

"Excuse me, señorita, but it's coming out. Could you take

me to the bathroom, please?" asked the very old woman who was bald.

"A poem?" Juan Peineta was astonished. "Do you eat that with ice cream?"

"If you've pooped your underwear, I'll make you swallow it, you disgusting, doddering old man." The nurse with a mustache became furious.

"It tastes better with rice." The male nurse laughed out loud. And he imitated a solicitous waiter: "Would you like a poem with ice cream or with rice, sir?"

"Put a little ketchup on it instead," Juan Peineta ordered, very seriously.

"Well, at last," Luciano welcomed them. "It's about time, ladies."

"I thought you'd passed out in the sauna," said Quique.

"You would have liked that, my dear husband," Marisa joked, tousling his hair. "To be a widower and dedicate yourself to we-all-know-what, right?"

"Look how red you've made poor Quique," Chabela said with a laugh, smoothing his hair. "Don't be so evil, Marisa. Don't torture him with those bad memories. Or perhaps they weren't so bad, Quique?"

"Quique likes to be tortured every once in a while," replied Marisa, kissing her husband on the forehead. "Isn't that so, darling?"

"You're like a geisha, Marisa," said Chabela. "If you keep fondling him like that, he'll become unbearable, you'll see."

"And put on a little mustard, too, if you can," ordered Juan Peineta. "But above all, serve it to me nice and hot."

"He isn't doddering, he's totally crazy," concluded the male nurse, placing a finger against his temple. "Or he's really fucking with us and having a wonderful time at our expense."

"Chabela and I are planning a weekend in Miami," Marisa said suddenly, with absolute naturalness. "Chabela needs to do some things in her Brickell Avenue apartment and she's asked me to go with her. What do you think, darling?"

"I think it's terrific, darling," said Quique. "A weekend in Miami, away from all this. Fantastic. Why don't you take me along? I could look at some boats and see if I finally buy the yacht we've talked so much about, Marisa. Why don't you come too, Luciano? We'll go to that Cuban restaurant that's so good, the one where you can get that delicious dish: *ropa vieja*, isn't it?"

"Yes, of course," said Chabela, not showing too much joy. "The restaurant's called the Versailles and the dish, *ropa vieja*, I remember very well."

"Did that madwoman Marisa have this all planned?" she thought. "For how long? Then it's certain, Marisa has told Quique about us. I'll kill her, I'll kill her. This pair of smart alecks planned it with all the bad intentions in the world, of course." She was very serious, her large black eyes darting from Quique to Marisa, from Marisa to Quique, and she felt as if her cheeks were burning. "He knows everything," she thought, "the two of them planned this little trip together. I'm going to slap this madwoman's face a couple of times."

"Do you think I can allow myself that luxury with the mountains of work we have at the office?" said Luciano. "You go, you're all so lazy. But at least bring me back a little gift from Miami."

"A tie with palm trees and parrots in eighteen colors," said Quique. "And by the way, Chabela, do you have room for me in your Brickell Avenue apartment, or shall I book a hotel room?"

"There's plenty of room for you, too." Marisa looked into Chabela's eyes with complete malice. "A multifamily bed where at least two couples can fit, ha-ha. Isn't that right, darling?"

"Absolutely," said Chabela. And she turned to Quique: "I have a nice guest room that's completely independent, with its own bath and a painting by Lam on the wall, don't worry about that."

"And if not, you can have Quique sleep in the doghouse," joked Luciano. "And if you find that yacht, be sure it has a cabin for guests. We'll see if that's how I'll finally learn to fish. They say it's the most relaxing thing in the world for one's nerves. Better than Valium."

"She's told him everything and it must be true that it gets him excited. I'm positive the two of them dreamed up this little trip together," Chabela kept thinking, smiling all the while. "And they thought that in Miami the three of us would go to bed together, of course." She was surprised, intrigued, curious, enraged, somewhat frightened, and a little excited, too. "This madwoman, this madwoman Marisa," she was thinking, looking at her friend, who in turn looked back at her with a mocking, defiant gleam in her light, almost liquid blue eyes. "I'll kill her, I'm going to kill her. How dare she."

"Congratulations, Shorty," said the Doctor. "The issue dedicated to Deputy Arrieta Salomón was downright delicious. It took him down a peg and now the poor devil is begging for mercy."

"But he's filed a suit against us, Doctor," said the editor of *Exposed*. "We've already received a summons to appear before an examining magistrate."

"I'll take care of it," said the Doctor. "You can wipe your little dog's ass with that notice. Send it to me and I'll see that it's lost in the mass confusion of our Judicial Branch."

"And what's going to happen to Deputy Arrieta Salomón?" asked Shorty.

"Overnight he's lost his balls," the Doctor replied. "Now, instead of attacking the government, he goes around trying to convince the Fathers of the Nation that he isn't a rapist of servant girls or a faggot who's fucked by his chauffeur. Speaking of dogs, Shorty, do you have one? Would you like to have one?

I can give you a dachshund pup. My dog has had several litters."

"A conversation alone, Ceferino, you and I," said the editor of *Exposed*, taking the photographer by the arm. "I'm inviting you to lunch. Not in Surquillo but far from here. Let's go to the Seven Deadly Fins, in Miraflores. Do you like shellfish?"

"I like everything, of course," said Ceferino, disconcerted. "You inviting me to lunch, Julieta? What a surprise. We've known each other for a thousand years and this is the first time you've extended an invitation like this."

"I'm not going to try to seduce you, you're not my type," joked Shorty, still holding him by the arm. "We'll have a very, very serious conversation. Your jaw will drop when you hear what I'm going to tell you. Come on, let's take a taxi, my treat, Ceferino."

"How nice Miami looks," said Quique, looking at the skyscrapers in amazement. "The last time I came here was about ten years ago. It was nothing, and now it's a big city."

"Shall I pour you some champagne, Quique?" Marisa asked her husband. "It's delicious, nice and cold."

"I prefer a whiskey on the rocks, with lots of ice," said Quique. He was examining the paintings and objects in Chabela's apartment, admiring her good taste. Why was Luciano's wife so prim?

"That's it, let's get drunk," Chabela laughed, raising her glass. "Let's forget about Lima at least for one night."

"It's clear you're at the top, Julieta," Ceferino said with a smile. "Is it true you left your little alley in Five Corners and moved to Miraflores? I imagine they've doubled or tripled your salary. And we thought just a few short months ago, when they killed Rolando Garro, that our world had come to an end and we'd starve to death."

"Come, sit here, darling," Marisa said to her husband.

"There's plenty of room between Chabela and me, don't go so far away."

"You'd think you were afraid of us, Quique," Chabela said mockingly.

"I'm delighted to be in such good company," Quique laughed, moving to the sofa where Marisa and Chabela were sitting. He sat between them. Beyond the railing was a silvery sea, sparkling with the last lights of dusk. A silent sailboat was in the distance. "Really, it's beautiful. What marvelous peace."

They ordered cold beer, two corvina ceviches, Julieta asked for a stew of meat, potatoes, and hot peppers with rice, and Ceferino a spicy chicken chili, also with rice.

"What shall we drink to, Shorty?" asked Ceferino, his glass raised, smiling, vaguely intrigued by this unexpected invitation from his editor. "The new *Exposed* and its successes?"

"To Rolando Garro, its founder," said Julieta Leguizamón, clinking glasses with the photographer. "Tell me frankly, Ceferino. What did you think of him? Did you respect and admire him, or at heart did you hate him, as so many others did?"

"Now that we're getting high, I'm going to ask you a question, Quique," Marisa said suddenly, facing her husband in the half-light of the spacious terrace. "Answer me honestly, please. Do you like Chabela?"

"What kind of question is that, Marisa?" Chabela gave a forced laugh. "Have you lost your mind?"

"Tell me if you like her and if you'd like to kiss her," Marisa insisted, not taking her eyes off her husband and pretending to be put out. "Answer me honestly, don't be a coward."

Before responding, Ceferino tasted the ceviche, chewed, and swallowed the mouthful, showing signs of satisfaction.

There weren't many people yet in the Seven Deadly Fins. The morning was damp and gray, a little melancholy.

"Who wouldn't like to kiss so beautiful a woman," Quique stammered. He had turned as red as a beet. Was Marisa already drunk, asking nonsensical questions like these?

"Thanks, Quique," said Chabela. "This conversation is getting dangerous. We ought to tape up your dear wife's mouth."

"Of course she's beautiful, and besides, she has the most delicious mouth in the world, Quique," said Marisa. And stretching both arms above her husband, she took her friend by the cheeks and pulled her to her. "Watch and die of envy, hubby dear."

Chabela tried, but without much conviction, to move her face away, and finally allowed Marisa to kiss her cheek and begin to bring her mouth close to her lips.

"I didn't hate him, though at times he treated me very badly, especially when he had his fits of temper," Ceferino Argüello said at last. "But Señor Garro gave me my first opportunity to be what I wanted to be: a professional photographer, a graphic reporter. Of course I admired him as a journalist. He knew his trade and had great courage. Why are you asking me this, Shorty?"

"Let me go, you madwoman, what are you doing," Chabela said at last, blushing and confused, moving her face away from Marisa. "What will Quique say about these games?"

"He won't say anything, isn't that right, Quique?" Marisa caressed her husband's face with her hand, while he looked at her openmouthed. "Remember, he's an expert in orgies. I assure you he's dying of envy. Go on, hubby, enjoy yourself, kiss her. I give you permission."

Instead of answering him, Julieta Leguizamón, who hadn't tasted her ceviche yet, asked him another question:

"Did his death make you sad, Ceferino? Were you sickened by the terrible, brutal way they killed him?"

Quique didn't know what to do or say. Was his wife speaking seriously? Was she really saying what he had just heard? A half smile was frozen on his face, and he felt like an idiot.

"What a coward you are, Quique," Marisa said finally. "I know you're dying to kiss her, you've told me so, so often when we're alone, and now that you have the chance, you don't have the courage. You set the example, darling. Kiss him."

"Are you really giving me permission?" Chabela said with a laugh, now more in control of herself. "Well, sure, of course I have the courage."

She stood up, walked past Marisa, dropped onto Quique's knees, and held up her mouth to him; he gave a fast, sideways glance at his wife, and finally kissed her. Bewildered, his eyes closed, he felt Chabela's mouth trying to part his lips, and he parted them. Their tongues became confused in a vehement encounter. As if at a distance, he seemed to hear Marisa laughing.

Ceferino held up his fork with his second mouthful of ceviche, which he had prepared carefully, adding pieces of corvina, onion, lettuce, and hot pepper. Very serious now, he nodded.

"Of course it left me horrified, Shorty. Of course it did. May I ask what all this is about? Damn, you're very mysterious this morning. Why don't you tell me once and for all the reason for this meal. Say it openly, Shorty."

"We're very uncomfortable here and there's no reason to be," Quique heard his wife say. Chabela's face moved away from his and he saw that she was aroused, her eyes very bright and her full-lipped mouth wet with his saliva. But Marisa had taken her by the hand, both women had stood, and he watched them move away toward the bedroom. "Come, come, darling, let's get more comfortable."

Quique didn't follow them. It had grown dark, and the faint light on the terrace came from the street. He was stupefied. Was all of this really happening? Wasn't it a hallucination? Had Marisa and Chabela kissed each other on the mouth? Had his wife said what she'd said? Had Luciano's wife sat on his knees and had the two of them kissed with so much passion? He began to feel an excitement that made him tremble from head to toe, but he didn't have the courage to get up and see what was going on in that bedroom.

Julieta agreed: "You're right, Ceferino." She had to lower her voice, because the waiter had just sat a couple at the next table, where she could be overheard. They were very young, rather stylishly dressed, and held hands as they studied the menu, exchanging romantic glances.

But finally, leaning on the sofa with both hands, Quique rose to his feet. He was shocked and happy. He had dreamed about this but never imagined it would be possible, that it could pass from dream to reality. Walking on tiptoe, as if he were going to surprise them, he walked slowly down the dark hallway. In the bedroom a faint light, probably the bedside lamp, had just been turned on.

"Well, yes, I'll tell you the truth and nothing but the truth, Ceferino," Shorty declared. "It was an unlucky hour when you agreed to take photographs of that orgy in Chosica to earn a few pesos. That's where it all began. If it hadn't been for those damned photos, Rolando would be alive, this conversation wouldn't be taking place, and I probably never would have invited you to lunch or said what I'm going to say to you."

From the door to the bedroom, Quique watched them: they were naked, lying on the bed, their legs intertwined, embracing and kissing each other. "One dark and the other blond," he thought. "One more beautiful than the other." In the circular half-light of the lamp their bodies gleamed as if oiled. Neither woman turned to look at him; they seemed given over to their pleasure, having forgotten he was there observing them, that he, too, existed. His hands, as if independent of his will, had begun to unbutton his shirt, lower his trousers, remove his shoes and socks.

"Well, well, Shorty, this gets more and more intriguing." The photographer spoke as he ate, quickly, as if someone were going to snatch away his ceviche. "Go on, go on, excuse the interruption."

When he was naked he moved forward, still on tiptoe, and sat on a corner of the large bed, very close to them, not touching them.

"You both look very beautiful like this, it's the loveliest thing I've ever seen," his mouth murmured in a mechanical way, without his being aware that he was speaking. "Thank you for making me feel at this moment like the happiest man on earth."

His penis was stiff, and in the midst of the happiness he felt, he was terrified by the idea that he wouldn't be able to sustain it and would ejaculate too soon.

"That foreigner who hired you to take the photographs must have been a gangster." Shorty's motionless eyes looked with disgust at how Ceferino ate: chewing with his mouth open, making noise, dropping fragments of food on the tablecloth. "If he disappeared suddenly, it must have been because he had to escape suddenly or because his pals or his enemies killed him. He had you take those pictures because he planned to blackmail the millionaire for lots of money, of course."

Quique saw that Marisa had moved her head away from Chabela and was looking at him. But she spoke not to him but to her friend, in a low, thick voice that he could hear very well: "Let me suck you, darling. I want to swallow your juices."

He saw that the women's bodies separated, that Marisa had crouched down and, squatting, had buried her head between Chabela's legs and she, on her back, an arm covering her eyes, began to sigh and pant. Very slowly, taking infinite precautions, he also lay down on the bed, and with the minimal, sinuous movements of a reptile, began to approach the couple.

"I always knew that, Shorty," Ceferino interrupted. "I never believed Señor Kosut had me take those photos so that he could jerk off with them."

"When I advised you to consult with Rolando about what to do with the photographs, thinking he'd use them for a good article in the magazine, I made a terrible mistake, Ceferino," said Shorty, filled with remorse. "Without meaning to, I myself set in motion the events that ended with the murder of our boss."

Quique moved the arm that Chabela held over her eyes, and now, her timidity and shame conquered, he kissed her furiously while his hands caressed her breasts and then stroked Marisa's hair, and his entire body struggled to get on top of them both, rub against their skins, trembling from head to foot, blind with desire, happier than he had ever been in his life.

Ceferino, having finished the ceviche, wiped his mouth with the paper napkin. The pair of young lovers had already ordered lunch, and now he was kissing her hand, finger by finger, looking at her, enthralled.

"Why, Julieta?" Ceferino asked. "What do you mean? Why like that?"

"Rolando was working for the Doctor and went to ask him what to do with your photographs," Shorty explained.

"For the Doctor?" Ceferino put on a surprised face. "I heard that from time to time and always doubted it, I never wanted to believe it. Did he really work for him?"

"The way we work for him now: you and I and the entire staff of *Exposed*, Ceferino," said Julieta, slightly angry. "You know that very well, don't play the asshole. And you also know that if it weren't for the Doctor, you and I wouldn't earn the good salaries we do now, and the magazine wouldn't even be published. The best thing would be for you not to distract me with stupidities and for us to get down to what really matters, Ceferino."

He felt he was ejaculating and remained with his eyes closed, thinking it was a shame he couldn't have held on a little longer and penetrated Chabela, whom he was holding around the waist, caressing one of her breasts. He felt his wife slithering up his back, reaching his face, biting his ear, and saying: "There you go, Quique, you've had what you dreamed about so often, you saw Chabela and me making love." Keeping his eyes closed he turned, found his wife's mouth, and kissed her, murmuring: "Thank you, my love. I love you, I love you." And he heard Chabela, beneath him, laughing: "What a nice love scene. Shall I go and leave you two lovebirds alone?" "No, no," murmured Quique. "It's just that I couldn't hold back and I've finished. But don't go, Chabelita, wait a little while, I have to make love to you." And he heard Marisa laughing: "Didn't I tell you, sweetheart? He seems all man, he gets excited, and when the good part's about to begin, then wham, it's wilted away." "Don't worry," responded Chabela, "I'll make sure this little bird sings again."

Shorty had to pause because the waiter came to take away Ceferino's plate. He asked whether the lady hadn't liked the ceviche, and she said yes, but she wasn't hungry. He could just take it away. And she continued:

"But the Doctor categorically prohibited the boss from publishing the photos of the millionaire in the magazine or trying to blackmail him for money. Don't ask me why, I'm sure your little head is capable of guessing the answer. The Doctor didn't want to antagonize one of the masters of Peru, someone who, if he decided to, could do him a lot of damage. Or maybe because, who knows, maybe he was getting money from him another way. Rolando was crazy enough to disobey the Doctor. And he went to blackmail Cárdenas to get him to put money into *Exposed*. He dreamed the magazine would improve, grow, become the best in Peru. And also, perhaps, he wanted to be independent of the Doctor. He had his dignity, he wouldn't want to keep being the drainpipe for the Fujimori regime, the toilet for all the government's shit."

"Is that what we are, Shorty?" asked Ceferino. His voice had changed and the euphoria he'd felt earlier because of the lunch disappeared. He hadn't even tasted the chicken chili that had just been brought to the table. "The shit the government uses to soil its enemies?"

"That and worse, Ceferino, which you also know very well," Shorty agreed. "The vomit, the diarrhea of the government, its dung heap. We serve it by stuffing the mouths of its critics with filth, especially the enemies of the Doctor. To turn them into 'human garbage,' as he says."

"Better end the story soon before it makes me even more depressed, Julieta," Ceferino interrupted; he was pale and frightened. "So, then, Rolando Garro . . ."

"He had him killed," murmured Shorty. The photographer saw a terrible gleam in her round, unmoving eyes. "Because he feared the millionaire. Because of arrogance, because nobody disobeys him without paying for it in spades. Or because he was afraid that Rolando, in one of his temper tantrums, would announce to the public that *Exposed*, instead of being independent, is nothing but a tool of the government to shut the traps of its critics or to blackmail those it wants to rob and swindle. Got it now, Ceferino?"

Quique thought he wouldn't get aroused again but, after

a moment in this position—with Marisa squatting over his face, offering him a reddish sex that he licked conscientiously, and Chabela kneeling between his legs with his penis in her mouth—he suddenly felt his sex beginning to harden again and that delicious tickle in his testicles, a sure sign of excitation. With both hands squeezing Chabela's waist, he lifted her and sat her on top of him. At last he could penetrate her. For a few moments before he ejaculated again, the idea passed through his head that he was so happy at this moment that the entire horrible experience of the last few weeks, few months, was justified by the pleasure he was experiencing thanks to Marisa and Luciano's wife. The blackmail, the fear of scandal, his time in prison, the humiliating interrogations, the money spent on judges and lawyers, it was all forgotten as he felt that his body was a flame that burned from head to toe, that made his body and soul burn at the same time in a joyful fire.

"I've got it, except I still don't know the most important part," said Ceferino Argüello, swallowing. "I know my voice is trembling and that I'm dying of fear again, Shorty. Because I don't have the balls that you use in life. I'm a coward, and proud of it. I don't want to be a hero or a martyr, I want to live till the end, with my wife and my three children, and not be killed before my time. Why the hell are you telling me these things? Don't you see that you're messing me up? Now that I finally was feeling safe, you put me up against the wall again. What do you want from me, Shorty?"

"Eat your chicken chili and drink your beer first, Ceferino." Shorty had sweetened her voice and even her eyes had thawed, they looked at him now with a mixture of affection and compassion. "What you've heard is nothing compared with what I'm going to ask you."

"I'm sorry, but I'm shitting with fear, Julieta," said Ceferino's tremulous voice. "And though it may surprise you,

I've lost my appetite and don't feel like finishing this beer, either."

"Fine. We're even. Let's talk, then, Ceferino. I mean to say, listen to me very carefully. Don't interrupt until I finish. Then you can ask me all the questions and make all the comments you want. Or stop and break that bottle of beer on my head. Or denounce me to the police. But first, let me talk, and pay close attention. Try to understand clearly, very clearly, what I have to say. Got it?"

"Got it," Ceferino Argüello stammered in agreement.

"It's obvious you owe me a roll in the hay, darling," Marisa said with a laugh, not moving. "Well, well, Quique, who would have ever thought you'd fuck my best friend right in front of me."

"With your consent," said Quique. "Now I love you more than I did before, thanks to you I've had some marvelous moments, Marisa."

"And didn't I add my grain of sand, you ungrateful wretch," laughed Chabela, not moving either.

"Of course you did, Chabelita," Quique said quickly. "I'll be eternally grateful to you, too, of course. Both of you have made the dream of my life come true. I dreamed about this for years and years. But I never thought it could become a reality."

"Let's sleep a little and recoup our energy," said Marisa. "And be ready tomorrow to enjoy Miami the way we should."

"The bed is all smeared with this gentleman's pleasure," said Chabela. "Shall I change the sheets?"

"Don't bother, Chabela," said Quique. "I, for one, don't care if they're wet. They'll dry by themselves. To tell the truth, I like the smell."

"Didn't I tell you my husband is just a bit of a pervert, Chabela?" Marisa laughed.

"How was your trip, how was Miami?" asked Luciano,

who had come to the airport himself to pick them up. "Did you have a good time? Lots of shopping? Did you eat the *ropa vieja* at the Versailles?"

"And I brought you your tie with palm trees and loud colors, brother," said Quique.

Julieta Leguizamón began to talk, in a very low voice at first, worried about the couple at the next table, but becoming louder when she realized they were more interested in caressing each other and no doubt saying silly, pretty things in each other's ear than in listening to what was being said at the neighboring table. She spoke for a long time, without hesitations, her large, cold eyes seemingly frozen on Ceferino's face, and she saw him redden or become livid, opening his eyes in surprise or half closing them, overwhelmed by panic or looking at her in total disbelief, frightened and astonished at what she was telling him. At times he opened his mouth, as if he was going to interrupt, but then he closed it immediately, perhaps recalling that he had promised not to say anything until she stopped. How long did Shorty talk? A long time, because as she spoke a good number of people came to enjoy the Peruvian dishes and seafood at the Seven Deadly Fins and then left, and the restaurant began to empty out. A surprised waiter came to take away Shorty's and Ceferino's untouched plates— after inquiring if the lady and gentleman hadn't liked something—and he asked whether they wanted dessert and coffee and they shook their heads no.

When Shorty finished speaking and asked for the check, she told Ceferino that now he could ask her all the questions he'd like. But Ceferino replied, in a quiet voice, his head down, that for the moment he wouldn't, because he felt demolished, like the only time he had tried to run a marathon and had to stop at kilometer seventeen because his legs were trembling and he felt he was going to collapse. He would ask her questions later, or perhaps tomorrow, when he had digested everything he'd just heard her say and his head cleared a little, because it had turned into a labyrinth, a pandemonium, a volcano. Shorty paid the bill, and they left and took a taxi back to the editorial offices of *Exposed*. They both knew that from then on their lives would never again be what they had been.

21

Special Edition of *Exposed*

POLITICAL-CRIMINAL EXPOSÉ

In this issue, for the first time, our weekly abandons show business—the world of the plasma screen, the stage, acetate, and the silver screen, which is its world—and dedicates all its pages to reporting on crime and politics in order to denounce, in all its scabrous detail, the truth regarding the monstrous crime that brought down its founder, the late eminent journalist, Rolando Garro.

EDITORIAL

WE KNOW BUT WE'RE DOING IT
By our editor, Julieta Leguizamón

We know that this may be the last issue of our beloved magazine. We know the risk we run publishing this special edition of *Exposed*, which denounces as a murderer and a corruptor of the Peruvian press the man who has, perhaps, accumulated more power, increased more corruption, and caused more destruction in the history of our beloved nation, Peru: the head of the Intelligence Service, known to all factions by his famous pseudonym: the Doctor.

We know that I might lose my life, as did the lamented Rolando Garro, the eminent journalist and founder of this weekly, and all the reporters, employees, and photographers of *Exposed* might, like me, lose their jobs, their salaries, and be the victims, they and their families, of a merciless, savage pursuit by the bloodthirsty power of the Doctor and his master and accomplice, President Fujimori.

We know this, and yet, without hesitation, we are doing it: we are putting out this incendiary issue of *Exposed*, demonstrating explicitly, conclusively, and categorically that with the murder of Rolando Garro—one of God alone knows how many others—the current government has committed one of the most atrocious murders of liberty in the history of Peru (perhaps of the entire world) and one of the cruelest violations of freedom of expression committed against a journalist, one who was polemical, that's true, but respected even by his worst enemies, who recognized his talent, his guts, his testosterone, his professionalism, and his love for our ancient country.

Why do we do it, risking everything?

First of all, and above all, because of our love of freedom. Because without freedom of expression and freedom to criticize, power can commit any outrage, crime, or theft, like those that have darkened our recent history. And because of our love of truth and justice, values for which journalists must be prepared to sacrifice everything, including their lives.

And because if acts like the cowardly and base murder of Rolando Garro, and the equally vile and grotesque falsification of justice signified by attributing the murder to a poor old man without all his faculties—we refer to the veteran and esteemed reciter Juan Peineta—if they go unpunished, Peru will sink even deeper into the infernal abyss into which it has fallen because of the authoritarian, kleptomaniac, manipulative, and criminal regime that dominates us.

And we do it because, by expounding these stinging truths, we help to impede—though with a tiny grain of sand—Peru's becoming, because of the Doctor and his master, President Fujimori, a banana republic, one of those caricatures that damage our America. The die is cast. *Alea jacta est.*

Julieta Leguizamón
(Editor)

THE BEGINNING OF THE STORY

A PERVERTED FOREIGNER
AN AMBUSHED MILLIONAIRE
AND THE ORGY OF CHOSICA

*(CONFESSIONS OF CEFERINO ARGÜELLO,
OUR VALIANT GRAPHIC REPORTER)*
by Estrellita Santibáñez

The story of the murder of the journalist Rolando Garro, ordered by the strongman in the regime of Engineer Fujimori known as the Doctor, begins a little more than two years ago. A mysterious foreigner named Kosut (undoubtedly a false name), about whom the Immigration Service has no data regarding his entering or leaving the country, which might indicate that he is a gangster, a member of an international mafia, hired our workmate at the editorial offices of *Exposed*, the distinguished photographer Ceferino Argüello, to photograph a supposed social event that would take place in a house in Chosica.

"I was miserably deceived by this individual, who seemed to be a respectable businessman and was in reality a liar, a cheat, and probably an agent for international cartels," Ceferino tells us. "He hired me to photograph a supposed social gathering that was, if truth be told, an orgy with prostitutes."

How many whores were at the orgy, Ceferino?

Four, I seem to remember. Or maybe five. I didn't have a good view of the gathering because I was taking pictures from concealed locations, so that my view was somewhat limited. But my cameras did have a broad perspective and were working well.

Could you describe for us the characteristics of the orgy you photographed, Ceferino?

Well, everybody ended up taking off their clothes and practicing coitus, or the sexual act, at times in the correct way and at times in the rear. As the respective photographs I took show.

Do you mean, Ceferino, that the whores, the mysterious foreigner, and Engineer Don Enrique Cárdenas took off their clothes and fornicated right there, like animals, getting together indiscriminately?

They not only fornicated, if with that verb you mean they made love, Shorty. Because there were also other positions, vulgarly known as going down and sucking off, and, I believe, even an attempt by Señor Kosut to sodomize, if you'll permit me the highfalutin word, one of the whores; but, apparently, it was only partially successful because it hurt her, she screamed, and Señor Kosut became frightened and stopped. My pictures bear witness to all this, except for their shouts, though I heard them very well.

What was the attitude of Engineer Enrique Cárdenas at the beginning of the orgy?

He was surprised. Clearly he had been deceived, too. He didn't know it was an orgy. It was obvious he thought he'd been invited to a social gathering. He found something very different. But in the end, breaking down his initial reserve, he took part. And then he didn't feel well, perhaps because of the countless alcoholic drinks and lines of blow Señor Kosut persuaded him to consume. He didn't seem familiar with those practices. In any case, Señor Kosut had to take him to Lima in the chauffeured car that he had hired, because the engineer was in no condition to drive his own automobile.

Why do you keep calling Señor Kosut a swindler, Ceferino?

Because he never paid me the five hundred dollars he was supposed to pay me for my photos. In fact, I never saw him again after that day. At his hotel, the Sheraton, they told me he had checked out without saying where he was going.

And what did you do then, Ceferino, with the photographs of the orgy?

I kept them safe, thinking the swindler would show up one day and pay me for the work he'd hired me to do.

And why, more than two years later, Ceferino, did you decide to reveal to the editor of Exposed *that you had those photos?*

I was obliged by economic necessity. I'm married, I have three children, and I'm dead broke. One of my children, the youngest, came down with scarlet fever. I urgently needed income because my savings amounted to zero. Just what I said: I didn't have a goddamn cent left. Then I took those photographs to Señor Rolando Garro, editor of our weekly. And I told him the whole story. Señor Garro said he would study the matter and see what he could do with the pictures. And just a month and a half later, he decided to publish them and put out that special edition of *Exposed*, "Photos of the Orgy in Chosica," that was so successful. Unfortunately for him and for us and for national journalism. Now we know he was savagely murdered by order of the Doctor for having published photographs that placed Engineer Don Enrique Cárdenas in a compromising position.

(Follow the continuation of the story of the murder in the article by our editor, Julieta Leguizamón, on the following page: "The Hand That Moves the Killers and the Heroic Death of the Founder of Exposed.*")*

THE MURDER OF A JOURNALIST AND THE THREAT TO FREEDOM OF EXPRESSION IN PERU
by Julieta Leguizamón
(Editor of Exposed)

There are truths that hurt, and we would prefer them to be lies, but in this extremely serious case we try to present to our public the truth, pure, raw, and hard. Truths have to be said, clenching fists and teeth. And we're doing that.

Neither I nor anyone else in the editorial offices of *Exposed* knew that our founder, Rolando Garro—my teacher and my friend—worked for the Doctor and his sinister Intelligence Service. And for this reason, many of the exposés and campaigns of our beloved weekly were not born spontaneously of the journalistic instinct and investigative talent of our reporters, but were ordered and guided by the Doctor himself, from whom Rolando received direct instructions orally. This is confirmed by the secret recordings that we have placed in the hands of the National Prosecutor's Office and of the Judicial Branch, before whom we have denounced the murder of Rolando Garro by the instigation and order of the Doctor.

Why did Rolando Garro, like so many other journalistic colleagues, agree to receive stipends from the bloodstained hands of the strongman of the Fujimori regime? For an obvious reason, as clear as it is painful: the need to survive. Without the economic assistance of the regime through its Intelligence Service, *Exposed* and many other journalistic publications would have disappeared because of an absolute lack of advertising, in spite of the fact that some, including ours, enjoyed public favor. The need, the desire to continue to exist, fulfilling his journalistic and civic mission, undoubtedly led Rolando to place himself at the mercy of the sinister strongman of the Fujimori regime, not suspecting that with this sacrifice, which saved the life of the weekly, he would sacrifice his own.

What is this really about? When our colleague, the graphic reporter Ceferino Argüello, told me about the scandalous photographs of Chosica (and then showed them to me), I naturally advised him to take them to our director and editor and explain to him the entire story of the treacherous Kosut. That is what Ceferino did, following my advice. Only afterward did we learn (this is also documented in one of the recordings turned in by me to the authorities) that Rolando Garro quickly showed the photos to the Doctor and asked him for instructions with regard to them. The aforementioned Doctor categorically forbade him to publish or publicize them in *Exposed*, or attempt with these photographs to exercise any kind of pressure or extortion on Engineer Don Enrique Cárdenas, the main participant in that orgy. The Doctor would explain to me later, in his own voice (see the transcription of the corresponding recording that I turned over to the authorities), that he had forbidden Rolando to do this because he knew that one should not meddle with those more powerful, the rich of Peru, among whom one finds the outstanding and upright mining engineer Don Enrique Cárdenas.

But Rolando Garro did not obey these instructions and tried to coerce (blackmail) Señor Cárdenas, taking him the photos and asking him to invest his money and prestige in *Exposed*, so that the magazine could improve its content and presentation, and so the publicity agencies, thanks to the good name of Engineer Cárdenas on the board of directors, would take out advertising that would assure its survival. Since Engineer Cárdenas refused to be coerced, he rudely threw Rolando out of his office, threatening to kick him; our founder, seized by one of those rages that tended to overwhelm and blind him, published the special edition of *Exposed*. Then the Doctor decided to punish him, and had him killed.

(See the transcription of the secret recording I made of the Doctor's confession to the author of this article, a kind of preventive threat so that she—that is to say, I—would know the possible consequences of disobeying his orders.)

This is the sad story of the tragic death of Rolando Garro, the reason for our public denunciation that covers the pages of *Exposed* this week, which we have dared to place before the eyes of our readers at the same time that we have presented the corresponding accusation to the authorities, confident that our upstanding judges will determine that the killer of Rolando Garro should be judged and duly sentenced for his calamitous action.

(*See, below, how the author of this article, brimming over with audacity and courage, managed to record the compromising confessions of the head of the Intelligence Service, when he met with her in his office or in his secret house on*

the southern beaches to give her instructions regarding oper-
ations to discredit critics or adversaries of the regime, which
was the price for the necessary economic assistance offered
to us for the existence of this magazine.)

We cannot prove the rest of the story now, but we can
deduce and guess it. To invent an alibi for the brutal murder
of our founder, those responsible—the Doctor and his thugs—
found a poor, sclerotic old man, the retired reciter Juan Peineta, very well known for his longstanding rancor toward and
hatred of Rolando Garro, documented by repeated, insistent
letters and phone calls attacking him, which he sent to newspapers, radio, and television stations in the belief that Rolando's
criticisms were responsible for his having lost his position
on the well-known program *The Three Jokers*, of América
Television, where he had once worked. The Doctor attempted
to hide the crime with a slanderous accusation against the
veteran practitioner of the ancient art of recitation. This is the
true story of the death of Rolando Garro.

Julieta Leguizamón
(Editor of *Exposed*)

THE SECRET RECORDINGS
(RUNNING RISKS TO SERVE
TRUTH AND JUSTICE)
Reporter: Estrellita Santibáñez

Before beginning the interview, I tell our editor, Julieta Leguizamón, that I'm not going to interview her as my boss on
the weekly where I work, but with the freedom and boldness
with which I would treat any stranger who might be important
to current events. And she responds: "Of course, Estrellita.
You've learned the lesson. Do your duty as a journalist." With
no further preambles, I formulate the first question:

When did you get the idea of carrying a small recorder hidden in your clothes in order to record conversations with that important individual known as the Doctor?

The second time I saw him. The first time, to my great surprise, he confessed to me that Rolando Garro had worked for him and that he wanted *Exposed* to survive the death of its founder and for me to be the new editor. From then on, I decided to take the risk and record all our conversations.

Did you know what you were exposing yourself to with that decision?

I knew very well. I knew that if he discovered that I carried the small tape recorder between my breasts, he could have me killed, just like Rolando. But I decided to take the risk, because I never trusted him. And, thanks to that, I discovered what I know and what all of Peru knows now, thanks to the courageous support given to me by all the reporters on this weekly and the accusation we have filed with the authorities: that it was the Doctor who ordered the murder of Rolando Garro for having disobeyed him by publishing the photos of the orgy in Chosica. I thanked God the day that he, on his own, without any urging on my part, told me what he had done to our friend and teacher, the founder of *Exposed*.

And why do you think that the head of the Intelligence Service made so stupid, I mean so serious, a confession, which could have sent him to prison for many years? The Doctor is known for many things except for being stupid, isn't that so?

I've asked myself that very often, Estrellita. I think there were several reasons. Since I had already begun to work for him, and very efficiently, creating the exposés and discrediting campaigns he ordered, he had confidence in me. But, even so, he wanted to be sure I'd never dare to betray him. It was a way to warn me so that I would know the revenge he could take against me if I betrayed him. I've also thought that he did it out of satanic vanity. So I would know he had supreme powers, including the right to take the life of those who rebelled against him. Don't they say that power eventually blinds those who hold on to it unlawfully?

What did you feel when you heard the Doctor say that he had ordered the killing of Rolando Garro, whom you loved so dearly?

Terror and panic. As we say in vulgar language, I was shitting with fear, Estrellita, excuse my language. My knees trembled, my heart beat faster, and at the same time, though you won't believe it, I was seized by a secret happiness. I had found the real killer of Rolando Garro. He was there in front of me. I prayed to God, the Virgin, and all the saints that the recorder had worked well that day. Sometimes, because the tapes were worn or defective, it didn't, it was difficult to hear, and sometimes it simply didn't record anything. But heaven heard me, and that day the recording was perfect.

How many tape recordings have you handed over to the Office of the Prosecutor and the investigative judge?

Thirty-seven. All the ones I recorded, including those where the recording is poor, almost inaudible. Of course, first I took on the responsibility for making a careful copy of those thirty-seven tapes, in case the ones I turned over to the Judicial Branch were lost.

Do you believe the judges will dare to make proper use of those recordings? Aren't you afraid they might allege that testimony taped secretly, that is, illicitly, cannot be used to accuse the head of the Intelligence Service of murder?

That, of course, will be the argument the Doctor will use in his defense to impede being charged and sentenced for the murder of Rolando Garro. But he would have no basis for doing so. I have consulted with well-known attorneys in this regard, and all of them have said there is no juridical or moral basis for utilizing a shyster's trick like that. Public opinion would be totally scandalized and the country wouldn't permit it. In any case, if something like that did occur, it would demonstrate that the independence of the Judicial Branch doesn't exist, and that the judges, like so many journalists, are nothing more than tools of the masters of Peru's bodies and minds, which is what Fujimori and the Doctor have become.

When you went to see him, didn't the soldiers or police who protected the Doctor search you first?

They searched me, very superficially, only the first time. But without touching my breasts, which was where I had hidden the small tape recorder. The other times, they let me pass without any checking. Otherwise, I was forbidden to see him if he hadn't called me. Each time I saw him, except the first time in the bunker he constructed on the southern beaches, it was in his office at the Intelligence Service.

Aren't you afraid of suffering an opportune accident, for example being run over by a car or truck, or having your food poisoned, or having them pick a fight with you on the street and knifing you, et cetera?

I take every precaution I can, of course. But you shouldn't forget that at this moment, the regime of Fujimori and the Doctor no longer has all of Peru on its knees. Opposition to the dictatorship has gained strength, every day there are meetings against Fujimori's insistence on having himself elected for the third time, and it's obvious he would achieve this only by means of a monstrous fraud. The defenders of human rights are going to wash the Peruvian flag every day at the doors of Government Palace. In general, because of these new circumstances, the media are less servile and submissive, and some dare to criticize the regime openly—Fujimori and especially the Doctor, head of repression, censorship, and assassinations. Let us hope that this context of opposition increases and sends the Doctor to the dock, and then to prison. For me, the great danger is that he'll flee first to another country, where he and Fujimori keep all the millions they have stolen.

Do you think that Exposed *will survive this latest scandal or will the Doctor take charge of closing it down forever?*

I hope it continues to live, now on its own responsibility and risk, without gifts from the regime. I'll do the impossible, with the help of my valiant collaborators, to keep the killers of Rolando Garro from also killing our weekly. In our defense, we count on public opinion, and the longing for justice and freedom. We have confidence in our readers.

(See the inside pages for the photographs that Ceferino Argüello, the photographer for Exposed, *took of our editor, Julieta Leguizamón, and the recorder hidden between her breasts, helping to hold it in place with her bra, which bears witness to the crime ordered by the Intelligence Service.)*

(See the inside pages for the biography of the notable journalist Rolando Garro; all that is known of the adventurist and criminal life of the Doctor, the head of the Intelligence Service; and the shameful dictatorship suffered by Peru.)

(Also see, in the center pages, a summary of "The Scandal of the Photos of the Orgy in Chosica" and the sad history of the well-known bard and reciter Juan Peineta, forced by those responsible for the Rolando Garro crime to declare himself guilty, and then sent to an old-age home where, because of his senile dementia, he has been able to live all this time without even being aware of the drama of which he has been the innocent, unconscious victim. Also see the survey carried out by our weekly in which 90 percent of those consulted believe that Juan Peineta should be pardoned, because they doubt that in his physical and mental state he could have committed the crime for which he was condemned.)

22

Happy Ending?

"I can't get it out of my head that Luciano knows, darling," Quique said suddenly, and Marisa, who was beside him in bed, leafing through the latest *Caretas*, gave a little start.

"He doesn't know, Quique," she declared, sitting up against the pillows and turning toward her husband. "Get that damn idea out of your head once and for all."

Quique, who had been reading a book by Antony Beevor about the Second World War, placed the heavy volume on the night table and looked at his wife with a worried face that he hadn't had until that instant.

It was a sunny Sunday morning, and summer had finally really begun in Lima. They had woken early with the idea of spending the day in the little beach house they had in La Honda and having lunch there with friends, but after breakfast they had decided suddenly to go back to bed to read and have a quiet morning. Perhaps they'd go to a good restaurant later for lunch.

"It's just that he isn't the same, Marisa," Quique insisted. "I've been observing him for some time. He's changed, I assure you. He keeps up appearances, of course, as a gentleman should. Because that's how he is. Would you like to know how long it's been since we've had lunch or dinner together?

Two months. Has so much time ever gone by without the four of us going out for dinner or lunch?"

"If Luciano knew, he would have stopped speaking to us, Quique. As conservative as he is, he's capable of challenging you to a duel," said Marisa. "And he would have left Chabela immediately. Do you think he would stay with her after finding out that his wife made love to both you and me?"

Marisa had an attack of laughter, blushed like a girl, and, turning on her side, curled up against her husband. His hands caressed her naked body, going under her light silk nightgown.

"Yes, yes, it's what I tell myself, too, to reassure myself, darling," Quique whispered in her ear, slowly nibbling her lobe. "The way he is, Luciano would have fought us to the death and no doubt would have divorced Chabela. And taken the girls away from her as well."

Suddenly Quique felt that Marisa was holding his penis. But not with love; she was squeezing it, as if she wanted to hurt him.

"Listen, listen, that hurts, darling."

"If I found out that you saw Chabela alone, that you fucked her behind my back, I swear I'd cut this off the way Lorena Bobbitt cut off her husband's," said Marisa, pretending to be furious; her blue eyes were flashing. "You remember the story of Lorena Bobbitt, don't you? That Ecuadorean who castrated her gringo husband with a knife and became a heroine to Hispanics in the United States."

"Are you really thinking about that?" Quique said with a laugh, taking her hand and moving it away. "That I could be seeing Chabela behind your back? You're crazy, darling. I like what the three of us do together. It excites me to see the two of you make love. And afterward to fall on you like a heavy rain."

"Well, the last time you fell only on Chabela, you wretch, and left me high and dry."

Quique turned and embraced Marisa. He gave her a long kiss on the mouth, pressing her against his body:

"Are you making a scene with me over Chabela?" he murmured happily, trying to take off her nightgown. "You've gotten me all excited, Blondie."

She moved him away, laughing. Her blond hair was tousled, and to Quique her long neck seemed even softer and whiter than her cheeks and forehead.

"I don't know if it's jealousy, Quique," she said, curling up against him again. "It's a very strange feeling. When I see you making love, and I see you so passionate and so excited, and she's the same way, and you're entwined, touching each other, holding each other, I feel something like anger. And at the same time I'm excited and get all wet watching you. Doesn't the same thing happen to you?"

"Yes, yes, just the same," said Quique, putting his arm around Marisa's shoulders. "Especially when I see the two of you entangled, sucking each other. I feel as if suddenly you had expelled me and I'm left an orphan. It makes me angry, too. But the truth is, Marisa, ever since this story began, our sex life has been greatly enriched, hasn't it? Don't you agree?"

"That's absolutely true," Marisa agreed. "Soon it will be three years since that first time the three of us were together, there in Miami. Do you remember? We have to celebrate. The other day Chabela and I were talking about it. She was insisting that we do it right there, in her apartment on Brickell Avenue."

"Three years," Quique recalled, moved. "Everything that's happened since then, right, darling? Of all the things that have happened to us, do you know the only one that matters to me? That since then, I love you more than ever. Now our

marriage has really become unbreakable. Thanks to everything we went through, now I live madly in love with the marvelous woman I was lucky enough to marry."

He turned and kissed Marisa on her lips.

"It's incredible," she said. "Who could have imagined that
terrorism would disappear, that Fujimori and the Doctor would
be in prison, that Abimael Guzmán and the other one, the one
from the other group, what's that man's name—"

"Víctor Polay, of the MRTA," said Quique. "They're the
ones who kidnapped and killed poor Cachito. I hope that
gang rots in jail for that savage piece of cruelty. By the way,
don't be so optimistic. Terrorism hasn't disappeared completely. There are still groups at large in the jungle. And the
army can't manage to finish them off."

"And what if Chabela had told Luciano everything and
he'd gotten excited over the story too?" Marisa laughed to see
how what she'd said made Quique turn pale and filled his eyes
with fear. "I'm joking, silly, don't be afraid."

"It's just that sometimes I get the same idea," said Quique.
"It's impossible, isn't it? With Luciano, absolutely impossible.
But always, deep down, the doubt remains. Sometimes he looks
at me in a way that makes me start to tremble, Marisa. And I
say to myself: 'He knows. Of course he knows.'"

"Chabela has sworn he doesn't even have the slightest suspicion," said Marisa. "Luciano is so pure, so much a gentleman, he can't even imagine that anyone could do what you
and I do with Chabela."

They were interrupted by the telephone vibrating on
Marisa's night table. She picked up the speaker. "Hello?"
Quique saw her smile from ear to ear. "Hello, Luciano. What
a surprise. Fine, fine, but missing you, we haven't seen you for
so long, Lucianito. Yes, of course, always so busy, just like
Quique. Life can't be all work, Luciano. We have to have a

little fun, too, don't we? Lunch? Today?" (Quique signaled yes.) "The four of us? Great idea, Luciano. Quique's right here, he says he'd love to. Terrific, let's go there, then. How's two o'clock, what do you think? Fantastic. And afterward we could see a movie in that little private cinema you've built yourself. All right? Great! Kiss Chabela for me, and see you soon."

Marisa hung up the phone and turned to her husband with a triumphant expression; her blue eyes were flashing.

"You see, you were just being apprehensive, Quique," she exclaimed. "Luciano was very loving. He thought about our having lunch together because they ordered some very fresh corvina and are going to make a ceviche. And we never see one another and that can't be . . ."

"Just as well, just as well," Quique said gaily. "Just my foolish ideas. I must have a bad conscience over what we're doing, that's the explanation. What good news, darling. I'm very fond of Luciano. He's my best friend and I've always admired him, as you know. What's happened with Chabela hasn't lessened the affection I feel for him at all."

"Do you know what you are, Quique?" Marisa said with a laugh. "An out-and-out cynic, my dear husband. The most cunning man the world has ever seen. You're very fond of him and he's your best friend, but you don't hesitate a second to deceive him with his wife."

"It's your fault, not mine," he said, embracing Marisa and lying on top of her. He spoke into her ear while he caressed her body and rubbed against her. "You corrupted me, darling. Weren't you the one who invented all this?"

"I was never in a *partouze* like that one in Chosica," she said into his ear. "So we'll have to decide who corrupted whom."

"I've asked you so often not to talk anymore about what

happened in Chosica." His voice changed as he moved away from his wife, and turned his back on her again. "You see, I was hot, I was going to make love to you, and with that joke about Chosica you left me as cold as an iceberg. A stab in the back, Marisita."

"I was joking, silly, don't be sad, this morning you were nicer than other days."

"I beg you, Marisa," he repeated, very seriously. "One more time. Let's never talk again about that damn story. I implore you."

"All right, darling, forgive me. Never again, I swear." Marisa brought her face close to his and kissed him on the cheek. She tousled his hair, playing. "Do you know you're the most contradictory person in the world, Quique?"

"Why?" he asked. "How am I contradictory?"

"You don't want me to remind you even in a joke about Chosica, and every night you watch that ridiculous program with that vulgar little woman."

Quique broke into laughter.

"I don't suppose you're going to tell me that you're jealous of Julieta Leguizamón and *Shorty's Hour.*"

"Jealous of that awful midget? Of course not," Marisa protested. "But you, you must hate her. Didn't she accuse you of having had Rolando Garro murdered? Wasn't it because of her that you had to spend those horrible days in prison with bandits and degenerates? How can you see her and listen every night to all her revolting gossip? You should be ashamed, Quique."

"*Shorty's Hour* is the most popular program on Peruvian television." Her husband shrugged. "Yes, yes, I know, it's gossip and pretensions, you're right. I wouldn't know how to explain it, I don't have a convincing answer for you. To me there's something fascinating in that woman in spite of what she did to me."

"That midget, who's as ugly as a bogeyman, is fascinating?" Marisa said, mocking him.

"Fascinating, yes, Blondie," said Quique. "She accused me because, like practically everybody else, she believed I'd had Rolando Garro killed because of the scandal he got me involved in. But afterward, when she found out that the real murderer was Fujimori's right arm, she denounced him, too, risking her life. And don't forget, that accusation was key in the downfall of the dictatorship. Fujimori, the Doctor, and company will rot in prison for who knows how many years because of that woman. They didn't have her killed, as many of us thought they would. She's still here. She was nobody and now she's a real star of Peruvian television. She must be making a fortune, in spite of being, as you say, an ugly little midget. Don't you think it's a fascinating story?"

"I've never been able to stand the pretensions of her program for even five minutes." Marisa made a gesture of disgust. "All that gossip about poor people. Can you imagine if she found out what we do? She'd dedicate an entire program to us: 'The happy, perverse trio,' I can see it now. Just thinking about it makes my hair stand on end. Well, let's not be late. I'm going to shower and get dressed for lunch."

Quique watched her jump out of bed and go into the bathroom. He passed his eyes over the painting by Szyszlo: What did that room, that totem mean? At certain times it seemed to shoot out flames. Sometimes it frightened him a little to look at it. On the other hand, Tilsa's desert with a serpent calmed him. There was no mystery at all there; or, perhaps, there was, the slimy eyes of that snake. He kept thinking. Yes, of course, the fascination that Julieta Leguizamón held for him and that moved him to watch *Shorty's Hour* every night he could. That little woman had made history without proposing to, without suspecting it. With her audacity she had provoked events that changed the life of Peru. Wasn't it extraordinary that an inconsequential girl, a nobody, on the basis of pure courage, had caused an earthquake like the fall of the all-powerful Doctor? He would have liked to know her, talk with her, find out how she spoke when she wasn't on TV, playing the part of someone who rummaged through intimate secrets. Bah, what foolishness. Get up once and for all, shave, and shower. How nice that Luciano had invited them to lunch and to see a film in the screening room he'd built at his house in La Rinconada. He didn't know anything, and they would continue to be the good friends they had always been, what a relief.

Quique brushed his teeth, shaved, and showered. After soaping himself, when he was rinsing off under the stream of water, he realized that he was humming a song by John Lennon. He remembered: the tune had been very popular when he was studying in Cambridge, Massachusetts, at MIT. "You, singing in the shower?" he asked himself. "That's a first, Enrique Cárdenas." He was happy. The invitation from Luciano had put him in a good humor. He was very fond of him, really, he'd always had great affection for him. And the truth was that in these three years, he'd often felt remorse whenever he and Marisa went to bed with Chabela. In spite of that, it never occurred to him to cut off that relationship. He derived immense pleasure from their making love together. "A strange story," he kept thinking as he chose from the large closet the sports clothes he would wear to Luciano's house: loafers, linen trousers, the Texan red-and-white checked polo shirt that Marisa had bought him on her last trip to the United States, and a light jacket.

The truth was that until the damn blackmail that Rolando Garro attempted to inflict on him, his sexual life with Marisa had been withering, turning into a gymnastic exercise without fire. And then, with no warning, during the days of their separation following the scandal of the pictures in *Exposed*, and during their reconciliation, he had experienced that rebirth of relations with his wife, a second honeymoon. The same thing had happened to her. Not to mention later on, when he finally found out about Chabela and Marisa's affair. It would soon be three years since the triangle had begun that had given them back the energy of adolescents, a new vitality. How wonderful that Luciano hadn't learned about it. Breaking off that friendship would have been a misfortune for Quique.

When he came out, Marisa was ready, waiting for him. She looked very attractive in a low-cut blouse that revealed her perfect white shoulders, and very close-fitting orange pants that emphasized her delicate waist and high buttocks. He leaned down to kiss her on the neck: "How pretty you look this morning, señora."

As Quique drove the car toward La Rinconada, Marisa said:

"I love the idea of watching a movie in the screening room Luciano and Chabela have built for themselves. Don't you think it's fantastic to have a theater at home and to see the movies you want, whenever you want, with whomever you want, in those big, comfortable seats?"

"A cinema wouldn't fit in our apartment," said Quique. "But if you like, we'll sell it and build a house with a garden and pool, like Luciano's. And I'll build you the most modern theater in Peru, my love."

"How gallant," Marisa said with a laugh. "But no, thanks. I don't want to be bothered with a big house and all its complications, or have to live at the end of the world, like they do. I'm happy with my Golf Club apartment, close to everything. Well, you seem very happy, Quique."

"I'm enormously pleased that he hasn't found out about

anything," he said. "It would make me very sad to fight with someone who's been like a brother to me ever since we were kids."

Luciano and Chabela received them in bathing suits. Because it was hot, they were in the pool with the two girls. It was a splendid morning, with a vertical sun in a cloudless sky. They didn't want to swim, and they sat under umbrellas in the easy chairs around the pool, drinking Campari and eating yucca with *ocopa* sauce, which the cook had prepared for them, knowing it was Marisa's favorite canapé.

Luciano was full of good humor and more affectionate than usual. He complimented Marisa, saying that recently she was suspiciously good-looking—"You must have a lover tucked away somewhere, Marisita"—and congratulated Quique because he knew he had just acquired another mine, in Huancavelica, in association with a Canadian company. "I mean, you want to keep getting richer. Will your ambition to be King Midas and turn everything you touch into gold ever end?" They talked about politics and acknowledged that all in all, in spite of the ferocious attacks against him, the new president, the mestizo Toledo, was doing pretty well. Things were improving, the economy was growing, there was stability, and, thank God, the abductions and assaults had stopped.

Luciano told them that his firm was now legal counsel to the leading film-distributing chain in Peru, and he was happy; thanks to that relationship, they sent him all the new films so that he and Chabela could watch them in the brand-new screening room in the garden. Sometimes he and his wife stayed up till dawn on Friday or Saturday nights, watching future premieres. Marisa and Quique were invited to those movie nights whenever they liked.

When they sat down at the table, it was close to three o'clock. In fact, the ceviche and the grilled corvina were fresh and delicious, especially with the French white wine, a well-chilled Chablis.

The afternoon was relaxed, amusing, and pleasant—the girls had left to play with the dogs—and lemon cake with coconut ice cream had just been served—when Luciano, in the same casual, nonchalant tone in which he had spoken and joked throughout lunch, suddenly exclaimed:

"And now I'm going to give you all a big surprise: I've decided to go with you to Miami so I can celebrate this third anniversary, too!" And after a brief pause he smiled and added: "In fact, it's time I took a vacation."

Quique, at the same time that he noticed how Chabela's dark face reddened, felt that a solar panel was unexpectedly burning in his brain. Had he heard correctly? He looked at Marisa, his wife was blushing too, and a flash of panic appeared in her eyes. Now Chabela lowered her head, unable to hide her confusion. She kept mechanically carrying to her mouth the small spoonful of ice cream that she returned to her plate without tasting it. The atmosphere seemed leaden. Quique didn't know what he should say, and neither did Marisa. The only one who was calm, unchangeable, and cheerful was Luciano.

"I thought I was going to make you happy, and you all have funereal faces," he joked, holding his glass of wine, bursting into laughter. "Don't worry. If I'm not welcome at the celebration, I'll stay in Lima, sad and abandoned."

He burst into laughter again, raised the glass to his mouth, and drank some wine with a very satisfied expression.

Quique's hands and legs were trembling, and he only managed to observe, right in front of him, Chabela's black hair; she kept her head lowered. And then he heard Marisa, sounding passably natural in spite of how slowly she pronounced each syllable:

"What a good idea for you to come to Miami too, Lucianito. You're right, it's time for you to take a vacation, like
everybody else."

"Thank goodness, at least somebody in this group loves
me." Luciano thanked Marisa, taking her hand and kissing it.
"I know we'll all have a good time up in Miami."